Eleanor Dark was born an
married Dr Eric Dark and
Katoomba.

Eleanor Dark published stories and verse during the twenties, and her first novel, *Slow Dawning*, appeared in 1932. Her other novels are *Prelude to Christopher* (1934), *Return to Coolami* (1936), *Sun Across the Sky* (1937), *Waterway* (1938), *The Little Company* (1945), *Lantana Lane* (1959) and the historical trilogy, *The Timeless Land* (1941), *Storm of Time* (1948) and *No Barrier* (1953).

Eleanor Dark died in 1985.

Also by Eleanor Dark
and available in Imprint Classics

WATERWAY
THE TIMELESS LAND

IMPRINT CLASSICS

RETURN TO COOLAMI

ELEANOR DARK

Introduced by Barbara Brooks with Judith Clark

A division of HarperCollins*Publishers*

AN ANGUS & ROBERTSON BOOK

First published in Great Britain by
William Collins Publishers in 1936
Sirius Quality Paperback edition published in 1981
by Angus & Robertson
This Imprint Classics edition published in Australia in 1991
by Collins/Angus & Robertson Publishers Australia

Collins/Angus & Robertson Publishers Australia
A division of HarperCollinsPublishers (Australia) Pty Limited
Unit 4, Eden Park, 31 Waterloo Road, North Ryde
NSW 2113, Australia

William Collins Publishers Ltd
31 View Road, Glenfield, Auckland 10, New Zealand

Angus & Robertson (UK)
16 Golden Square, London W1R 4BN, United Kingdom

National Library of Australia
Cataloguing-in-Publication data:

Dark, Eleanor, 1901–1985
Return to Coolami
ISBN 0 207 17052 5
I. Title
A823.2

Cover illustration: Trees *c. 1926 by Grace Cossington Smith*
Oil on plywood 91.5 × 74.3 cm. Collection of the Newcastle
Region Art Gallery. Reproduced with permission of Ann Marshall
Mills, Trustee of the estate of the late Grace Cossington Smith.
Printed in Australia by Griffin Press

6 5 4 3 2 1
96 95 94 93 92 91

INTRODUCTION

Return to Coolami begins with Susan and Bret about to leave Sydney on a long car journey. They are with Tom and Millicent Drew, Susan's parents, in Drew's flash new car. A dangerous accident narrowly avoided, a drive over the mountains, a tense night of mountain climbing, a lot of country and a lot of thinking lie between them and their destination. Their destination is not only the property, Coolami, but also the resolution of conflicts and longings. As they turn west, over the mountains, the country and their own preoccupations flash past.

> About sunset they'd come to it—up the crest of a long hill with the sun in their eyes, so that until the car began to swoop downward they couldn't see anything. And then like magic it would all be there, the great valley glowing with opalescent light . . . (p.314)

Any journey is a kind of time out, a physical and mental space to think and re-evaluate. This one is 'an interlude between two lives'; not just a car journey but a 'heading away from security into unimaginable adventures'. And the end of the journey is not just a destination but a new beginning.

'Two days that changed four lives', the blurb on an earlier paperback edition says. 'A near fatal journey that changed their lives.' Four people in a car for two days, carrying with them their past and future. Susan and Bret are desperate to resolve an unpromising marriage. Drew and Millicent are at a low point in their marriage, a kind of mid-life crisis. For a moment you can see where the breathless blurb comes from, and the highly coloured, sensational, romantic cover with the tall, unbending figure of Bret, a cross between James Dean and a squatter, grasping the pliant and bending body of Susan, her anguished face against his broad chest. And behind them, the mountain . . .

But these images don't do justice to a novel about people in a process of change, a novel that came out of a decade that began with the Depression and ended with war. A novel that sees Eleanor Dark beginning to get into her stride as a writer. A novel that bridges a gap many of her contemporaries found hard to cross, between the innovations of European modernist writing and a growing awareness among Australians of a sense of country, nation, independence, national culture.

As much as *Return to Coolami* is a thriller, a romance, a pacy narrative with a surprise, a drama, an adventure around every corner; it's also more than that. It has the underlying flow of consciousness, of magic and dream. It's also a dreamlike journey where the characters see or sense something about their lives and the country where they're living. And the interconnections. The characters experience this and the reader experiences it as well—through Eleanor Dark's writing, through the memory and consciousness of the characters, through flashbacks, monologues. Moving from one consciousness to another, through states of shifting awareness, making time bend and become fluid, Eleanor Dark creates a sense of interplay and interrelation between the individual lives and their circumstances, a fluidity and an immediacy:

> As if they were all the time just one jump ahead of an illusory past, with a future coming endlessly upon them which was still not quite their future. So that in a dreamlike way their thoughts seemed actually to leave their bodies, to hover before them . . . (p.307)

By 1934 when she was writing *Return to Coolami*, Eleanor Dark was married and launched into her writing career. She and Eric Dark had been living in the Blue Mountains for twelve years, in a house on the outskirts of Katoomba with two acres of garden surrounded by bush. The reference in this novel to Coolami as a house that grows out of its surroundings could be to Varuna, the house Eleanor Dark designed. She, like Bret's mother, had abandoned the European idea of a garden in favour of 'a new and more difficult beauty':

> So she'd planted the trees of the country, the flowers of the country and fought them into living. That was how she'd described it herself . . . 'I'm still at war with my garden.' For they hadn't easily capitulated, the wild flowers, defensive behind their sharp hard leaves, their prickles; they resented their captivity as a nervous animal might; bitter, mistrustful, they had died to elude her. (p.139)

The Darks spent much of their spare time driving, walking, hiking and climbing in the bush. Eric Dark was one of the best rock-climbers in Australia, and Eleanor's experience makes the description of the moonlight climb up Jungaburra precise and accurate and vivid.

Eleanor and Eric Dark had established a comfortable and rewarding life for themselves in Katoomba. *Return to Coolami,* published in 1936, belonged to the optimism of the mid 1930s—a time of changing relationships between men and women, of rebuilding lives after the war, of a growing sense of what it meant to be living here in Australia, with this country as the centre of their lives and not an outpost, cultural or political, of the Empire. This was the decade she was to describe later as 'the uneasy thirties' which carried them all towards the climax and catastrophe of the Second World War. She and Eric Dark saw the effects of economic depression, and like all thinking people were moved by it. This, and the sense of urgency as war came closer, marked the beginning of a changing political consciousness which made them both more active and more outspoken in the late 1930s. It shifted her commitment as a writer. She started out in the 1920s as someone who wrote to be published, in the 1930s she had begun to integrate her ideas into her story-telling, by the 1940s she saw the value of writing as social criticism.

In 1936, she had already published two novels. *Slow Dawning* (1932) is the story of a young woman doctor in a country town and her frustration with the limitations imposed on her sexuality and career by social conventions, a 'pot-boiler' she called it, a romantic and sentimental novel, with outspoken feminist ideas. *Prelude to Christopher* (1934) was 'her first legitimate brainchild', a novel about madness, motherhood, eugenics and utopianism. It was an experimental novel that won her recognition from her contemporaries. She decided to publish it in Australia, out of the cultural nationalism she shared with other intellectuals of the time, and it came out with P.R. Stephensen's press.

Reading *Return to Coolami* today, it's easy to forget that in the 1930s Australian writing was seen as a 'pioneering' literature. Writers, as Miles Franklin said, were popping up like mushrooms. And many of them women, writing about complex human relationships in the cities as well as the country. *Return to Coolami* was published in 1936, the same year as Jean Devanny's *Sugar Heaven,* Dymphna Cusack's *Jungfrau,* Barnard Eldershaw's *The Glasshouse,* Brian Penton's *The Inheritors* and Miles Franklin's *All That Swagger.* The year P.R. Stephensen published *The Foundations of Culture in Australia.*

Opportunities for publishing in Australia were limited. English publishers, agents and readers were making decisions that vitally affected Australian literary culture. Asta Kenney, an English literary colleague of Nettie Palmer, who acted as agent for Eleanor Dark, expressed these reservations about *Return to Coolami . . .*

> and when pulled up by the Australian names I hurry to make an appropriate setting for your characters . . . For the life of me I don't see why any action or any psychological process should seem to fit not quite naturally in Australian surroundings, but . . .[1]

Prelude to Christopher was regarded as gloomy, confusing, difficult to follow by the English agents she sent it to. It was an experimental novel, confronting both in subject matter—a woman with a family history of madness, denied by her husband the chance to have children, who eventually suicides—and in form—her first use of interior monologue, flashbacks and the compression of the story into a space of time. More than any of her other novels, it was a departure and ahead of its time.

After *Slow Dawning* was published, Eleanor Dark's English agent wrote offering advice. He'd written to Marjorie Barnard and Flora Eldershaw in the same vein. Strong human themes . . . sincerity . . . humour, he suggested, love stories, domestic stories . . . does life have meaning? Does marriage work?

In July 1934 she wrote to Molly, her stepmother, about *Return to Coolami*:

> It's a pleasant and inoffensive tale about ordinary people and it ends happily in the conventional way. So I might possibly make some money out of it.[2]

It wasn't as simple as that. Eleanor Dark was always self-deprecating about her work. She wrote a novel that looked like what they wanted. But she set it in Australia, taking her sophisticated characters out into the bush for their pioneering adventures, and making it part of the series of reconciliations in the novel that they came to terms with living there. Her characters debated war, feminism, the roles of men and women. The irony was not lost on her readers.

She set her novel in the Australian bush, and described that 'difficult and elusive' beauty that even breaks down the resistance of Tom Drew. That sense of the country, the bush and its qualities—the blueness of the Blue Mountains, the timelessness and enduring sense of the land, the surprising beauty of native plants—is part of all her novels. She develops her argument through the novels, starting from the awareness of the landscape, moving to its effects on the people, the relationship of the people and the country, ending with the examination of the history of settlement, as a history of the interaction between the land and the people, in her historical trilogy.

But if the novel is about a future in the bush, it's also about a present in the city, and the connections between them. Susan is a city girl, or woman—independent, articulate, self-aware, fun-loving and sophisticated. She sits in the back of a fast car wearing a smart hat and smoking cigarettes. She's a spoiled middle-class girl with a lot of pluck when life turns sour. She stands her ground, for independence, for an equal footing with men. In *Slow Dawning*, Eleanor Dark had looked at the problems of work and sexuality. In *Waterway* (1938), she looks at marriage and the intellect. Through Susan Drew in *Return to Coolami* Eleanor Dark articulates part of her argument about women and men; and Bret expresses the male reaction to women's sexual independence:

> he felt, suddenly, the whole male sex rear its head in his person and bellow angrily. She was upsurping its privileges, endangering its supremacy—actually attempting, heaven smite her, to kiss and ride away. (p.132)

Eleanor Dark's ideas about men and women are tied up with her attitudes to war. In the thirties the effects of the First World War were still being felt, and Colin, in this novel, is one of its casualties.

The connection between war, masculinity, and aggression is an argument that appears first in this novel and is developed further in *Waterway* and *The Little Company*.

> Let them take care, these irresponsible child-mates of womankind! Let them not hold too cheaply the life which she is growing tired of producing for such a senseless purpose! Let them not forget that of the fundamental differences between the sexes a difference of mentality is not one—that the feminine brain starved and hampered through the ages is fighting at last into its own. So that a day may come when she will say,

'No. I bear no more children into a world not fit to receive them—' (p.201)

She makes Coolami mean 'birthplace of heroes'. Was this serious, and a bit over the top? Bret as the first in a long line of Australian paragons? Or was she gently mocking the mythologies of Europe, the Old Country, of war, and the prejudices of those who saw Australia as the birthplace of second-generation convicts? What did she really think of those heroes?

Not only did she set her novel in the bush, but she mocked Drew's attitudes to the 'savage' place names—Parramatta, Kirribilli—gibberish, he said. This very smartly undermines any patronising attitudes the reader might have to the setting. '. . . one in the eye for the ignorant who still regard us as colonials.'[3]

At the beginning of the novel, Drew has no sense of himself, he has no sense of country, and has expressed his love for Millicent only by providing her with material possessions. He finds himself at fifty-eight without an identity, without a battle to fight. ' . . . an existence and a host of material possessions.' Millicent wonders, 'Could you make a life of those?' (p.281)

Return to Coolami is a challenge to Eleanor Dark's readers to reject materialism as well as colonial attitudes which defined everything Australian as second rate. It was only when Australians came to grips with their country that they could fully live here, know themselves a part of the place, and it a part of them, she was saying. Thinking about the country like this eventually led her to an awareness of the Aboriginal people and their culture.

Her commitment to writing about this place/Australia for these people/Australians comes through in *Return to Coolami* in the details like the placenames debate, and the descriptions of houses and gardens, that could be European ideas transplanted and imposed on a landscape, or things that grow out of it and blend with it. It comes through in the whole movement of the novel, the journey to the bush and the places that are past and future homes of the characters, part of their new beginnings. The changes that Millicent and Drew and Susan experience anticipate what she says later in *Waterway*—we haven't changed the land, it has changed us.

Her interest in what it meant to be Australian became more urgent towards the end of the 1930s and took over her writing in the historical trilogy that occupied most of her time and energy between the late 1930s and the early 1950s—*The Timeless Land* published in 1941, *Storm of Time* in 1948, *No Barrier* in 1953. In these she wrote an extensively researched account of the early settlement of New South Wales, from the point of view of the Aboriginal people, convicts male and female, as well as free settlers and government officials. Her interest was so far ahead of its time that it inspired the teaching of Australian history in Australian universities in the 1940s.

Her interest in Australian history seemed to develop out of her curiosity about the way to live in this country, out of her love for the bush—and also out of her fascination with the nature of time. The bush, the country, is 'timeless'; even in *Return to Coolami* Drew is struck by the 'antiquity' of the land, the age of the grass-trees. And a sense of history meant she could live with the past—of the country, of the people—as though in a kind of conversation with them, and could understand a possible future better. What memory is to the individual, she says, history is to the community. Time is not mechanical, linear, the way she understands it.

She had this complex understanding of time in the form of her writing too—telling the story of *Return to Coolami* in two days, constantly doubling back into the past through memory, but keeping a sense of immediacy by using a kind of stream of consciousness. It's there in Bret's idea of the minute when the car started to slide off the road being longer than any other minutes of the journey.

In 1936, the *Bulletin*'s Red Page reviewer called it 'a perfectly modern novel'. In many ways it still is.

There she was, in 1934, after the confused and mystified reactions she got to *Prelude*, perhaps trying to write a story that wouldn't startle her readers (or was it her publishers?) too much. Relax, she might have said, I'm going to tell you a story. Slightly melodramatic, a kind of romantic novel, with a happy ending. But a story about this place where we live. I want to take hold of this place and describe it to you in a way that makes you understand what it means to live here.

> So when people are searching for an understanding of their problems, they turn naturally to their literature, which gives—or ought to give—a reflection, and perhaps an interpretation, of themselves and their community.[4]

There she was, in the 1930s, writing about issues that still touch our lives. Eleanor Dark was a socialist, a radical historian, a feminist, and an environmentalist. 'Man has only one wealth,' she says in *Waterway*, 'the earth and its fullness.'

There she was, in 1934, writing about war and masculinity, in a way that anticipates the 'take the toys from the boys' slogans of the 1980s.

> She saw the whole world suddenly as a gigantic nursery full of delights for half of humanity that has never grown up. Not only the weapons that his own ingenuity had conceived, but there to his hand an inexhaustible supply of enemies and victims to annihilate . . . (p.200)

One of the pleasures of reading this book is the enjoyment of the story. There is even deeper pleasure in the ideas sparked off, ideas that are timely now. Beyond that is the satisfaction we gain from the possibility of re-reading Eleanor Dark's work—regaining our sense of continuity with the women writers of the 1930s—and further back than that, with the successful and forgotten 19th-century women writers in Australia.

BARBARA BROOKS AND JUDITH CLARK
SYDNEY 1990

(1) Eleanor Dark papers, Mitchell Library, State Library of New South Wales (ML MSS 4545 box 24)

(2) Eleanor Dark papers, Mitchell Library, State Library of New South Wales (ML MSS 4545 box 15)

(3) May Roseby to Eleanor Dark. Eleanor Dark papers, Mitchell Library, State Library of New South Wales (ML MSS 4545 box 24)

(4) Eleanor Dark papers, Mitchell Library, State Library of New South Wales (ML MSS 4545 box 10, Australian Writers Speak Series, interview with Eleanor Dark 7.10.1944)

Quotations from the Eleanor Dark papers are made with the kind permission of the Eleanor Dark estate and the Mitchell Library, State Library of New South Wales.

CHAPTER ONE

I

Bret came out of his wife's room carrying her two suitcases and went slowly down the stairs. He was alarmed at his own anger.

Anger, he assured himself, stung by the memory of Susan's white face, not so much at her as at the grotesque and impossible situation in which they were both struggling. Anger that with all his efforts at decency, at forbearance, with all her fierce and determined honesty they hadn't managed to do better than this——

Well, anyhow she was coming home. It might be, as she had half admitted last night, that this long absence of hers, these months which had amounted, really, to a kind of artificial return to her unmarried life, had been a mistake. And yet it had seemed reasonable enough at the time. Their brief marriage had, so far, been pretty awful, and after the baby died she was naturally run down, nervy, at the end of her physical and emotional strength. He hadn't forgotten the look of almost frantic appeal in her eyes when he went to see her in the hospital. "I'd like to stay at home for a while, Bret—for a couple of months or so—I—I don't want to go back yet—to Coolami——"

The "at home" he realised, was illuminating. Coolami, to her, was not a home but a place where she was working out, with a courage that he couldn't but admire, a dreary, heartbreaking expiation. Well, if she felt like that——

So he'd gone home next day, alone. Of this visit of his to bring her back, he didn't want to think any more than he could help. He stopped dead on the landing and stared absently in front of him, his face a queer mixture of amusement and despair. For tragic and impossible as the situation was when you were one of its chief actors, it had, undoubtedly, if you could sufficiently detach yourself to see it, a funny side. Susan, thank heaven, had an invincible sense of humour, and only her glimmer of a smile answering his through the murkiness of their problem as the lights of one ship might signal through a fog to another, had preserved for them a fragment at least of mutual respect and reliance. He had discovered it, he remembered, in the early days of their marriage. They'd come one night when they were travelling by car to a small country hotel where Bret's demand for a room with twin beds had met with no success. He had found Susan in the room looking pale and exhausted, and he had said, eyeing the vast white bed ruefully:

"I should have a drawn sword to lay between us—but I'm sorry I've nothing better than a mashie-niblick."

Her little spurt of laughter had relieved and reassured him. You could do a lot of patching, he thought grimly, going on down the stairs, with a joke or two!

But there were times of course when you didn't feel like joking—times like last night when the tangle you were in became unbearable, when you fought it, quite hopelessly because it was woven of subtle and incomprehensible things within yourself—of anger, of resentment, of aching desire, of an obscure sense of loyalty to Jim, of pity for Susan, of a vague disgust for the whole business, of a bewildered conviction of beauty to be grasped in it—somewhere—somehow——

All those warring impulses—and in Susan how many more, poor infant that she was, after all——

He paused in the hall to put down a suitcase, jam his hat on his head and pick it up again. He saw his own face in the mirror and stopped, suddenly remembering her desperate cry: "If you weren't so *like* him, Bret!" That had surprised him. He hadn't ever thought that there had been more than a family resemblance between himself and Jim. He could see now, searching for it, that the likeness was there—in the shape of the nose and mouth, and in the rather aggressively straight eyebrows. But his own eyes were of that light grey which looks so surprising in a sunburnt face, and Jim's had been dark; Jim had been young, moving like quicksilver; Jim——

He turned sharply away from the mirror and went out through the front door, his shoulders sagging a little under the weight of the suitcase.

The gravel of the path crunched rhythmically beneath his tread. Round the curve between the azalea bushes he saw his father-in-law's new tourer waiting outside the gate, its hood folded down, its luggage carrier laden, its green body shadowy, shining, like a mirror, like a limpid pool.

2

The sun, not yet over the tops of the camphor laurels, shot a stray gleam through them on to the polished nickel of Drew's new Madison. He himself, circling round and round it with a piece of chamois leather in his hand, caught the dazzle of it from the corner of his eye, and smiled. The lustrous olive-green of the bonnet, satin-smooth, mirror-bright, held his glance for a pleasant moment; from there it passed with a shade of reluctance to the silver-plated effigy on the radiator-cap. Funny how he'd come to buy that thing. Saw it with a lot of others in old Waller's office—he'd been importing them—and felt suddenly that he had to own one for his new car. Something about it——

Quite well done, probably, though he didn't know much about art. Cost enough, anyhow. But—fanciful. Unrestrained. Yes, that was it, he thought, pleased with his choice of a word, and looking, therefore, with increased severity at the little gleaming figure, unrestrained. To the solid opulence of the car it lent a note, incongruous enough but queerly exciting, of eagerness, of adventure. In the lines of it, of course, he told himself, eyeing it with what he hoped was critical detachment; in the perspective; and the pose. That lean, boyish-looking body—straining forward. The outstretched arm, the pointing hand, the lift of the head. A clever thing. Quite clever. But fanciful. That, after all, was the last word. You couldn't approve really of anything that was fanciful, and Lord alone knows what sudden impulse had made you buy it. But bought it was, with hard cash, for the radiator of your new car, and on the radiator of your new car it should stay. . . .

Footsteps on the gravel made him turn. Bret with two more suitcases. Well, they'd have to go in the back. The luggage carrier was full. Funny the things women had to cart around with them.

A good chap, Bret, even if you didn't quite know

what to make of him sometimes, or what to make of his attitude to Susan, or hers to him. Time, he thought ruefully, instead of unravelling a tangle had merely made turmoil of something which now, when you looked back at it, seemed to have been clear enough in spite of its distastefulness!

This "rest" of Susan's! Rubbish! Susan playing the invalid! Well, he wasn't going to interfere, it was women's business; let her mother handle it. But no one was going to tell him that Susan with her clear eyes and her clear skin, with her vitality and the lights that fairly crackled in her amazing hair, had to take four months' holiday to get over a perfectly normal childbirth. The child's death only a few days after its birth had upset her certainly—that was only natural. But it didn't make her stubborn and continued absence from her husband any more excusable.

Anyhow it was over now. She was going home to Coolami, and who had engineered that he supposed he would never know. Perhaps Millicent, whose gentle persistence was sometimes a match for even the steel and flame of her daughter's determination. Perhaps Margery. Perhaps, he thought, glancing at his son-in-law as he took the suitcases and stowed them in the back of the car—perhaps Bret? After all, he had his rights. After all, though neither Susan nor Margery nor Millicent nor Bret himself seemed to see it in that light, he'd been, in a way, magnanimous to marry her at all!

Stung by this thought as he had been for the past year whenever it obtruded itself, he said brusquely:

"Susan ready?"

"She said five minutes."

Drew said, "Good God!" in a resigned voice and

climbed into the front seat with an air of being prepared to wait an hour. Bret was walking round the car; Drew, catching sight of him in the driving mirror for a moment, found himself thinking for the hundredth time that you could always tell a countryman from his hat. Turned down and pulled forward over the eyes. Bret had a semicircle of unburned skin on his forehead——

He asked, without turning round:

"What do you think of her."

"She looks great. Have you finished running her in?"

Drew snorted.

"Made 'em do it for me. Can't bear this crawling round at twenty-five. No, I can let her out to-day. How far did you say it is to Colin's place—from here?"

Bret reflected.

"Round about a hundred and fifty. A very easy day's run."

"And about the same from there on to Coolami?"

"Yes, roughly."

Drew nodded and looked towards the house again.

Well, here was Millicent, anyhow. The faint scowl, that had settled round his eyes since he thought of his daughter's marriage, cleared away while he watched his wife coming up the path. Cool, she looked in that greyish-green dress; but she'd want her thick coat crossing the mountains——

He called:

"Where's your fur coat?"

She protested.

"Tom, I won't want that. I've a tweed one here—it's quite thick."

She stood at the gate which Bret was holding open for her, and looked at her husband and her husband's car. For she did not really think of the car as being in any way her own. Her fur coat even, she thought, with a smile flickering, was really Drew's fur coat. And he would be so disappointed, poor darling, if she didn't wear his fur coat to-day when she was going for her first drive in his wonderful new car. He said off-handedly:

"Oh, all right, all right, please yourself. But it'll be cold when we get up there near Katoomba——"

She agreed quickly.

"I expect it will, dear. Perhaps I had better have it. Bret, you wouldn't mind running back for it? Take this—just throw it on the bed. The fur one is hanging in my cupboard. Susan will know——"

Quite solemnly her eyes met the solemn eyes of her daughter's husband. But the laughter that passed between them warmed her heart as he turned away. Dear Bret! Lucky Susan! If only——

3

Coolami. Coolami. A word, thought Susan, and a mass of pictures. A word and an ache of memories, a chill of many fears. She stood at the window pulling her bright blue felt hat down over her hair, hoping that the breeze would fan from her hot cheeks, before she joined the others, traces of that brief and fiercely subdued burst of crying which had overwhelmed her just after Bret went out.

Coolami. About sunset they'd come to it—up to the crest of a long hill with the sun in their eyes so that until the car began to swoop downward they couldn't see anything. And then like magic it would all be there, the great valley glowing with opalescent light, the wheatfields quivering and flowing to the current of a vagrant breeze, the river like a mirror beneath a green deluge of weeping willows. Coolami; she rubbed the back of her hand across her forehead, as though she might clear in that way the obscure confusion of thought that the name roused in her. What did it stand for, that name of her husband's home, beyond the lovely picture that it flashed instantly to her mind—beyond her memories of Jim—beyond the unbelievably carefree months of her romance, the freezing horror of its ending, the dreary and humiliating mess which had somehow grown out of what had seemed so lovely and so gay——

It was no joke, she thought, living too intensely when you were very young. Crowding emotions and experiences into too short a space of time. Being pitchforked out of what was practically childhood into a maturity which had not yet found its feet. Loving and being loved, seeing death and giving birth and seeing death again—all in so short a time. Not two years yet since she had first met Jim. Then she had been nineteen and a child, but now she was twenty-one she hardly knew what to call herself. She'd been in love and she'd had a baby—surely if those things didn't make a woman of you nothing would. And yet for four months nearly, she'd been hiding here like a panicky child behind her mother's skirts! All the same, she defended herself with unhappy honesty, it wasn't so much fear as just confusion—a muddled, miserable feeling of having found herself in a situation that was too complicated, too tangled, too——

But if Bret meant what he had said——

She couldn't blame him, after all if he did. She'd

thought of demanding the divorce often enough herself, and really it did seem under the circumstances the only decent way out. But when it came to the point—when you felt it really near you, this cutting adrift from Bret, from Coolami——

It would be like hacking a piece out of yourself—— Too much of your life, not in time but in essence, had been bound up in Coolami——

"Ready, Susan?"

She swung round from the window, hoping that with her back to the light the tear stains wouldn't show. Not that she could tell from his quite expressionless glance whether they did or not. He had his hat in his left hand and her mother's fur coat over the same arm, and he stood in the doorway with his right hand on the knob barring her way. She picked up a bag, glanced in the mirror and said, "Quite. Come on." But he didn't move.

She flushed angrily. He didn't know perhaps (or perhaps he did, but she wasn't going to give it away anyhow!) that the unfair advantage of his physical size and strength was a perpetual irritation to her. She would have given anything, at that moment, with the full flare of her red-headed temper burning her up, to have been able to push him aside, to send him spinning against the opposite wall while she walked victoriously down the stairs! The knowledge that she could brace her feet against the doorway and shove till she was tired without moving him an inch made her so angry that she could hardly see, so she turned her back again and strolled over to the window, and from there spoke airily:

"When you are."

"I was bluffing about the divorce," he said.

Relief ran like a cool tiny trickle of water amongst the flames of her temper and was consumed.

"What a pity," she said politely. "I was just feeling glad you'd saved me the bother of having to ask for it myself."

His hand was no longer on the doorknob. She walked past him, pulling on her gloves. He followed silently.

CHAPTER TWO

I

FROM where he sat in the front seat of his car, with his arm across the wheel, Drew could see the railway station at the foot of the hill. And dimming, as it always did, the pleasure he felt in his home, his neighbourhood, he could see, too, the last four letters of its name—tall and white on a black ground, pricking him to a faint exasperation.

"——LOOL."

He glanced sideways at his own house. To him it had always been perfection, and his wife's attitude towards it, of faintly amused detachment, had puzzled and disturbed him. To-day, he thought, wishing vaguely that Millicent instead of himself should have been the one to notice and comment on it, it looked particularly well; the sun glowed on the red roof and cream-coloured chimneys, and the dark brick walls were still in flickering shadow. The cypress hedge that he'd planted was growing well, and the pergola was fairly smothered in yellow roses. The lawn, he noticed with a slight frown, needed clipping round the edges, and he made a mental note that Stock the gardener must be brought to book not only for this but for the patch of dandelions which, even from here was visible, marring the immaculate smoothness of the turf. A good house, he thought, refusing with some inward defiance to harbour memories of his wife's rapture in their first home—that little place with the straight stone path and the neglected orchard, foaming with pink peach blossom—the little place he'd got cheaply because it was next door to a cemetery!

Here, he thought, looking along his own high brick wall towards the high brick walls of his neighbours, there was dignity, security. Roads were smooth for the passing of costly cars; footpaths were well-kept; gardens—gardens were properly looked after, they were assets, they were frames for the houses, not, as Millicent seemed to think they should be, rather in the nature of joyous accidents——

Yet there on the station was that name—that somehow unsuitable and undignified name—Ballool.

He said over his shoulder to Millicent:

"What's it mean, that name? Ballool."

She shook her head.

"I don't know, Tom. Why?"

He grumbled. "Must mean something, I suppose. Where the devil are those two? We won't get away before lunch at this rate." He blew the horn violently.

Millicent, passing her daughter's room, had heard her crying. Not for the first time in these last four miserable months. She said gently:

"Don't hurry them, Tom," and he, with a sudden outburst of impatience and long-concealed anxiety, demanded:

"What's the matter with the girl, anyhow? He—— treats her all right, doesn't he?"

She said warmly:

"Bret's a dear. But—it's been a bit of a mess, Tom—— Give them time. Sometimes I've wondered if we were right to allow it."

He grunted. "Too late for that now." And turned his head towards the sound of their approaching footsteps.

More than ever when they came in sight they bewildered and annoyed him. Side by side, just finishing as they came round the corner some apparently amiable and trivial conversation, Susan smiling, Bret quite unperturbed—What the devil did they *mean* by not being as carefree as they looked?

Susan said, patting his hand as she passed:

"Sorry to keep you waiting, Dad. I'm going to sit behind with Mother."

But at that Drew's vaguely pricking disquietudes became transformed into a rich and satisfying anger. Damned young fools with their silly squabbling! "Going to sit behind with Mother," was she? Well, he'd show her what a marriage was, the spoilt little devil! And he said with determination:

"Nothing of the sort. Your mother's sitting in front with me!"

There! He simmered in the gently subsiding glow of his indignation, and held the rug for Millicent, who climbed meekly in beside him with lowered eyelids and a funny expression round the corners of her mouth. From the back of the car, silence. Serve them right! Let them stew in their own juice for a while! He wasn't going to have his day spoilt for them—his first long run into the country without Millicent at his side——

And Susan's voice bubbled out behind him:

"Bret, darling, just move that suitcase over the other side, will you?"

2

Now that they were actually moving Bret's faintly nagging impatience became suddenly a blaze. Something, he wasn't quite sure what, lent the journey a rather exciting tang of adventure. It might be simply the thought of Coolami, lying like a promised land three hundred miles away; it might be the deserted, still-sleeping appearance of the streets which made one feel one was perhaps rather picturesquely enterprising to be abroad at all; it might be even—yes, it was possible—because Susan was beside him and bound too, however unwillingly, for Coolami. Or, as a last guess, perhaps it was that surprising little gadget of Drew's on the radiator—that simple and primitive figure straining forward incongruously from the sophisticated bonnet of a new Madison!

Whatever it was it made him feel better. It pushed into the background of his mind the depressing psychological tangle that his life had become, and brought forward the refreshing physical simplicities of his work and his home. He began to enjoy in anticipation a hundred small things he would do and see within the next week—his crops springing up rich and green after last week's heaven-sent rains—his favourite horse, Ranger—the cattle-stop he had told them to put in while he was away in place of the old gate by the creek—Desdemona's new foal——

But there his thoughts tripped and crashed painfully into a memory of Jim sitting on the fence and laughing and claiming the next offspring of Desdemona as his own. Not much more than a year ago. And by some freakish twist of unprepared emotion it now seemed the most poignant and unbearable of all the results of Jim's death, that he should not be able to have the foal now that it was born.

Gaps. Gaps. Everywhere you came up against them. Weak places in the structure of your life. Like walking a carpeted hall, not realising the rotten boards till your feet went into them! Jobs that Jim had always done—suddenly you had to find some one else to do them; a realisation one night of a piano always silent; a letter from a tailor who wanted another fitting—how subtly horrible that was!—from a Jim who would never again swank about in clothes to which he lent an intriguing air of mixed Beau Brummel and Tom Mix!

Well, it was over—*over*, he told himself violently, angered again by the dark slow-welling tide of resentment against his wife, Susan, which he could not control with any amount of carefully fostered mental justice. He told himself wearily what his mind, from constant repetition, found no sense in any longer, that it was no use thinking about it, no use wondering or regretting, or resenting. The thing had happened and it was over. Some one else did Jim's work, the piano was silent, and there were no more tailor's bills for Jim. Even the baby had died. And he thought for the first time that, in a way, it was not till that scrap of humanity drew its last breath that Jim had made his real, his final exit.

Leaving Susan——

Drew called over his shoulder:

"Where do we strike the Great Western Road?"

Bret answered, leaning forward:

"Parramatta."

3

Drew thought irritably:

"There's another of them!" Parramatta. It had a silly sound, a jabbering sound, the kind of sound that a child might make experimenting with vocal noises!

And over there to his left still another—Kirribilli! Well, they sounded just exactly what they were—the language of savages!

And he thumped his hand heavily on the horn. The note of it, deeply and mellowly austere, the chastened alacrity with which a lesser car slid to the left while he roared past it consoled him slightly. He called back to Bret:

"Well, tell me where to turn off. I don't know this road at all."

He glanced sideways at his wife. He had remembered, even as he spoke the words, that she did know it. Or that she had known it, years ago. Queerly reluctant he'd always been to talk to her or to allow her to talk to him about her girlhood in the country. Jealous, perhaps. Fiercely touchy about a time when she'd had far more than he could give her. Resentful of a home more impressive than the one with the peach blossoms and the cemetery next door! Such things stung and goaded you when you were a youngster with energy and ambition and precious little else; and a good thing, too! They'd stung you into the best house in Ballool, goaded you into the latest model Madison, brought your wife fur coats and your son a country property and your daughter——

Well, confound it, what more could he have done? Was it his fault she'd got these damnable modern ideas from God-knows-where and dashed off——

His memory thrust at him suddenly a picture of four-year-old Susan galloping down the beach in a blue bathing-suit, her arms outstretched to a colossal curling breaker in a gesture that was at once a fearful welcome and a pathetic attempt at defence—— He remembered feeling, as he rushed to the rescue, a pride in her that was vast and painful. So small and so intrepid and so damn silly! Just exactly like that she'd rushed into life—where he couldn't follow and pick her up and comfort her because she'd had the breath knocked out of her and her feet swept off the firm ground——

And he remembered again the one small circumstance at which he had been able to grasp for comfort in those dreadful days after it had happened—he had never wanted her to go to Wondabyne; and if she hadn't gone there she'd never have gone to Coolami either, and if she hadn't gone to Coolami she wouldn't ever have met this—this Jim——

Yes, it had given him some slight easing, rescued him from too overwhelming a feeling of failure as a parent, to be able to say, stamping up and down the room, "I said at the time I didn't want her to go—— I was always against it——" But of course he hadn't thought—couldn't have foreseen——

As a matter of fact he hadn't had any real reason for opposing the visit—except that always, ever since his marriage, he'd felt this obscure jealousy of the country. He'd been jealous of its pull on Millicent, jealous of its pull on his two children, jealous of something they felt which he couldn't share, didn't know anything about. And didn't want to. What a game! He'd learnt a good deal about it, indirectly, since his marriage, and whoever wanted it could have it! No stability to it, no certainty, no chance of letting up for ever and ever amen! Good seasons, bad seasons, endless work, endless anxiety. When you weren't praying for rain you were being flooded out! Rust in your wheat, fluke in your sheep, rabbits and droughts and bush fires. Hell!

And in the end, what? Peace for your old age? Security? Not on your life! Just look at Millicent's family and Wondabyne! Rich and prosperous in her parents' time—passed on, still rich and prosperous to her brother. He dies, and what then? Comfort for Agatha his widow and money well invested? No such thing! The money you make on the land goes back into the land—what you don't spend on your periodical sprees to the city. Back it goes, and the land eats it up and demands more. Then wool's down and wheat's down and Depression arrives on the scene and you're beaten—finished. You've got to sell out and live on next to nothing in a little flat, and all you've given your life to is yours no longer. Look at Agatha. Adrift, alone, and this stranger, Mortimer, at Wondabyne driving it back again to a new prosperity. Oh, yes, it was there all right, the money. The richness, the essential value. But how many got it out and stuck to it? Not one in a hundred—not one in a thousand——

And he began to wonder and to worry about Colin.

4

Round a corner the fresh breeze from the harbour leapt at them suddenly. Susan clutched at her hat. Bret took his off and held it on his knee. Millicent, who didn't mind looking old-fashioned and had tied hers on with a veil, lifted her head up and sniffed blissfully.

She had been feeling, very much as Bret had felt, that a momentous journey, a momentous undertaking of any sort perhaps, should always begin in the very early morning. Hours before you were, on ordinary days, awake at all. You came to it then with the extra freshness and eagerness of novelty. You felt clean and the day felt clean, and you had a cheering sensation that everything was beginning anew. Rather like the feeling when the desk-clerk at a hotel turns over a page, and you are the first to inscribe your name on it; and you write neatly and clearly because you are leading off a whole pageful of heaven only knows what other people on what other diverse and extraordinary occasions, and it behoves you to set an example of order and seemliness——

Yes, anything begun like this would surely lead to pleasant things. A time when you saw streets empty and shops closed; a time dedicated, it seemed, to milk and magic and morning papers. Susan must be feeling it too. Bret must be. And they were both young. When you were young and felt good the natural outlet for the good feeling was to love some one. Why there—even Tom, bless him, had suddenly put out his hand and patted her knee! And spring, too. Bret, what are you thinking of! Susan, Susan! Forget it all, put it away, be happy!

"In the spring a young man's fancy——" How old was Bret? Thirty-fiveish? Well, that was young. Jim——

The thought ran over her mood like a small cloud-shadow over a sunlit plain. Jim of course was only twenty-five. That was spring, too. Last spring——

Poor children. Youth, difficult and lovely. Susan, Colin, both gallant and impetuous and mad. Never mind, she thought fiercely, I *like* my children mad! God save us from cool and calculating young people!

But not war—that wasn't fair. Susan had come to grips with Life and been worsted—temporarily. That was one thing; one grieved, worried, tore oneself to bits with pity for her, but one felt all the time that it had been at least a clean fight. War was different. There wasn't anything clean in that; there wasn't anything there that was worthy of having such a wealth of courage, such a flame of selfless youth matched against it. It wasn't a fight any more than the ancient sacrifice of little children into the molten jaws of the god Moloch. It was something obscene that grabbed and devoured, or where it couldn't devour, maimed or warped or mutilated——

And there, like her husband, she could remember that she had cried tormentedly: "He mustn't go! He can't go! Eighteen—Tom, he's a child! You went, you got your leg smashed up—isn't that enough?" But, unlike her husband, she found no comfort in the memory. Nothing but a bitter self-reproach that she had given way in the end. Nothing but contempt for a mother who had been taken in even for a little while with fine phrases spun to cover abominations——

A boy had gone away, very cheerful, very excited, very particular about his buttons and the shine on his belt and boots. There had come back a boy wrapped in a strange, bleak maturity that sat on him like an ill-fitting garment; a boy with restless eyes and hands, sharp tongue, sudden laughter, long silences——

And dreams. Nightmares. Things that crowded on him in the night and tortured him and flung him, shuddering and wet with perspiration, out of frightful sleep where these horrors had been false into still more frightful wakefulness when he knew that they'd been real——

The trouble was that before it all happened, one's ideas of war had been so wrong. One's thoughts were a sort of hotch-potch of second-hand ideas, mostly poetical and all so very out of date. One thought: "On, on, you noblest English," and "'Charge for the guns,' he said," and "What can I do for thee, England, my England." Yes, even out of the heart of it had come a cry, the spiritual descendant of those old-fashioned cries, the cry of the warrior who was still a warrior out of war that was no longer anything but butchery: "Now God he thanked who has matched us with this hour——"

They had had that—they had had it in thousands and they matched it with what? Glory and valour of days gone by? A charge, a battle, real anger, real action, triumphant conquest, honourable defeat? No—but mud and vermin and waiting. Boredom. Disease. And then an orgy of organised and nauseated killing. Not in anger, not in any hot outburst of natural hostility, but coldly and mechanically, from afar; death from the air, from under the sea, out of tanks, out of machine-guns, out of gas-bombs——

And Colin in the midst of it——

But now there was Margery. And little Richard——

Millicent sighed and began to see again. She came back painfully from this blind excursion into her thoughts, and looked at the harbour like a pearl in its early morning veil of mist. Sandals—something about sandals, wasn't it? Her mind groped among rhymes and metres. "The still morn——" Yes, yes, "and the still morn went out with sandals grey——"

She lifted her head a little, and it went back suddenly and she was staring upward. Oh, lovely, lovely! She was wildly happy again. How much more delightful it was to see beauty where you didn't expect it! You looked at the harbour knowing it would be lovely, and it was lovely and you drank it in and said, "*That's* all right."

But this sudden miraculous beauty curving and spinning away over your head, this cobweb wizardry of steel, of soaring arches just touched by the first sunrays to a faint golden warmth – this was something you hadn't expected, hadn't looked for – it was an extra, given free with the morning——

Her husband said:

"Better than the punt, old lady?"

She laughed excitedly, far less at his remark than for joy at her recaptured happiness. She said:

"Oh, yes, darling, better than the punt – much, *much* better than the punt!"

CHAPTER THREE

I

But Susan was only twenty-one, and for her places were not, save from her own association with them. The last year with all its burden of tragedy and joy was still vivid enough to make places connected with it queerly poignant, touched for ever afterwards in her mind with a sharpness, an intimacy that other places could not have. Across that year she looked back as one might look across an angry bar to calm water beyond, at a time which seemed curiously remote; and to a Susan so gaily and energetically sure of herself that the present Susan could only think of her with amazement —and envy—and a faint pitying contempt——

Envy—yes, you couldn't but envy any one so blindly and deliciously certain that she knew all about life and could lead it round like a little dog on the long leash of her theoretical knowledge! A marvellous feeling, while it lasted! Perfectly marvellous until your leash suddenly snapped and you discovered that your poodle was a lion after all—or a gorilla or—what was bigger and fiercer than a gorilla——?

"Bret?"

"Yes?"

"What were those animals—you know—lizardy things only as big as a house—prehistoric beasties—?"

"Ichthyosaurus, do you mean? Or rather I suppose it's Ichthyosauri."

"Yes, those are the things."

That was what it was like. But the picture she instantly saw of herself standing aghast before its devouring jaws turned out to be comic instead of tragic, and she giggled suddenly.

"Are they funny?" asked Bret.

"This one was."

And then she saw it all allegorically again and felt sick with shame, remorse, misery. Funny? Jim's death; those dreadful months before the baby lived and died. Bret and their hopeless sort of marriage—funny? And she remembered the first few moments when she'd known that her theories had failed her, the first glimpse she'd had of a life that wouldn't run to the charming pattern she had shaped for it, the first sickening, panicky feeling of being trapped——

Bret asked conversationally:

"What did it do?"

She looked at him dubiously. You couldn't explain all that to your companion in the back seat of a car, shouting a little because the wind was in your face—even if it weren't so muddled and incoherent and absurd. So you just said, "It ate some one," and looked away at the road again and felt a fool——

No comfort though in the road. Not because it was, anyhow, depressing road now—jumbled shops and houses, cheapish, resentful-looking even in this early morning freshness—but because she had travelled it so often with Jim in those lovely lunatic months before it all was spoiled——

No wonder, she thought now, Bret had looked at her so much askance. They'd torn up and down, she and Jim, from Sydney to Coolami, from Coolami to Sydney, as though the three hundred odd miles were across the road and back; starting out early in the morning, roaring along at sixty for a while and then crawling at twenty-five while they argued it out all over again. Jim pleading, raging, expostulating, herself all reasonableness and determination, not knowing that there were things that could make your reasoning like a whisper in a hurricane, your determination of no more importance than the defiance of an ant beneath a steam-roller.

Yes, here—just here one day when they'd been a few seconds too late and the railway gates of the level-crossing had barred Jim's impatient way, he'd slumped back in his seat, all glum and glowering and said:

"Well, if you won't—it's over. We can't go on like this. I won't stand it."

And she'd just said:

"All right. That's that."

And meant it, too. Not being in love gave you an awful power, a detached merciless power. She knew that well enough now that Bret had turned the tables on her so neatly. And yet she'd tried to be kind to Jim—not to take advantage of this strength of hers. It wasn't her fault that it had all become so dreadfully serious to him and remained for her the charming and jolly adventure it had been in the beginning. She hadn't ever, not for one moment, pretended, or led him to think or expect she was going to love him some day as he loved her. She had tried, really very hard, though Bret didn't believe it, to stop the whole thing when she saw how Jim was beginning to take it. But it wasn't any good. He'd only followed her to Sydney, tortured her with arguments and beseechings, sworn that he understood, that he knew she couldn't force her love for him——

And she couldn't. No one could. Love happened to

you or it didn't, and it wasn't any use your telling yourself what a dear Jim was, how strong and young and jolly and good-looking, how thoroughly eligible in every way—you just simply went on not being in love with him.

Oh, and why should you be? A little flare of defiance made her move sharply in her seat. She stared angrily at the back of her father's head and told herself again that she didn't care *what* had happened, her theories were good theories, and if the world wouldn't allow them to work then the world was wrong and stupid—and unfair——

And she remembered Bret's angry, unfamiliar-looking face, its tan smeared over with a queer pallor, staring at her across a flower-laden table.

"It isn't fair," she'd cried, "that the baby should have to suffer too."

And he'd answered contemptuously:

"You're young enough to be surprised, I suppose, when things aren't fair."

Well, a year had cured her of that, anyhow. She knew now that unfairness was in the day's work—everywhere, all the time people were unfair because they hadn't understood; like Bret the night he'd found Jim in the car——

Could you ever make anything decent of a life begun in such bitterness, such ugliness and hostility? Wouldn't you always have pictures at the back of your mind——

Swinging Japanese lanterns on the long verandah of Wondabyne; dancing; lovely air, cool and smooth with a smell of freshly-cut grass and the morning's brief spring shower; happiness brimming in you—happiness you couldn't account for now and didn't bother to account for then; a feeling of being tremendously well, and tremendously vigorous, and glad that music sounded as it did, and the country smelt as it did, and that silk slid against your bare skin with just that elusive and delicious touch——

And then Bret at her side:

"Can you spare me a minute? I want to show you something."

She'd said, "Yes——" and looked up at him doubtfully. She hadn't known him very well then, and she thought that in the barred light and shadow from the lantern overhead his face looked rather startling—distorted, almost as though it were mutilated with vast horizontal scars——

But she'd walked with him down the drive to the car. He opened its door. She was rather bewildered and peered at him through the darkness.

Jim had said once, grinning. "Bret's a fish. He'll never marry," but at that moment she had wondered with the rather pathetic wordly half-knowledge of the pretty flapper whether he was quite such a fish after all. She said:

"What is it?"

And he answered harshly:

"Jim's in there—drunk."

She said nothing. Stood for a rather whirling, blackening moment staring into the car. Then she leaned forward, groped into the darkness and the faint smell of whisky and cried miserably:

"Jim! Jim!"

Bret said shortly from behind her:

"Don't try to rouse him, please. I'm going to drive him home now. I just wanted you to see your handiwork."

She flared round at him, shaking with anger.

"What do you mean?"

He said, shutting the door, speaking over his shoulder:

"Don't be so absurd. You're a pair of young fools. Do you think I'm going to watch Jim go to pieces, because a vain flapper wants his scalp to add to her collection?"

She said, calmly enough:

"I'm not responsible for this.

He shrugged and got into the car.

"You know best what you've done or said to him to-night to make him drink. It isn't one of his failings."

The car was gone. She stood in the drive watching its red tail-light disappear, and then she began to cry painfully, silently, with her hands over her face, because some loveliness was gone out of the night, and she didn't quite know why it should have or whether it would ever come again——

From beside her, Bret said, conversationally:

"But of course they're extinct now. *Quite* extinct."

She looked round at him sharply, but his face was as wooden as ever. And suddenly irritated, determined that, for once, he should be forced to explain himself, she demanded:

"What do you mean by that?"

He looked at her too now and for a few horrible seconds the thing she was always trying to avoid happened. They stared straight into each other's eyes and she could see in his, all over again, the jarring clamour of a year-old war. She supposed, dully, that he could see things in hers too, and that in a moment or two they would be both struggling alone like swimmers flung violently apart by a tremendous wave. She'd found that out quite a long time ago. So long as they didn't look at each other things weren't so bad. They could laugh and joke and make amicable conversation. They could even, when people were about, fling in a "dear" or a "darling" that sounded quite convincing. They could create an illusion of intimacy which was at least good enough to make it possible for them decently to pretend that they believed in it themselves——

But the things they saw when they looked at each other were—were——

But not a smile. Not a smile like that—mechanical smiles, sometimes; pitying, mocking, cruel, or really amused. But not smiles like this one that Bret was suddenly giving her—not——

"You seemed to be bothering about it," he said. "I just wanted to remind you they really are extinct."

And then he leaned forward and called to her father:

"This is Parramatta we're in. The turn off comes pretty soon—to your left."

2

Millicent looked over her shoulder to speak to Susan and looked quickly back again. She mused pleasantly for a few moments on the quaintness of her own Anglo-Saxon temperament. Perhaps it would be more satisfying, at all events from the material point of view, if one were a Latin? Perhaps it would be nice when one saw in the faces of one's children intense joy, intense sorrow, to be able to plunge into it with them, to lift one's voice in lamentation or to cry the praises of the blessed Virgin? But no, she thought regretfully, glancing down at her fragile body, one must have the figure for that kind of thing as well as the temperament. One might conceivably lash oneself into the required emotional frenzy, but one could not acquire the bosoms! So one glanced round and saw one's daughter looking as though heaven and all its angels had appeared before her; and one glanced away again quickly so that no one should be embarrassed by the acknowledgment of too deep an emotion——

But there it was. Oh, lovely day! Susan looking happy, and here before them, mile after precious mile, the Western Road!

CHAPTER FOUR

I

DREW settled down to his driving with a freshened interest. This, you might say, was the beginning of the country; here you began to see bits of vacant land, and there were grassy banks by the roadside, and the scattered shops had that gauche but rather engaging appearance unknown to city shops, of not being quite sure what it was they were really there to sell. Drew began to feel benevolent; he began to feel expansive and kindly and tolerant, and he liked the mental picture which he had of his large, gleaming, powerful car rocketing along through this naive and humble countryside.

It was pleasant, he thought, to feel the velvety throb of the engine, the effortless power of it soaring them up the crest of this hill ahead. Pleasant, too, not to know what was coming. Pleasant—and of them all, he thought, rather grimly, he was the only one who could be knowing that particular pleasure—to come to it without memories, quite fresh to a fresh adventure.

They swooped at the sunny crest of the hill, sank away from it into lavender coloured shadow, and the road raced on ahead of them to another hilltop. Yes, this was fine! Good road, straight, just enough ups and downs to keep it from being monotonous, and a car that purred like a cat newly fed on fish and cream! You could let her out a bit on a road like this—turn the purr into a roar, the cat into a tiger!

Up into the sun again, down into the shadow and still the road lay in front vanishing like a thread over yet another distant hill! Forty-five and you hardly knew you were moving! Fifty. Fifty-five. A miracle really, this conversion of a few gallons of petrol into annihilated miles! A liquid, a vapour that could spin you like the carpet of Bagdad from Ballool to Coolami!

A longer hill, this one—but she rose to it like a bird! Funny, the effect of movement the glittering sun gave to that little silver figure in front; if it weren't so damned fanciful, so definitely one of the miracles that *don't* happen, you'd say that all the power of this headlong flight came from its wild, forward-leaping body and followed its forward-pointing hand——

And here was the top coming at them, behind them—and still the road straight as ever, and still another green softly rising hill ahead!

That was pretty, he thought, glancing out of the corner of his eye at a tiny cottage, a vast flame-tree, a green garden with children in it. And a peach tree in blossom. Funny that he'd never thought of putting in peach trees at Ballool? Milly might like it better if——

But of course, naturally, she did like it. Rotten damp little place that one near the cemetery. No conveniences. She had those now. Hot-water service, all the electric gadgets you could buy—more comforts than she'd ever had even at her wonderful Wondabyne! And here was another of those damn hills!

He said crossly:

"How long does *this* go on?"

Millicent said, peering at him round the edge of her veil:

"Well, dear, it's like that rhyme of Hilaire Belloc's:

"The road went up,
The road went down,
And there the matter ended it."

But presently she added comfortingly:

"Not *all* the way. Wait till we get on to the mountains."

He snapped:

"I know the mountains as well as you do. Been there by train dozens of times."

She said: "Of course, darling, I'd forgotten," and patted his knee.

2

So she thought about it now, and wondered how it could happen that a man like Tom should be so–so *circular*? He was rather like one of those dear, busy toy trains you have when you're little, she reflected, the ones that run round and round and round and bluff themselves that they're getting somewhere. And it was odd that Tom should be like that, because he wasn't really unimaginative. Every now and then he did something, said something which made you feel that he'd got on to the circular track by mistake–that if some one or something could juggle with the what-do-you-call-thems?–joints?–points, yes, that was it–and straighten the line out he'd be off with a rattle and a roar, whistling and puffing and spouting steam——

Well, you'd think the war might have done that, but it hadn't. He'd gone and he'd come back, and immediately, except for Colin, it was as if the war had never been. But that, probably, was because he'd had to leave things unfinished when he went, and he did so hate unfinished things. Yes, she knew well enough though he hadn't actually told her, that until he'd provided her with every comfort and convenience that money could buy he wouldn't even look up from his unsparing self-imposed slavery.

Oh, the poor darling! Impossible to tell him how little she cared for anything beyond a quite modest and reasonable comfort. Worse than impossible—harmful, dangerous. Because that was the test he'd set himself right from the day of their lovely, ridiculous elopement—to outdo her old life in happiness, her old home in comfort, her old possessions in opulence! A test he wouldn't ever let himself forget, not even, as it should have been forgotten, in those fairy-tale days when they'd lived like a pair of babes in a wood of unbelievable peach blossoms!

And the result had been, ironically and pathetically enough, that no home she had ever shared with him had seemed to her as truly home as Wondabyne. That, of course, she hoped he didn't know. It was one of the freakish practical jokes Life played sometimes, jokes not in the best of taste, which one tried to ignore. But it had been, always, a kind of restless pilgrimage with, God help us, Ballool for its Mecca! "This will do for the present, Milly. We'll get something better later." So they had got something better. And still better. And now, at fifty-seven, they were in the best at last, and the best was——

Oh, rubbish, rubbish! The best was beautiful! Not because, as Tom seemed to think, it had three bathrooms and a hundred guinea billiard-table, but because Tom was triumphantly still Tom, and because fifty-seven or not she'd elope with him again to-morrow——

And this trip, really, was significant. What did it mean, beyond that he wanted to have a good long play with his new toy, the Madison? She glanced at him rather ruefully, wondering if it could possibly mean that he'd forgiven the country at last for having been her home before he knew her? For having taken both his children? For having been, in the back of his mind for nearly thirty-seven years, a vague, intangible enemy and rival which he must vanquish or die?

And then she realised that she'd been staring without seeing it at the effigy on the radiator-cap, and she found herself thinking with an irrational confidence:

"But of course he'll love it when he gets there——"

3

Bret, perturbed, fished in his overcoat pocket for cigarettes. Then he thought:

"Oh, hell, I couldn't light it if I had it." And sat gloomily, his hands still in his pockets, staring at the countryside. Amazing, he reflected, the things that could happen between two people without any words at all!

Susan——

You glanced at her and she looked so wretched that you were sorry. So, as was right and natural, you said something, stupid enough, Lord knew, but meant to be comforting, and she looked at you and you looked at her and suddenly things began to happen. A kind of warmth, an expanding, a surprised, relieved, but elusive feeling that everything was really very simple after all—and on her face a dreadful and disturbing joy——

Then it was gone, like a fitful gleam of sun on a drizzling day. Other things began to drip, drip through your mind obscuring a radiance too fleeting and uncertain——

The Coolami verandah and his own voice speaking from the dark to Jim reading in a patch of butter-yellow light.

"Jim, what are you at with Susan Drew?"

"What the devil has it to do with you?"

That, he remembered thinking, while he watched a moth crawl up the page of the book Jim was pretending to read, was the sort of tone he had to expect. So he shrugged and went on deliberately:

"Just that if her father found out about your little affair there'd be a row—and I don't want a row."

Jim flicked the moth away and said angrily:

"What do you mean by 'affair'? And if there was a row it would be my row, not yours."

Bret said wearily:

"Oh, don't be an ass." And then lost his temper.

"And you know what I mean. Do you think I don't know about your idiotic flat in Sydney? And if I know there'll be plenty of other people who know too——"

Jim said hopelessly.

"She won't marry me."

Bret laughed outright and then sobered. The boy was too obviously unhappy to be really amusing. He said shortly:

"Why should she? She only wants a few sensations."

And there it was. That was a conversation you had had. Nothing could alter it. You'd said those things, you'd thought them, believed them, about Susan. Now——

Even though you didn't believe them any more, even though you'd come slowly to a very different conception of her, those things which had happened and which, therefore, were irrevocably a part of your knowledge of her, remained.

So many of them. That night when he'd found Jim, tight, in the car. Another time a few days later beside the sun drenched tennis-court at Coolami, when Susan had turned to him suddenly, cool, polite, dangerous:

"You don't often play tennis, do you?"

"Not often. But I wanted to be here to-day."

"I see. Police supervision?"

"Possibly."

"Will you tell me how you knew about our flat?"

"I found out accidentally. But I'd have known sooner or later. You don't keep those things dark for long."

"Apparently not."

"I want to ask you something."

"Yes?"

"Will you give it up now?"

"The flat?"

"Yes—and Jim too. The whole business."

"Why?"

"Because it's a rotten waste of time—and other things that shouldn't be wasted."

"That's a matter of opinion."

He looked at her curiously.

"Do you know Jim's in love with you?"

"He's often told me so."

"You don't care two hoots for him."

"I like him very much."

"Don't you feel you're being unfair to him?"

"No. I don't feel that."

It was then he'd realised for the first time that she wasn't, anyhow, doing this in the heedless butterfly fashion he'd imagined. He looked at her with new interest and increased dislike. He saw that she'd thought it all out; that she was playing the game rigidly in accordance with some rules which, rightly or wrongly, she believed to be fair. He was startled; he was even for a moment, through a veritable blaze of resentment, amused by his own reaction. For he felt, suddenly, the whole male sex rear its head in his person and bellow angrily. She was usurping its privileges, endangering its supremacy—actually attempting, heaven smite her, to kiss and ride away!

And then he'd voiced a threat and she'd answered it—two brief sentences which he'd often found himself remembering since:

"You'll burn your fingers."

"You won't hear me yell if I do."

A cheeky face it had been in those days. A pair of brown eyes with a gleam in them defying him from beneath her copper coloured hair. He'd gone away into the house rather hurriedly. He'd always suspected that if he had stayed a moment longer she'd have put her tongue out at him——

He looked at the two heads in front of him. Drew must have been a fine-looking fellow when he was young; even now though the contours of his face had thickened, you could see a good line of cheek and jaw, a glimpse of handsome, if rather arrogant nose. And Millicent, of course, must have been quite bewitching. It wasn't any wonder when you thought about it, that Susan was—Susan. The vitality of her, springing like grass after rain, the flame of adventurousness flickering fascinatedly towards danger was pure Millicent. The Millicent who had snapped her fingers at Wondabyne and married a bank clerk she'd known for a week——! And yet, in Susan there ran too the streak of obstinacy, the conviction of her own rightness, the arrogance that he'd seen just now, in her father's nose!

Life had hammered that out of her, poor kid! He glanced at her, troubled, knowing how much and how unwillingly he'd helped with that hammering. And yet she wasn't quite flattened out, even now! Judge her as you would, you couldn't deny her courage. Nor that queer, absurd, heroic honesty she'd taken for her only standard——

She asked him suddenly:

"Will Kathleen and Ken be at Coolami? When we get there?"

He said, "Not that I know of." And added presently:

"Did you see her show?"

"Yes—we all went."

"Like it?"

"Yes. Dad bought the one of Wondabyne Pool for Mother, but she doesn't know yet. For her birthday."

And that, thought Bret, was just about as unfortunate a choice as he could have made. Not that he knew, of course, how much of his daughter's love-affair was bound up in that spot—the spot where two generations of young people from Wondabyne and Coolami had swum, and picnicked and flirted——

He suddenly found that he didn't want very much to think of it himself, and he wondered, looking at the long range of mountains now visible, remote, intangible as a bank of cloud across the plain, whether what he felt was jealousy.

CHAPTER FIVE

I

SUSAN pulled her hat off and sat on it. The wind and the sun leapt into her hair, blew it out behind her and burnished it so that it looked like the flame of a grass-fire, flickering, crackling. She was nervous. There was a kind of constriction in her throat, a swollen feeling behind her eyes and she was uncomfortably conscious of her breathing. It was the road that was doing it, this road which had always seemed to her to fall naturally and topographically into three sharp divisions. There was what she always thought of as the city-side and then, like a vast wall, the mountains. And on the other side of them, the country. Bret's country. Jim's country—Coolami.

While they were here, on the city-side with the mountains still ahead, but so much nearer every moment, she could cling to the queer detached life of the last four months—feel herself not quite Susan Drew and not quite (how queer it still sounded!) Susan Maclean, but a Susan who had drifted numbly in a present which couldn't last, but which, while it did, was peaceful so long as she could keep herself from thinking——

But soon now the car would rush upward. Incredibly soon after the road began to climb they'd be able to look backward at the plain they were now on and see it far below as a soft pattern of greens and browns, remote and tranquil beneath a grey-blue film of morning mist, the long curves of the Nepean lying so still that the trees fringing its banks were no more perfect in detail than the trees mirrored in its dark water——

And that, thought Susan, her hands clasping rather tighter on her lap, would be the end of the city-side. They'd be climbing the wall. And on the other side she'd have to begin to realise things again, to face certain questions, to make certain decisions; to be, finally and irrevocably, Susan Maclean of Coolami.

It would be hard, very hard, to feel that. Perhaps men didn't realise that among the many difficult adjustments a woman must make on marriage the changing of her name is not negligible. It wouldn't be so bad, perhaps, she thought, if you were really—if you were able to feel altogether a sense of belonging to each other.

But there was something confusing, something that made you feel you had lost your psychological bearings, in finding yourself no longer the Susan Drew you had known from babyhood, but an unfamiliar Susan Maclean, standing like a shy and forgotten child at a party, in the midst of a strange life. It wasn't even as if you had been properly invited. You were a sort of unwilling gate-crasher——

Not that Bret, she acknowledged quickly, had done anything to make her feel like that. Nor Kathleen. Ken—yes, a little, perhaps, but more teasingly than unpleasantly. There hadn't even, in that perfect and perfectly-run home, been any particular work for her to do. You couldn't when you were twenty, and lucky if you boiled an egg properly, tell anything to Mrs. Dobbs who had taught Bret to use a spoon. You couldn't dictate to Matty who had learned her housework under the eye of Bret's mother herself. No one attempted to, not even Kathleen. Domestically, for many years the house had functioned under the rule of these two with a beautiful noiseless and invisible efficiency. So that, feeling rather awkward, and very nervous, and acutely unhappy, there had been nothing for it but to live there for seven endless months, in the family but not of it—not a wife exactly, or a friend exactly, or a guest exactly——

Feeling at first while Matty swept and dusted in her room and then passed on with expressionless eyes to Bret's, a seething under that naked and bony forehead of conjectures, of austere and bitter condemnation. Seeing, a few months later, with new-born super-sensitiveness Mrs. Dobbs' speculative eye on her figure. Forcing herself, through the growing lassitude of her body, the nervy grating of her mind, to remember that she'd played a game and lost and was now paying her forfeit——

She had, indeed, made for herself a little Litany of a scrap of conversation she had had with Bret. It began after a while to have, by sheer force of repetition and reaction a steadying influence:

"*You'll burn your fingers.*"

"*You won't hear me yell if I do.*"

No yelling, therefore. Not even when it became most awful. Not even when they were both discovering that the mind, soul, psyche or what you will of a human being is a fathomless wood where he may lose himself indefinitely—where he may find green glades with sun in them and banks of violets, or bogs of viscous slime smelling heavily, sickly-sweet of menace and corruption——

Not so simple to be clean in a wood like that. To be rational, honest, controlled, just—everything which, they had tacitly agreed, would save this dreary marriage of theirs from total failure. You were in a bog before you knew it was there, floundering, struggling, crawling out to lie breathless and befouled, wondering just where and how you had lost your footing. Rational—no, not always possible to achieve that, either, when you were lost, quite lost, quite confused, your nerves screaming with the panic of your utter solitude. Not honest either when your every action came from motives so obscure, so primitive and tangled that you could not always recognise them yourself——

But no yelling——

Not even when sometimes it had seemed that the ultimate destruction was coming. Sometimes Bret started it—a look—a touch—— Sometimes she started it herself, goaded on by an obscene devil of perversity to endanger the only treasure she had left—to risk the defilement of her last remaining shrine——

The shadowy range loomed over them. Drew called to Bret:

"What's the grade like?"

And Bret said:

"Good."

The Madison roared and leapt at it. The hill dropped away behind them.

2

Bret was thinking about the thousand sheep he had to get, somehow, by the end of next week, from Coolami to Manton's place out of Gunnedah. He was wondering, with a faint corrugation of worry between his brows, who he'd send with them now that Giles was needed for the shearing and Jim—and there wasn't Jim any longer.

A pity in a way that Ken—and yet, no, it wouldn't have been any use his sticking to the land when he wanted the law. He was cut out for law, too—his sharp inquiring mind, his precision of thought, his fluent, caustic tongue. All the same, Bret realised uneasily, he himself had been finding something a bit blank, a bit solitary about life and work, since Jim's death. He'd been restlessly aware during the past year that he no longer had any one to talk to about Coolami. Ken and Kathleen, of course, had their share in it. They were fond of it, too, as a home, as a background. But they didn't run it, plunge themselves into it, know it and understand it to the last of its seventy thousand acres as he did—as Jim had done.

An odd thing really, that of the four of them he, the eldest, should have had more in common with Jim, the youngest, ten years his junior, than with either of the other two. It had begun, probably, after their father's death when he was 24, and Jim, home for holidays, had mustered sheep with him and fenced paddocks and slept near him at night in a rolled blanket by a camp fire. It must have been then, too, that he began to rely on the boy, half-unconsciously, for companionship. There hadn't really been any one else. Their mother was like a pale flame flickering just before it goes out. She'd been ill, then, for years, and her husband's death had finished her—only ten months after him she'd died——

And Ken had been at the university, very absorbed, appearing rarely, disappearing suddenly—not really minding very much what happened to the goose that was Coolami, provided his golden egg reached him promptly each quarter——

And Kathleen—twenty, in the thick of her first love affair—very stormy, very hectic, very brief. Love had got her that way at the beginning and had gone on getting her that way, till now, at 31, she'd learnt to take it a bit more casually; he grinned, thinking of her standing in front of her easel in a blue overall, brushes bristling from her fingers, the floor littered with bits of this and that, paint in her dark hair where she'd pushed it fiercely back from her lovely face, which was lovelier now, he thought, by a good deal, than it had been when she was twenty. Kath, certainly, was one of those women who improve with age. The clamours and impetuousness of youth had subsided now, and her eyes had a laugh in them instead of a blaze. She'd learnt a certain very valuable detachment; her discarded amours strewed the path of her life in very much the same cheerfully haphazard way that her rubbish littered the studio floor. And her pictures grew better and better——

So that she hadn't had much time either to think of Coolami. Only Jim, in scrawled impatient letters from school, demanded whether there'd been rain yet, and how many of the sheep had been shorn and if Bret was putting in corn or lucerne down on the river flats? And what the hell was the use of his staying on for the Leaving when he wasn't going to the 'varsity? When he was just coming straight home to Coolami? Why shouldn't he leave when he was sixteen? "You know very well I'm a blob at exams, anyhow."

And so on. Yes. Bret acknowledged now, they'd both talked the same language, he and Jim; loved the same——

Now that was funny. He hadn't been thinking of Susan at all, and suddenly in a queer back lane of words which could suggest what they hadn't really meant, his thoughts bumped her suddenly. There she was in the middle of them, barring his way. They tried angrily to pass, dodged, doubled, protested.

"The same *things*! The same *land*—the same work——!"

And the same woman?

3

What *was* this love, anyhow? He could say quite honestly that he didn't know—and get strangely little satisfaction from the statement. There'd been Myrtle, bless her, just before the war, when he was eighteen; Myrtle, four years his senior, big and rosy and kind. Myrtle, whose father had been a share farmer on Coolami until he died and whose husband, a good chap called Roberts, had taken his place; Myrtle, who now, nearly forty, broad in the beam, but still rosy and hearty, would look at him over the heads of her five small Robertses with a grin which told him she remembered as kindly as he did a long summer evening by the creek on Coolami——

That was all right—pleasant, wholesome, something you could look back on without a sour taste in your mouth. Not like the war episodes—not like Lilian, either, for whom he'd lived six feverish months before he discovered she was engaged to some one else all the time——

It must have been that, he supposed—the jar of feeling himself very badly and callously let down, which had kept him unmarried so long. Not that he'd cared, a year later, what happened to Lilian. He'd never known till it was all over how very shallow a feeling it had really been——

And after that nothing—except Coolami. And that, undoubtedly, the most satisfying, the most lasting. He'd been content with that. Nothing complicated about it, nothing dark and difficult, no tearing of yourself by many warring impulses, no plungings into sudden unsuspected emotions, no reactions of weariness and disgust——

Just work—a deep absorption, a passionate interest. Triumphant hours, anxious hours, even despairing hours. They didn't matter, the ups and downs of your mood. Through them you knew the land was there, and the feeling that knowledge gave you was not to be put in any words. It was something indefinable, fed by the memories of all your senses; it was something you smelt, grass and earth, bales of wool—something you saw—a hillside moving as a thousand sheep poured over its horizon, white, their backs golden with sunlight, swaying upward to a blue sky. It was the early morning sound of magpies, the hot midday sound of the reaper and binder in the five-hundred-acre-paddock. Not a sharp emotion, not gusty and ephemeral, but something that lived with you, and made a background of contentment to all your days——

And if, he thought cynically, the love of or for any woman could equal that he'd admit there might be some excuse for all the talk about it! The trouble seemed to be that it had to be both of *and* for. And that, heaven knew, was a fluke! One-sided it became dangerous, explosive, something that muttered beneath the surface of your life like a volcano. Yet it must be, nearly always, like that. The French faced it in their practical way, commented on it with their usual airy cynicism—"il y a toujours un qui baise, et l'autre qui tend la joue!" And which had the worst of it he was damned, now, if he knew! A year ago when Jim was kissing, feverishly, the cool turned cheek of Susan, he'd been afire with indignant sympathy for his brother. But now, he was learning painfully, as no doubt Susan had learned, that it is as difficult to be the loved as the lover.

More difficult perhaps. For there are many other tributes you can give besides love, but they are all rejected. Many good things which he could feel quite honestly of Susan, pity, admiration, yes, and respect—but to her they were only so many blows in the face——

And he remembered knocking at the connecting door of their rooms one night, hearing her call, "Come in," and entering. She'd swung round to the sound of the door with a look of startled fear that checked his words and movements. She'd snatched her wrapper from the back of her chair and clutched it round her. In the mirror opposite he could see the line of her cheek, her bent head. She said with an effort:

"I thought it was Kathleen at the other door. Did—did you want to speak to me?"

But he was feeling literally sick with pity. A compassion engulfed him which had nothing in it but tenderness. It had been one of those illuminating moments when one feels for the first time something one has always known; the sight of her slender body, its swiftness and litheness and the graceful vigour of its youth being slowly and relentlessly obscured by her coming maternity, had given him an instant's poignant recognition of ordeal. He'd had a moment of uncannily clear perception. Pretty awful it must be, in a way, for a woman, this sharing of her own body with another life. Mustn't they feel sometimes that they wanted to escape? Mustn't they thirst for a solitude, physical, mental, spiritual, which they couldn't ever have while the small parasite within them drew its life from theirs——

He was beside her, his arm round her shoulders. She began to shake violently. He said incoherently:

"You poor kid! Never mind——"

She twisted away from him. She flamed at him, cheeks, eyes, hair. Her voice was hoarse, stammering with anger and some indefinable pain:

"Go away! How dare you pity me! Go away——!"

4

He began to wonder where they were, and to look at the country again. Already the air was colder.

CHAPTER SIX

I

THE road just now, to Drew, was bare road and no more. It was twenty-five feet of good metalled surface, greyish, prickled with faintly glittering points of light, bounded on either side by a tearing streak of reddish earth. For the hill, that long, well-graded pull which formed the first step up from plains to mountains, was far behind them now, and ahead there was a good straight bit——

The speedometer climbed. The car, beneath Drew's hands, felt like a powerful animal. He watched the road ahead and took his foot regretfully from the accelerator. Pity that curve was coming—she'd had heaps in reserve—heaps——

Forty-five seemed like a crawl, but there were plenty of curves now. He said quickly:

"Look, Milly—what's that shrub—flowering?"

It seemed to float towards them out of the soft sage-green of its surrounding bush, a smother of cloudy pink, bloomy, greyish like the young feathers of a galah. The sun tipped it with pale furry gold——

It was behind them. Drew said, puzzled, slightly aggrieved:

"They weren't flowers at all!"

He began to look about him. A strange thing, he thought in surprise, that the sun could create flowers like that where none existed! A confoundedly peculiar thing that now, when he came to look really carefully, it was doing it everywhere—yes, he'd be hanged if it wasn't——! Everywhere he looked! The speedometer dropped to thirty. To twenty-five. Drew studied the bush.

There were flowers too. You could see them here and there—a glimmer of wattle, a flicker of amethyst over a fallen log, something white and starry near the ground. But it wasn't the flowers that were lighting it all to what was (when you looked with eyes suddenly opened by the miracle of a flowerless flowering shrub) a veritable blaze of colour. It was the sun doing things to the leaves. Turning a young gum sapling into something that dripped rubies. Flaming suddenly behind a dead leaf so that it became a topaz. Plunging into a bush with dark glossy leaves and finding purple there—bursting out again leaving streaks of silver in its wake. Silver was everywhere; the landscape glittered with it. Every gum leaf, hanging motionless with its edge to the sun, looked burnished——

And here was the railway line again and a funny little station—new-looking with another of those names——

Warrimoo——

Oh, well——!

And he said rather reprovingly to Millicent:

"There's no real need to hurry, you know. We've made a good time to here."

2

Millicent said absently:

"Yes, we've been very quick," and went on wondering.

Whether it had been rather rash even at fifty-seven to believe oneself *quite* resigned? Whether it wouldn't have been as discreet as it would certainly have been valorous, to stay at home? At Ballool? To say, "Oh, no, darling, let them go home by train, and Margaret and Colin can come down and stay with us soon"? To repudiate utterly that strange ache so suddenly resurrected, for the country—for Wondabyne——

It had been, on the whole, pretty comfortably smothered for so many years. Smothered—yes, that was a good word, suggesting peat fires, banked up smouldering—but very far from dead. There'd been a flicker when Colin went to Kalangadoo, a hungry little flame of envy and excitement. And then Susan—to Wondabyne itself. Susan coming home from time to time looking as though she were lit from within by some fierce million-candle-power vitality. Susan, nineteen, sitting on the end of her mother's bed and saying things—long, long things which for Millicent were meaningless sounds with disconnected words shining jewel-like here and there:

"Those old round stones in the creek——" "Wondabyne——three steps up to the verandah——" "Jim came over from Coolami——" "the funny clackety noise the windmills make——" "Wondabyne——" "only six shearers——" "Wondabyne——"

Well, she supposed she'd been a very bad mother——

No, she hadn't. Your children had to live their own lives. That was a cliche, a truism, but not many parents managed to put it into practice. And now here she was preening herself because she was one of the few. Whereas it had not really been because she had schooled herself not to interfere, but because interference just naturally revolted her. They were so much more interesting, the children, going their own way. And life itself became exciting—an adventure——

Behind her veil Millicent blushed.

She always blushed a little when she remembered that day. She'd behaved—oh, atrociously. Just for a minute. And then, not being used to speaking insincerities, she hadn't quite known how to go on behaving, and had sat stupidly, guiltily, staring at her daughter, until Susan, bless her, suddenly began to laugh——!

Really——

"Mother, I'm going to have a baby."

"But, *darling*! How excit——!"

And there you sat, the bitten-off word thundering in the air, the appalling truth confronting you that in this imperfect world it was not going to be exciting at all, but merely disturbing and rather unpleasant——

So that there had been nothing to do but put out a hand and feel it grabbed, and watch a frozen young face crumble into laughter and incoherent words——

Words—but they weren't only words then. They were pictures and sensations you'd thought dead, buried these thirty years. Suddenly in the rush of Susan's explanation they'd come to life. You had felt a new enthralling kinship with your daughter. Not mother and daughter now—not even fellow women by virtue of a common maternity—but two people who had drunk the country like a strong wine; who had felt it rising in them, warm, swimming, an intoxication. The beautiful country——

Oh, what matter, some part of her had cried, if Susan had found the wine too heady? It was all a question of paying fairly for what you got. There were moments in life for which you could go on paying in misery till you died, and still end up indebted! Not nature forced these payments on you—only the clumsy adjustments of a fumbling civilisation. Still, she acknowledged with a rather satirical twist of her lips, if you were going to enjoy such luxuries as electric light and wireless and the talkies and, presently, television, you must be prepared to sacrifice something—and if the sacrifice demanded happened to be your moral integrity, well, as those same talkies would have it, that was just too bad——

Never mind though—there were some left, how many one could not know, who beneath the lip-service they gave to an established order, kept their own inner selves fiercely alive and waiting. Susan was one of those. She'd left the track, and the gods of the established order had snatched her back and boxed her ears and sent her off, staggering, along their appointed road again. Prickles and thorns, prickles and thorns, dust and a deadly monotony; that was her path, but she was walking it fed by an inexhaustible conviction that all this nastiness was smeared over something fundamentally lovely—— And for Susan in particular, Millicent thought, the nastiness was really only such a thin veneer. With Bret's help she'd propitiated the gods, and now so little lay between her and the loveliness below. A few teasing cobwebby, psychological shreds, a few clinging wisps of pride, resentment, a queer tangle of vague masculine prejudices and inhibitions—things insubstantial but dangerously strong——

She found herself inconsequently remembering Bret's mother when George Maclean had brought her home to Coolami, a slender little thing with fierce straight brows and a smile which flashed abruptly and was gone before you could respond, so that you were left grinning feebly into her serious dark eyes. And the very first thing she'd done had been to pull down the house. Just as well, Millicent reflected, that there had been good years; that George had been able to satisfy her very considerable demands!

She half turned in her seat.

"Bret!"

He leaned forward:

"Yes?"

"Did you ever know what your father paid for the house at Coolami?"

"No. Must have been a good deal. The stone came from Kalula. You remember it being built, I suppose?"

She laughed a little.

"I was going to tell you what your mother said to your father one day when I was over there. She was a very definite person, Bret, wasn't she?"

"Yes."

"She said, 'George, there are houses that look like architect's advertisements and there are houses that look like acts of God. In this landscape every house should look like an act of God. Anything else is a crime.'"

Bret thought a minute, smiling. Millicent supposed, watching his face, that he was trying to imagine his mother and herself as quite young women, standing on the verandah of a Coolami he had never known. He said at last:

"I suppose that's what it does look like."

"It might have grown there," she answered.

3

Drew, driving idly, basking with a new enjoyment in the sun, watching the bush with one eye and listening with one ear to Millicent, felt a little shock, a sharp and bitter pain. It made him angry. His brows drew together and his fingers tightened and his right foot went down, down——

The road became a grey streak again and his mind a confused whirl of thoughts, of protests, of accusations and defences——

Acts of God, eh? Architects' advertisements? Well, that was a dig at Ballool, sure enough. No, it wasn't, either; Millicent didn't give one left-handed digs like that. But there it was—he knew now what she thought of the house he'd built for her. And he wondered vaguely how he knew also so suddenly and certainly that she was right; that it *was* like an architect's advertisement——

It had, he felt sure, swinging round the well-dished curves, some obscure connection with other discoveries he'd made that morning—a moment of perception, flashed and gone, when he'd noticed the peach tree; other moments more lingering and queerly pleasant when he'd been seeing, for the first time, his native bushland; some half-formed understanding as the pink, flowerless shrub faded behind him, of beauty as something not necessarily obvious. Of beauty as a fugitive, fragile, ephemeral, incredibly elusive. Not even real, sometimes; an illusion—an emotion, perhaps—a mood——

Fanciful, fanciful——

And there before him was that other fanciful thing—

that silver bit of nonsense and absurd expense! He was troubled. Disturbed by a new glimpse of some other Tom Drew than the successful hearty chap he knew so well and so sincerely respected.

"Act of God!" Stone, eh? Probably like a prison. Well, if that was what Milly liked, what she wanted——

But it wasn't. It couldn't be. Thirty-seven years it had taken him to make his money, and not even Milly knew quite how much of it he'd made. So that the house at Ballool which was, after all, the culminating outward and visible sign of his victory, *must* be perfect.

Mustn't it——?

Because if not——

It was possible, of course, that he should have allowed her more say in the building of it. But that—it would have been—it wouldn't have had——

He wrestled with his thought, which was that he hadn't wanted his gesture spoilt. His final, magnificent gesture. To take her by the hand and show it to her—a thing accomplished, perfect in its every detail, the last, the *very* last word in comfort, efficiency. *Now* are you glad you eloped with me? *Now* are you proud? *Now* do you see that there's other enterprise than country enterprise, other endeavour, other achievement——

And he *had* let her furnish it herself.

"Architect's ad——"

He took a corner so sharply that Susan called out gaily from the back, "Are you feeling suicidal, Daddy?" Because he'd suddenly remembered that Travers, coming for a final inspection with him, had actually said complacently, "Quite my best, Mr. Drew. I'm proud of it. It's a credit to us both!"

Oh, blast the house! Blast all houses! The road swung round and a signboard leapt out before them, vastly lettered:

"BULLABURRA."

"*Hell!*" though Drew furiously, roaring past it. "Jabber-jabber, confounded gibberish——!"

Millicent glanced sideways, cautiously, at his crimson face.

CHAPTER SEVEN

I

BRET looked at his watch and Susan asked him idly:

"What's the time?"

"Eight o'clock."

"Heavens! Only just breakfast time!"

"Hungry?"

"No. But I'd like a smoke."

"I've been wanting one ever since we started."

She called:

"Daddy!" and her father answered with a grunt and a movement of his head.

"We're both suffering for a cigarette. What about a halt?"

He said crossly:

"You smoke too much." And then he asked Milly. "Where do you want to have breakfast?"

She thought for a moment. She was feeling rather miserable. It was inevitable that sooner or later out of that phrase remembered from so long ago should arise a picture of the house it so justly described. "Fool! Fool!" she cried angrily at herself, staggered and humbled that she could for even a second be so forgetful, so hideously and cruelly tactless——

How strong was it—that satisfaction of Tom's? That conviction of a triumph of which his house was the symbol? Strong enough to shield him from the appalling and quite accidental justice of that stark description? She hoped feverishly that it was, and then, confusedly, that it wasn't. For Tom, the Tom she loved, was not a man of dull perceptions and she could not wish him so; he was only a man obsessed and driven. She hadn't dared, yet, to admit even to herself how much she had hoped that now, with his goal achieved, his obsession satisfied, she might find another Tom whom she'd seen so far only in glimpses—rarely—

And now she had done, perhaps, irreparable harm. Something had made him angry, hurt. You don't live with a man for one year, let alone thirty-seven, without learning to read storm-signals on his face! It could only be that. Even now his mouth looked grim and his eyes gloomy. A dozen slick remarks in praise and admiration of his house flashed into her mind but she thrust them out hurriedly. She couldn't say things so blatantly insincere, nor was Tom the man to be mollified by them. He hadn't guessed before, she was very nearly sure, that she didn't share his admiration and his pride. It had been easy enough at first to take refuge in her gratitude, her love—these went deep, and she had used them without shame to cover a dismay and a dislike which would have come near to breaking his heart. Yes, it had been very easy, confronted with one perfection after another, to turn her back on a mingled despair and amusement fast mounting to hysteria, and to follow the more fundamental cry of her heart: "How *good* he is! How kind! How hard he has worked to get all this—for me!" Her kisses, her eager gratitude had not, she knew, lacked conviction then. It hadn't really mattered at all that what he thought was gratitude for the house was really gratitude for himself——

She said slowly

"Just anywhere where there's a view, dear."

"Better go on a little farther then."

Millicent put her right hand on his knee, and for a moment his left came down from the wheel to cover it. She said eagerly:

"I've never felt so much as though I were flying," and took the little smile he gave her to her heart for comfort.

It did really, she thought, feel rather like flying, especially when, as now, you were swooping down a brief hill to climb the longer one opposite. A cemetery. Strange things, cemeteries; strange creatures, human beings, who made their ultimate terror as bleakly terrifying as they possibly could! How charming it would be if instead of white stones every grave had a tree – a flowering tree——

Her mind's eyes saw it – a wild profusion of spring blossom, a triumphant rebirth of vigour and beauty from bare winter branches. Odd that no religious sect had ever seized on that very simple and obvious allegory of resurrection——

Down again, under a railway bridge, up another hill. Houses were almost continuous, now, and away to the left, the world opened out suddenly into blue, magnificent distance.

Millicent said, staring:

"It's always lovelier than you expect it to be." And Drew slowed down so that he could glance from time to time.

They slid into the town and stopped before closed railway gates. Over the roofs of half Katoomba they could still see that serene and luminous blue, bounded by a line of strange reddish-golden cliffs.

Millicent said to Bret, who had got out to stretch his legs and was standing beside her door:

"How queer they must look from the air, Bret. All the little mountain towns buried away in this—this vastness. I'd like to see it from the air."

He nodded.

"But it's bad flying, you know. Air pockets and what not."

Drew asked:

"Is this where you want to stop? Shall we go down to—what's their show place——? Echo Point, isn't it?"

"Well," said Millicent reflectively. "I think we could find—— Perhaps Bret——" and she called to her son-in-law who had gone over like a small boy to watch the train come roaring into the station: "Bret, could you guide us to a blue view without railings?"

He came back, considering.

"Without railings? Well——"

"Or seats," Susan amended, "or notice boards."

"I see. Strictly no modern improvements. Yes, I know the place. Just go on a little way through the town and there's a turn-off to the left. I'll show you."

Susan said:

"How far is it? I'm hungry after all."

And a man in shirt sleeves coming at his leisure to open the gates, heard her, and announced, grinning:

"Every one's 'ungry 'ere. It's the hair."

Drew scowled a little, pressing his self-starter, but Millicent laughed. They bumped across the line and out on to the road again. The mountains were lost now, and they ran between railway and houses till Bret, with a: "This is where we turn off," sent them lurching up a steep hill on to a red earth road shut in on either side by bush.

He directed, leaning forward to his father-in-law:

"Just go a bit slower here—we have to turn off again on to a sort of track—I don't want to miss it."

Drew asked suspiciously:

"Track?"

"Yes, just a rough cart track. I think this is it—yes, there, on your right—see it?"

The Madison slowed ominously and stopped. Its owner stared at the track with surprise and disapproval.

"Do you expect me to take a car in there?"

Bret who had driven many cars where there was not even a track, suppressed a grin and said judicially:

"It's not bad you know, really. Just take it slowly and it won't hurt the springs."

"It couldn't," Susan asserted tactfully. "They're such marvellous springs. We haven't felt a bump all the way."

Millicent intervened:

"No, Tom, not if you'd rather not. We could follow on to the end of this road. I can see blue through the trees. We'd find somewhere nice——"

But the Madison was snorting contempt, lumbering its great front wheels up the gutter on the side of the road, climbing disdainfully on to this contemptible highway whose like it had never yet beheld, setting off along it, lurching and swaying, while Bret and Susan ducked their heads from overhanging branches——

Millicent said with genuine admiration, clinging to the side of the door:

"It's really—surprising—— It—doesn't jar one—at all."

And Drew, manœuvring gingerly among water-washed chasms, thought proudly that the rocking was like the rocking of a cradle——

2

It came, Millicent thought, suddenly, but peacefully. There was something dream-like about it, and you came to it in rather the same way that you came to a dream. You found yourself in the midst of it with no clear conception of time either before or behind you. You felt only a sense of spiritual expansion, a rapturous absorbing of unbelievable colour, as a flower might open to take in draughts of sun.

"If," thought Susan, "you'd been blind from birth, blue wouldn't mean anything to you. And then you'd get your sight and they'd point to the sky and say, 'That's blue.'" And she felt, her eyes incredulously staring, that until this moment she'd been blind and now knew for the first time what blue was really——

Languorous, unfathomable, it drowned the valley in an other-worldly light of living colour. Yes, living, and that was strange because of its stillness, its far-away silence, its infinite and dreaming calm.

It hurt, she thought, feeling a sudden wave of misery and pain, it was nerve-racking, agonising; it had that quality of emotion which some music has—she couldn't look at it—couldn't bear to look at it——

She jumped out of the car and went quickly away towards the bush, her back to a loveliness that had become unendurable. She began to pick up sticks for the billy, seeing them blurred and distorted through a haze of sudden tears.

3

Bret watched her go. Drew and Millicent were still staring wordlessly down into the valley. He got out of the car, took the hamper and looked round for a spot to picnic. A doubt in his mind was beginning to worry him acutely. Yes, he'd been bluffing about the divorce. It had been simply one of the reckless things one says when one is half silly with anger, weariness, desperation. And he'd taken it for granted that when she had said, "What a pity—I was just being glad you'd saved me the trouble of asking for it myself," she'd been bluffing too. Just letting off steam because she'd been miserable and was furious that he should have caught her crying. But now——

He was amazed that he hadn't thought of it months before. Realised that it might be, to her, a veritable deliverance. Because he'd never been able to take quite seriously that staggering assertion of hers, made so calmly and deliberately in the garden at Ballool, the day before their marriage——

And he wasn't quite sure, knowing nothing at all of women and their odd reactions, whether, taking her love for him as a fact, it made the position better for her, or worse?

He found two big stones near him, and brought a third to complete his fireplace. He rummaged in the bottom of the car for the billy and filled it from the canvas water-bag swinging muddily on the luggage-carrier. Then he got out his pocket-knife and went off to cut a green sapling.

Well, if she did want it, what then? She must have it, of course. There was nothing against it except the rather unpleasant details. The baby had died, and with it had gone the whole reason for their marriage, the whole basis of their compact. It was quite obvious to him now that as soon as she was out of the hospital he should have offered to free her legally of an obligation from which she had already been morally released. His failure to do so—his failure even to think of doing so, puzzled him. It must have been that somehow in the months she had spent with him at Coolami she had grown into the pattern of his life more closely than he'd realised. Miserable months they had been, strained, nerve-racking months, and yet, he acknowledged now, he'd felt at the time some undefined promise beyond them——

Something, too, in the thought of the child had stirred him. He'd begun to think past his own life and to realise that Coolami would remain. So that with Jim's child other children of his own should grow up.

Yes, there, he thought, cutting a neat rod and trimming it, he'd put a finger on part at least of his problem. He did want children, and it seemed, surely, rather roundabout and unnecessary, having a wife already, to divorce her, and hunt laboriously for another whom he probably wouldn't like half so well——

For he did like Susan. She was game and she was honest and, he thought, glancing at her building her sticks deftly into his fireplace, confoundedly pretty. And that was another thing. You couldn't, if you were human, live in the same house with a pretty young woman for seven months, nothing but an unlocked door between you, without wanting—yes, wanting like hell, a closer intimacy——

That, because of Jim's baby, had been, for him, quite

unthinkable. But now – when they'd somehow adjusted their lives, when they'd got the purely physical aspect of their marriage straightened out into normality – wouldn't it all right itself——?

This love business. What was it? Surely if he hadn't it already he had the ingredients! Liking, respect, admiration, physical desire. Was there anything else?

He supposed there must be. Susan had had all that for Jim and yet she'd never ceased to deny him the love she'd given so incomprehensibly to his elder brother. No, quite obviously, he admitted, hanging the billy in a notch of his stick and propping it over the back of the fireplace with a stone to weight its end, his mixture wasn't right!

"Have you matches, Bret?"

He gave them to her, watched her crouch before the fireplace with the sun on her bent head and the nape of her neck, and the tips of her dark eyelashes. Smoke began to wreathe up through the twigs, there came a faint crackling, and the air was suddenly full of the lovely aromatic fragrance of gum-leaves burning. She looked up at him, and now the sun was on her brow and the end of her nose and her teeth and her white throat, and she was smiling. A disturbing smile with effort behind it, and determination and a strange uncertainty.

"It caught beautifully, didn't it?"

He said, "Yes," abruptly, and walked away with his hands in his pockets, wondering how the devil you contended, in marriage, with a smile like that.

4

He found a tiny path, rough and steep and rocky, leading down the hill to the cliff-edges. He followed it watching his feet, lost now in confused and troubled memories.

Hot it had been this time last year—unusually hot for the spring, even in Sydney. The air in the auction-room, crowded with buyers and sellers, had seemed thick, heavy with heat and excitement. He'd been excited himself that day, because the bidding for the last of the Coolami clip had mounted well beyond what he had expected; and from the look of the stolid German, Hesslein, and the small, swift Jap with the falsetto voice, it seemed as though it would go higher still——

He could remember, too, thinking that this auctioneer—one he'd never seen before—was a genius in his way. There was something like wizardry in the deftness with which he plucked out of pandemonium the voice of the first bidder; he had a perpetual faint smile and a trick of looking over his glasses; it made him appear indulgent, slightly disdainful, incredibly aloof——

It was peculiar, now he thought of it, how ridiculously detailed was his memory of that particular sale. Was he always so observant? Was it merely that impressions slid into his consciousness and out again because nothing happened to fix them there? It did seem now as if that scene must have been frozen into his mind indelibly by what followed it, because he could remember with photographic accuracy every face in the top tier opposite where at the moment he heard his name called, the little Jap was feverishly capering——

Some one had called him, and then several others had echoed helpfully:

"Mr. Maclean! Mr. Maclean!"

He looked along the row to a man whom he knew slightly and who was making explanatory gestures towards the door.

"Chap outside wants to speak to you," some one offered. "Says it's urgent."

He had pushed his way out of the room.

He hadn't ever known who the man was, but no face in the world was more clearly driven in upon his memory. He could see it now, lean and brown, all twisted up with embarrassment and a queer frightening pity——

"It's your brother, Mr. Maclean—car accident—he's in the Sydney Hospital. He said we'd find you here——"

Ken had been in Melbourne at the time, so he'd known at once it was Jim. He didn't think he'd spoken at all. Not in the lift, not in the street. Only once, in the taxi, he seemed to have a vague memory of his own voice saying: "Serious?" and the man's answering something that made his mouth go dry and his head throb with a sudden violent headache——

It hadn't looked much like Jim—the face half-covered with bandages, the other half yellowish white, sunburn without blood beneath it——

He'd said:

"Is that you, Bret? I can't see properly."

"Yes."

"Listen—something important. Are you listening?"

"Yes. Go on."

"Susan. Yesterday—she told me—she was going to have a baby——"

He'd stopped, his eyes closed as if gathering strength to speak again. In himself, like a spark in dry timber Bret had felt his dislike of Susan flame into hatred. Illogically enough, as he admitted now, he'd thought of her as directly responsible for the death that even now was shadowing Jim's face. It tore his heart with pity and resentment that, suffering, dying, his brother could think of her, could spend his last moments in worrying about her, his last breath in speaking of her——

"Of course—I've always wanted—marry her. She wouldn't. Now——"

"Yes," thought Bret, bitterly, cynically, "'now——'!"

"She—wanted last night to think it over. Said she'd meet me at the flat. To-day. I—was going there——"

Going there! To her. And if he hadn't been, Bret's thoughts had raved blackly, he wouldn't have been hurt, killed——

"Think it over!" Another night to torment him was what she'd wanted, the——

Staring at the blue valley he put his hand suddenly to his eyes. For his thoughts of her then had been so dark, so ugly with fury and contempt and bitterness that he couldn't even now remember them without shrinking.

Jim's voice had broken in on them, hoarse and dragging with effort:

"I want you—go there—tell her—see her through—look after the kid——"

He was glad now that he'd had enough control to say, "Yes. Yes, Jim, all right, I will." The boy hadn't been able to speak any more after that, or perhaps to hear either, and there'd been a ghastly interminable hour of sunlight and silence and queer hospital smells while he lay there and struggled with the breath that was so soon to forsake him——

CHAPTER EIGHT

I

FAR down in the valley between the tree-tops which looked, from here, like so much dark moss spread upon the ground, his eye caught a glint of silver. His eye caught it and his brain seized upon it too, feverishly seeking an escape from thoughts too torturing and profitless——

A creek down there. He tried to follow it but it lost itself among the trees. He looked farther across the valley at tiny scattered farmhouses and wondered vaguely what sort of a living they made. He sat down on a rock and realised with surprise that he hadn't had his cigarette yet, and decided he'd prefer a pipe after all. His thoughts began to dart about upon the immediate surface of *here* and *now*, like wary skaters on thin ice. He looked across towards the Black Ranges and regretted that he'd never, after all, found time to explore them as he'd always meant to when he was a boy. Wild country; they said there was gold there. You'd want to be in condition for it, and to have another good bushman with you. Jim——

And the Wild Dog Ranges out beyond the Cox. Queer names began to drift back to him, touched with the glamour of his boyhood. Tumbledown Mountain and Toppleover Peak. And the Cloudmaker——

High cliffs and tangled gullies dwarfed into deceptive flatness by the great expanses round them. Savage country, all but unknown, drowned in its mysterious and ineffable blue——

What a feat they'd performed, those chaps, those pioneers! Almost incredible that they should ever have got through at all! Miraculous, when you thought of the place they'd passed farther down where the road and the railway crawled huddled together along a ridge with the world falling away on either side.

A pebble rolled beside him. He looked up and saw Susan standing on the path.

2

Millicent left the car at last with a little sigh. Drew had climbed out rather stiffly a few moments earlier and was now hovering with the chamois-leather in his hand, rubbing and scowling at a faint scratch from a branch on one of the doors. Near the fire Susan was still crouching with a matchbox in her hand, watching the flames; and Bret's head and shoulders were just visible over there on the scrubby hillside.

She turned back ruefully to the blue view she had demanded and wondered if it had anything to do with the sudden illogical depression which had gripped her. Probably, she decided; almost certainly. Because a sight like that broke down your defences, opened your heart, made you in an instant mysteriously receptive. While you looked at it any small pleasure could become a joy almost unbearably poignant; and any anxieties could be transformed into veritable monsters of menace or despair.

So that now, for the moment, it had become unspeakably dreadful to be married to a cross man with a chamois-leather; to see your daughter with the wings of her youth drooping and bedraggled; to watch your son-in-law going off by himself to think and worry, not knowing how beautifully simple and how simply beautiful his life could be. To wonder about Colin, and whether, as Margery so stoutly maintained, he was really—had really given up——

And to live in a house at Ballool——

And to be fifty-six with life behind you—spirited away somehow when you weren't looking——

And to be made to feel, in the face of all this beauty and vastness, exactly like an ant, incredibly small, and quite ludicrously unimportant——

Oh, well——!

And anyhow, she concluded, making a swift grimace of defiance at the view before she turned her back on it, it was very possible that the divinest discontent might be unromantically allied with the emptiest stomach. So she went over to the fire and began to unpack the hamper, watching Susan out of the corner of her eye.

Susan hadn't even seen her. Heaven only knew what she was thinking, with her dark eyes fixed so absent-mindedly on the fire.

3

She was thinking that whatever else might be said for honesty it was, from her own experience, about as bad a policy as one could have. Perhaps her thinking had been wrong, but it had been honest; perhaps the very honesty of her actions had been the most foolish thing about them.

When you were nineteen and very pretty there were always lots of men about. That was all right, and quite enjoyable, but you couldn't help thinking that some day you had to marry one of them. And then what? You found yourself facing, at the end of this gaily lighted path of dalliance, mysteries, silence. It didn't help you very much to read the books which Mum, bless her heart, had always left so cleverly where you'd find them. Facts were better than nothing but they weren't feelings. When you married you wanted to feel *sure* it was going to be all right—you wanted to feel you could have your husband's children with joy that they were his as well as with joy that they were your own. And Love? What was that? You heard people say, "It comes after marriage." Well, if it did, that was all right, but supposing it didn't? You were in the soup, weren't you?

It did seem, however you looked at it, as if a girl were expected to buy a pig in a poke, which was to say the least of it a bit unreasonable, seeing that it was upon her fell all the weight of so many matrimonial miseries. And she'd thought of Mrs. Haversham, on crutches for a year, Mrs. Osban, three months in a hospital, having operation after operation—— She'd thought of young Mrs. Hunt, laughing with her over the front gate of her new cottage in Ballool, and four days later dead, with a dead baby at her side. And Daddy's sister, Aunt May, in her wheeled chair, drained and brittle and ghostly with her ten dreary children about her——

And they hadn't been sickly women. It was just that such things might happen to *you*—and you wanted to be pretty sure that you didn't dislike your husband before they began, because if you did you'd jolly well hate the sight of him before they were over!

And then Wondabyne—Jim. It was hard to believe, when you looked at Jim, that you weren't in love with him. You should be. What a pity that you weren't! Perhaps as they said, after marriage——? But by that time you'd be caught.

She remembered her mother saying once when she was a child: "But darling, just having a lot of red hair doesn't mean that you can make your own rules."

But she'd made them and she'd stuck to them. Even when she'd begun to discover that a situation you've been controlling may grow and develop and expand until it overwhelms you, till you're as helpless in it as a baby——

Because the love still hadn't come, but it was harder than she'd expected to retreat in good order. The tormented misery of the young man she wasn't in love with had become in the end as strong a tyranny as love itself. She was confused by it, vaguely frightened, desperately sorry for him. But not contrite, not remorseful. Never that. She hadn't pretended. She hadn't promised. She had denied and still denied responsibility.

"I don't love you, Jim."

"But you will——!"

"Possibly. I don't know."

And always, though in the end it had become to both of them a kind of torture, she'd reiterated desperately, half-asleep sometimes, with strain and exhaustion:

"I don't love you, I don't love you——"

Because she'd begun, by that time, to know something about love. It was still as mysterious, as unreasonable an emotion as ever, but it had begun to take shape, to solidify, to press down on her like some vast heavy shadow, to drug her mind with a dull weariness, to weight her body with lassitude. Because Bret so obviously disliked her. Because his contempt for her showed so plainly, and was so bitterly unjust. She must have been, she thought now, in a very queer mental state just then. Just as she had tried to fall in love with Jim, so she had tried, struggling helplessly, not to fall in love with Bret. Amazing that she should have recognised it as love, this dull, unpleasant ache, so different from her imagined ecstasies! It wasn't any use. There it was, heavy and leaden and oppressive; She knew well enough its utter hopelessness. But she had, driven by some obscure and not-to-be-denied instinct, cut adrift from Jim with a suddenness and a ruthlessness which surprised herself.

Until——

It had been an inspiration—that vague memory of a brother of Margery's practising somewhere in one of the eastern suburbs. He'd been helpful and kind and matter-of-fact.

"Can you—well, is the father in a position to marry you?"

"Yes—oh, yes, he could——"

"Well, that's the best thing to do, you know. For the baby's sake."

"Yes."

She'd gone out rather stupidly and sat alone for a long time in a park. She'd felt so muddled and tired that she'd actually slept for a little while in the sun with her head falling back against a tree behind the seat. And when she'd awakened there was a woman at the other end staring at her curiously.

"You all right?"

"Oh, yes—yes, thank you, I'm quite all right."

And suddenly she was. Not that the muddle and the misery were gone, but that she saw her way through them with clearness and decision. It wasn't any use blaming her theories; they'd been sound enough, and they had actually warned her. She could see the very sentence standing out at the bottom of a left-hand page: "*No method is 100 per cent. safe.*" Well, she'd been the hundredth. She'd taken a gamble and lost and the time was come for forfeits. No one, except possibly Mother, would believe that in marrying Jim she would be taking, for the child's sake, what was to her incomparably the harder way out. But there it was. If there was any suffering to be done it was only fair that the child shouldn't do it. So she'd stood up and straightened her hat, and gone off to ring up Jim——

A funny hot day, restless, feverish. When she'd opened the door of the flat there'd been a smell of faded flowers, and she wondered how long they would have stayed there if she hadn't had to come back. Till the lease was up probably, at the end of the month. Jim wouldn't have come here——

And she'd opened a window and sat at it staring out at the city skyline till she heard him come in. He'd stood at the door looking at her, some hope he couldn't quite subdue burning behind his eyes. It wouldn't, she reflected rather bitterly, have taken a great actress to play then the part which would have smoothed everything out so prettily! She could have done it without a word, and certainly as far as policy went dishonesty would have been the card to play! She hadn't played it—and here she was. And Jim dead, and Bret——

Poor Jim!

She moved suddenly, dropping the matchbox, her face puckered with remembered pain. The long hot afternoon, the droning rattle of trams far below, the slapping of a blind cord against the window-sill, their two voices——

"Susan, you'll see—this will make you feel different——"

"Perhaps it will, Jim."

"Susan, don't you hope it's a boy?"

"Yes—no—I—I don't mind much, Jim."

"This—Susan—this doesn't make you hate me?"

"Jimmy, darling, don't be silly. It wasn't your fault."

"When shall we be married? To-morrow?"

To-morrow! She'd never known a word to hit like a bludgeon before. To-morrow! And already the daylight fading outside the windows! Weariness and desperation and the panicky feeling of being cornered had swept her to her feet, to snatch up her hat, to fumble in the dusk for her bag. To-morrow! And she'd had a grotesque vision of the few hours between now and then shooting away like a tunnel into some fourth dimension to which she might fly, and hide——

"But, Susan, you're not going——?"

"Yes—I—I must, Jim."

"No—don't go yet. We haven't decided——"

"Oh, Jim, don't—let me go. It's so hot and I'm so tired. I want to think about it. I'll come back to-morrow. To-morrow afternoon. About three."

So she'd come back next day. But it wasn't Jim who had met her there——

4

Millicent said hurriedly:

"Susan, let's go down where Bret is. I'm sure the view's better from the cliff edge. The billy won't boil yet for a few minutes——"

The child mustn't be allowed, she was thinking anxiously, to stay *too* long among thoughts which painted her face so clearly with unyouthful anguish. So she put the sandwiches back in the hamper and shut the lid down and repeated:

"Come on, darling."

Susan said, "Ouch! I'm stiff! Give me your hand, Mother," and pulled herself to her feet. Drew joined them.

"Where's Bret?"

Millicent pointed. "We're just going down to see what he's seeing," and her husband, slapping a jumper ant from his trouser leg, grunted:

"No more than we can see from here."

"No-o," Millicent conceded it regretfully. "But it feels better from the very edge, don't you think?"

They went in single file down the steep track, Susan ahead. Millicent loitered, making difficulties for her feet where none existed. It had suddenly occurred to her that here possibly Susan and Bret might—might talk more clearly see more clearly, feel more clearly—whatever it was they needed——

For evidently during Bret's two days at Ballool they hadn't come any nearer to a solution. That she thought she could understand. They had met then for the first time under totally new conditions. Susan must now seem to Bret, Millicent thought, the third of a series of Susans. First the callous disturber of his brother's peace; second the mother of his brother's child; and now, simply his own wife. Difficult for him, no doubt, to keep up the necessary mental adjustments. And for Susan, unspeakably painful. She must have thought to herself many times in the months since the child's death, that nothing held him to her now but the bare legal contract. That wasn't a pleasant thought for any normal young woman. Susan had grown very quiet on it.

In that encountering of his uncertainty and her constraint, they couldn't possibly, she thought stopping dead, have done any adjusting at all!

"What is it?" Tom asked behind her.

Here, Millicent pondered hopefully, they were on—on neutral territory. Cut adrift for the moment from the externals of their everyday lives they might see each other, savingly, as individuals unhampered by past happenings. So she said:

"I'm tired and it's too stony. Help me back, Tom." And she called to Susan:

"Darling, I'm not coming any farther. My shoe pinches."

Susan stopped. She looked from her parents' already retreating figures to her husband's bent head.

She couldn't, as she'd seen lambs do at Coolami, run after her mother, bleating. So she went on slowly down the hill.

CHAPTER NINE

I

BRET looked up at her. She thought: "He's been remembering too." So many times during her months at Coolami she'd seen his face wither and close, his eyes blank, opaque, hiding his memories behind them——

And he said, taking his pipe out of his mouth and standing up:

"If you really want a divorce, Susan, it can be arranged." He didn't look at her.

Heights hadn't ever affected her before. But now she saw the blueness below begin to revolve faster and faster like a whirlpool and the rock she stood on seemed to tilt forward to meet it. She sat down suddenly on the ground and shut her eyes. Bret turned, and thought, troubled, how white her face looked against the cornflour-blue of her flannel frock and the impetuous red of her hair. He asked:

"Have you had your cigarette?" And she answered stumblingly:

"No–I–didn't–I forgot–thanks."

He lit it for her and felt her cheek against his cupped hands as he held the match. She said presently:

"I don't really want it–but——"

"Yes?"

"I think–in some ways it might be the best thing to do."

"In what ways?"

"Well–it isn't much good, is it, as things are now?"

He said with sudden harshness:

"It's utterly impossible as things are now. If we go on we've got to have some—some basis of understanding. I don't only mean that you've got to be my wife in the ordinary sense of the word, but that we must—somehow——" he made a helpless gesture—"clear the air."

She said nothing, flicking her cigarette-ash off with the tip of her finger. He went on slowly:

"No matter how much we talk there's always—there always seems to be—a constraint—the whole atmosphere's thick with things we're feeling and not saying——"

He stopped, looked at her and asked:

"Isn't it?"

She answered carefully:

"I don't think there's anything I've felt and left unsaid."

He knocked his pipe out on the rock beside him and considered this. He was inclined to believe she was right. She had been, from the very first of her affair with Jim, quite definite completely honest. As far as it was possible to make herself understood by words she had done so. It was himself who had shirked——

No, not shirked. It had been merely that the obscurity of his feelings had been too much for his powers of self-expression. He hadn't ever had to analyse himself before. He hadn't ever known that such confusion of thought and sensations could be possible to an ordinary and rational man——

Susan said lightly:

"Do you want another declaration from me?"

He turned on her sharply, his first reaction of anger fading into compassion and regret. There was no denying it, the kid had pluck, and there was a kind of splendour in her uncompromising honesty, disconcerting though it was——

He said, "You know I don't. Let's say the air's thick with things I've felt and left unsaid. It's not that I wouldn't be willing to say them if I thought it would do any good; it's only that I don't know how to – I don't see them clearly enough myself——"

"It all seems pretty hopeless. Perhaps there's nothing for it but the divorce."

"And yet there isn't much sense in that. You say you don't want it and I certainly don't. Why, then?"

She looked at him for a moment silently, curiously. At last she said:

"Hasn't it ever occurred to you that some day you'll probably fall in love, and then – well, it won't be very convenient to be married – really quite unnecessarily – to some one else."

He answered shortly:

"I don't seem to be the loving sort. I don't understand it. I don't think I want to." And added, half-defiantly, "I suppose that sounds brutal."

She shook her head.

"You can't give what you haven't. I know that." And he said with sudden fierce resentment:

"Why the hell do you keep on reminding me——? This devilish parallel——"

She said coldly:

"There is a parallel. We won't get anywhere by pretending to forget it." And she added, stung forward by her temper and the pain of her thwarted love for him, "I don't know why you aren't enjoying its poetic justice."

He put his pipe in his pocket and stood up.

"It's no good, Susan." He looked down blackly at her impassive face and lowered lashes. "We always end up with a row—bickering, hurting each other accidentally or deliberately, insults—other things——"

He paused for a moment. Each of them, in the rough, pebbly ground beneath their eyes, saw a long procession of unlovely incidents—of words forged by their speaker's pain into instruments of torture, of actions twisted with the inspired ingenuity of mental suffering, into veritable nightmares, of kisses like blows and caresses rotten with a taint of cruelty——

Bret said abruptly:

"It's ugly. It can't go on, Susan."

She agreed: "No," still without looking at him. And then she asked half-absently, "Why don't you want the divorce, Bret?"

He frowned, marshalling for her the reasons he had, not long ago, been discovering for himself.

"I like you, I admire you, I want you, and I want children."

It sounded, he thought, very adequate. But the bleakness of the smile in her quick glance flung up before him again baffling mysteries impenetrable to him. He said angrily:

"And sound enough reasons, too."

She said dryly:

"Very rational indeed."

"They don't satisfy you?"

"They don't satisfy me at all."

He said, "Hell!" under his breath and sat down again. He asked desperately:

"Then why don't *you* want it?"

There wasn't any bleakness in the smile she gave him

then. It warmed her pallor, lit her eyes, twisted something in him with sudden pain.

"I'm afraid I'm not very rational," she said.

He put his hand out and touched her foot.

"What a mess it is!"

"Yes. I'm sorry you got dragged into it."

"You meant," he said, at last with an effort, "that in spite of all the mess you—don't want to leave me. Is that it?"

She put her chin on her hand and began to scribble on the ground with a piece of stick. She said drearily:

"It isn't quite as simple as that. What it amounts to is that I—can't leave you. Even if we were divorced, even if I went right away, out of the country—I'd still be in love with you." And she added quickly, "Don't tell me I'm young and I'll get over it."

"I wasn't going to." He looked at her curiously. "Your point is that a divorce wouldn't free you at all."

"It wouldn't free me of what I feel for you, and—it would——"

"Well?"

"It would take me away from Coolami."

He stared.

"Would you mind that?"

She said angrily, blinking her eyes.

"Of course I'd mind it."

He stood up again and walked restlessly to the cliff-edge. It was there all round him again; Coolami. A possession which instinctively he snatched to himself, hearing some alien footfall—— He didn't know at all which of many warring emotions was uppermost in his mind; he didn't know whether the newcomer was an enemy, an invader to be jealously repelled, an admirer to be condescendingly admitted—a fellow-worshipper of his treasure—to be welcomed perhaps—to share——?

He said over his shoulder:

"For what it may be worth to you, a divorce would certainly free you in one way——"

And with his words pictures ran fiercely through his mind as he knew they were running, too, through hers. He remembered his visit to Ballool two months ago.

He remembered a drive back with her from a theatre when slowly mounting dark tides in him had broken into storm as he stopped the car in front of the steps——She was pulling her cloak round her, and he had put his arm across and re-closed sharply the door she had opened.

"Susan!" His voice sounded queer even to himself, but her little gasp and involuntary recoil made him suddenly furious. Blast the girl, what did she take him for? He said hurtfully:

"Why try this shrinking virgin stuff with me? Do you expect me to believe it?"

She answered bitterly, breathless:

"I don't expect you to believe anything good of me—ever!"

The faint scent which was always about her and all her belongings—camphor and something else, it smelt like, had forced back on his memory ever since, those ugly moments. She didn't struggle—only resisted, mentally and physically rigid, and at last her absolute passivity had chilled him. He could see her in the half darkness, sitting very still, crouching almost, in the corner of the seat with her hair dishevelled and her arms over her face. He'd realised, in a moment of acute shame and nausea, her utter helplessness. He'd leaned across her abruptly and opened the door, and she had pulled her cloak round her shoulders and disappeared without a word. He'd taken the car round to the garage and sat in it for a long time with his elbows on the steering-wheel and his forehead resting on his hands——

And he wondered now, looking moodily across the valley, which of several such scenes she was remembering——

But she had begun to laugh helplessly. She had a pretty laugh with an upward running inflection; it always called quite irresistibly to an answering smile in him. He asked, turning:

"What's the joke?"

She looked rather downcast. "I—it wasn't a joke really. It was horrid when it happened. It would be horrid, I suppose, if it happened again. But it suddenly seemed funny." She glanced at him apologetically.

He said: "Tell me about it," wishing that a mutual sense of humour were all that was needed for matrimonial felicity. But she hesitated. Because actually it had all been so definitely and abruptly unpleasant that she was not sure now where in its murky shadows she had caught her momentary gleam of the comic.

She'd been brushing her hair, and then in a second she was off her balance, the stiff bristles digging into her neck, her throat strained backward painfully beneath the violence of his kiss. In a panic of sheer physical pain she had fought insanely. The buckle of his wrist-watch had made a long crimson scratch on her arm. Misery and weakness had taken the fight out of her suddenly and she'd crumpled up with a sobbed appeal:

"Bret—don't—you're hurting me so!"

His hands had dropped to his sides and they had stood rather dazedly staring at each other. He looked at her arm.

"Did I do that?"

"It—was your watch, I think." She'd pulled her wrapper over it and laughed nervously. "It's nothing—it was just that I could hardly breathe."

He'd said, "What the hell's the matter with us, Susan?" And looked at her as if he expected her to know the answer——

And somehow, in that there had been a laugh. She said, "I was thinking—do you remember when you scratched me with your wrist-watch?"

He looked at her blankly. "Were you laughing at that?"

"I—Bret—if we—supposing you were in love you'd laugh too. It would seem so—absurd—so much a complicating of things that aren't really complicated—I don't suppose you see what I mean——"

He said grimly:

"I only see that I lost my head and my temper. It doesn't amuse me much. That's what I mean you'd be free of if we were divorced."

She said soberly:

"There won't be any more scenes like that."

And when he stared at her uncomprehendingly, she said with a sudden flame, "Well, I'm coming back with you, aren't I? We'll be home to-morrow. I'm not a fool, Bret."

He shook his head ruefully.

"If good intentions could make a marriage, Susan, ours would be a winner. We've both tried hard enough."

She stood up looking at him with a strange little smile.

"The tea's probably cold," she said. "Dad's been saying, 'Call them,' and Mother's been saying, 'Leave them alone.' Come on, Bret."

He followed her. Half-way up the path she paused and looked back at him.

"Trying's no good," she said. "I'm going to play-act."

He said sharply:

"Don't do that. At least you've been honest. Acting won't help us."

Her smile curled into open contempt.

"You won't know it's acting," she said.

CHAPTER TEN

I

No, Drew thought, sipping his mug of strong tea and watching them come up the path, Millicent's elaborately wangled tête-à-tête hadn't done much good after all. Susan walking ahead with her chin up looked—well, when she was a kid, her father thought grimly, that expression on her face had many times been followed by a spanking!

What the deuce, he wondered, passing Millicent two mugs for them, had she been saying to that husband of hers to make him look so white about the gills? And in a sudden surge of sympathy for a harassed fellow-male he decided that women were the very devil—and his daughter in the first flight of them——

So he made room for Bret on the rug, passed him his tea, offered him sugar, plied him with sandwiches and hard-boiled eggs, assuring him mutely of his moral support in a world most insufferably complicated by the moods and the whimsies of women.

Susan, disdaining the rug, had perched on a rock nearby. She was merry and voluble, talking at Bret and round him, her words darting, stinging, retreating, stinging again. There wasn't, Drew marvelled irritably, anything you could get hold of at all, and yet she kept you wincing, not so much from what she had said as from what you thought she was going to say next. You couldn't ignore her any more than you could ignore a wasp circling within inches of your head. Not that Bret wasn't making a very good show of it, looking at the valley, eating his way stolidly and silently through a large ham sandwich——

Drew looked helplessly at Millicent.

Lord how these women hung together. She was staring at her daughter with unmixed pity, and she said suddenly:

"Susan, bring your breakfast, and walk along to that point with me."

Susan stopped in mid-sentence and faded. It did really seem to her father as though Millicent's words had turned out a light somewhere inside her. Her eyes flickered for a moment, startled like the eyes of some one suddenly awakened. She bit into her hard-boiled egg, looked at Bret, looked at her mother, stood up:

"All right, Mother. Come on."

They went. Drew cleared his throat and said weightily to Bret:

"A queer thing, that blue. Never been satisfactorily explained, I understand——"

2

Bret said, "No?" refilling his mug from the billy. For the second time that morning he was staggered by his own capacity for silent fury. No one, nothing in the world had ever got under his skin as surely as Susan—or Susan's pride, or Susan's misery, or whatever it was that drove her when she had these devilish and impossible moods——

But this time beneath his anger some obscure, panicky doubt was pricking him.

"*You won't know it's acting.*"

There was, in that, an implied contempt for his perceptiveness that bit deeper because of an uneasy suspicion that it might be justified. Would he? She must, he reasoned, be pretty damn sure of herself to say that. As a burglar, who said, "I'm going to break into your house to-night by the kitchen window," would need to be pretty damn sure that his victim was a half-wit. "*You won't know——*"

Did she think him that? Emotionally half-witted? And with the phrase he was aware of a sudden revelation. Was that what it was—this confounded love business—a sixth sense? It sounded all right. I see, I taste, I smell, I hear, I feel, I love. Plausible, quite. Which meant, seeing that your emotions came to you through your senses, that you were, lacking that sixth sense, an emotional half-wit——

And if it meant that, it meant also that no emotion came to you complete. No music stirred you to the full range of its power; no beauty yielded you the completeness of its perfection. No flavour, no scent, no touch——

He began to see things, dimly. Susan backing away a step or two from him last night before she realised what she was doing. Susan standing still looking so desperately miserable that he'd sworn under his breath with uncomprehending exasperation, and gone out on the balcony to sit on the stretcher-bed so tactfully and casually left there by Millicent, and smoke, and think, and rage——

Well, he was seeing glimmers of what might be daylight now. He was getting very vaguely and uncertainly somewhere near her point of view. He remembered a fellow who'd come up with Ken, once to Coolami. Who'd gone round the place staring and appraising, who'd seen it all in the green bursting vigour of a good season, who'd watched the lorries loaded with wool-bales go out in file, as glamorous a sight as any treasure-laden fleet of Spanish galleons; who'd ridden with him over sprawling acres more securely his kingdom than the lands of many a crowned monarch. Who'd nodded reflectively at last and conceded: "Well, I suppose it pays all right——"

Was it from some such blundering obtuseness in himself that Susan had backed away last night? Could you blame her if it was? If an instinct she couldn't quite subdue withheld her from giving him something he hadn't the necessary sense—the sixth sense—to appreciate?

So that finally, of this obtuseness, this half-wittedness of his senses, she was driven to make an ignoble ally. When the time came, which was so close upon them, for the inevitable compromise, it would be these senses she would beguile—as one might beguile some shuffling moron—secure in the knowledge of his emotional deformity——

And he wouldn't know——

He stood up so suddenly that he upset his forgotten mug of tea, and began mechanically to brush away with his handkerchief a few splashes on his sock and trouser-leg.

The thought that her savage little gibe might be true appalled him. He wouldn't know, because he hadn't the sense to know with. Any more than he could know if he were blind, all the loveliness of Coolami, or hear if he were deaf that sudden far-away chorus of tolwongs from the valley——

Drew asked:

"What's wrong? Jumper ant bite you?"

Bret laughed:

"No—no thanks—nothing—I—I just thought I saw one on my leg——"

"There are some about. Painful, the sting, for a moment or two. Funny thing the way it starts to itch lik hell about a week after you've been bitten——"

"No," replied Bret absently, and his father-in-law said, "Hey?" glanced at him sharply and muttered, "Oh, well—better be getting on, perhaps——"

He called to Millicent and Susan, and began to repack the hamper. Bret said suddenly:

"It looks like rain over there."

Drew scowled at the bank of dark clouds lying like a distant smoke-screen along the western sky. "That means we'll have to put the hood up. Might as well do it now while Susan and Milly pack."

Bret, grappling with his side of the hood and side-curtains, was thinking that his discovery hadn't helped him much. There was still a very practical situation to be faced, and two long lives to be lived in whatever degree of happiness could be achieved——

But his anger against Susan was gone. That was something. And he smiled at her as she came up with the hamper, glanced at the still virgin glory of the Madison's bonnet and said with pretended apprehension, "We're going to get splashed!" to which she replied in an awed whisper, "Not God Himself would *dare*——"

After that, absurdly enough, he felt more cheerful. There began to creep over him one of those irresponsible moods which, because of his more usual soberness, swept him sometimes into incredible depths of foolery. It was at such times that he and Susan, clowning together, had always hit it off best. They had escaped into buffoonery as into the unreal sawdust world of a circus-ring, and there, forgetting everything, they'd capered and somersaulted and jumped through hoops in a kind of wild holiday abandon.

But Susan, somehow, didn't seem to catch his mood this time. She sat in her corner of the back seat, and though she smiled and chaffed her father's careful manœuvres through the scrub, she seemed, really, rather sober and withdrawn.

Drew came out on to the main road and turned westward again with obvious relief. He called back to Bret:

"We put in a solid hour there. Never mind, plenty of time. How far to Mudgee?"

"About a hundred. Take you over three hours, not knowing the road. Three and a half if it rains."

But Millicent protested:

"We've all day before us, Tom. And there's heaps of food still. We could have lunch by the road. It's only going to be a shower."

3

Susan was thinking that a year ago when she'd walked blindly out into the street from the block of flats, with Bret silent and inimical at her side, the sky had looked just as it did now. He'd put her into a taxi, said shortly, "I'll come to-night," and then she'd been alone with new refinements of suffering to face——

And nothing much to face them with. The half-hour she'd just been through with Bret had left her mind feeling as her body might have felt after being flung ashore from a heavy surf, aching, limp, helpless with exhaustion.

She'd gone down the passage to the door of their flat thinking, curiously enough, of Bret. Not thinking anything in particular about him, but just holding a mental image of him up before her mind as one will try in the midst of illness or pain to remember happier things. So that when the door had opened swiftly from inside, and she'd seen not Jim, but Bret himself confronting her, her little involuntary cry of his name had been only a continuation, really, of her thoughts. She must have looked, she supposed, rather ghastly, because he said at once:

"You know?"

But she'd only stared at him. He seemed malevolent, implacable, and the pallor of his face was like something smeared unevenly over its surface. She'd said with sudden tearing anxiety:

"Are—are you ill? What's the matter?"

He shook his head, and she with a flare of resentment that this hard thing should be made, by his presence, so unbearably harder, demanded sharply:

"Where's Jim?"

He'd crossed the room, flung a window up, turned and hurled the words at her as if he'd hoped they'd kill her:

"He's dead."

"*Dead*?"

Her repetition was the merest whisper, but it hovered and echoed about them interminably. Susan could remember putting her hands up vaguely, stupidly, as though there were something she could brush away——

Bret had turned back to the window; she wanted to speak to him but couldn't think of the words she needed. She could only wonder dully how she had come to be sitting on the end of the couch, and feel a rambling surprise that she had not fainted or screamed or fallen down——

But quite soon, if she wasn't careful, she'd go to sleep——

Her head sagged sideways, her eyes closed; with her last remnant of consciousness she tried to open them and couldn't——

It must have been only minutes, for when she woke again with a shiver Bret was still standing at the window with his back to her. But it had felt like years, it had felt like a whole blessed eternity, cutting her off as cleanly as a knife from the horrors on the other side. Nature, she thought now, watching the bush by the side of the road, its riotous colour subdued by the coming storm into a soft opaque grey-green, was extraordinarily ingenious. She cared less than nothing how you suffered until your suffering brought you to a point where your biological usefulness, either mental or physical, was endangered. Then, sharply efficient, she took things in hand. Sleep swooped like a black curtain between you and the shocks under which your whole brain and body were reeling. Not rest exactly but respite. Something that hid you for a few moments even from yourself. Probably, Susan reflected, it was a form of anæsthetic to keep you quiet while she went on doing things to you. Steadying your heart and smoothing out your nerves and making mysterious adjustments to all your too-rudely disturbed mechanism——

Anyhow, when she did wake again she was curiously calm. The few moments when she might have panicked had been deftly stolen away from her. She stood up and went steadily enough to the door.

"I'm going home," she said, but he turned so sharply

that she stopped with her hand half outstretched to the doorknob.

"No," he said, "I want to talk to you. Sit down."

She went back slowly to the couch. She wasn't thinking of him much now. Her whole mind, since waking from that brief black sleep, had been busy with the child. He came away from the window and stood facing her across the table. He said coldly:

"Are you all right? I've got to talk to you and it might as well be at once."

She said:

"I'm all right," and then wondering rather that it hadn't occurred to her to ask before, "How–what happened?"

"He was crossing the street–coming here." There was an accusation in the last words, she winced, not at it, but at his tone. "He–a car skidded and knocked him down; he hit his head on the corner of the pavement. They took him to the hospital and sent for me. He–didn't live long."

She twisted her hands together in her lap. Bret went on:

"He told me to come here–and tell you."

She looked at him dumbly, and he flared out with sudden savage brutality:

"Are you satisfied now you've killed him?"

The room, his furious, accusing face, danced crazily before her eyes but her voice was calm enough:

"Please don't say that. Don't think it. For your own sake as well as mine. It isn't true."

He said menacingly:

"He wanted to marry you. He wanted you in a way you didn't deserve to be wanted. All you could give him was–this——"

His little gesture swept herself, the flat, and all her hours in it with Jim, into a common limbo of unpleasantness. She sat up a little straighter and her voice had a crisper edge:

"'This,' whether you believe it or not, had its beauty—for both of us."

He retorted angrily: "Precious little for Jim."

She looked past him, seeing things he couldn't see. Jim on his knees by her chair, his vivid face alight with happiness, Jim with a towel round his waist helping her to wash up in their tiny kitchen. Jim reading aloud to her, Jim coming in with his arms full of parcels and flowers, Jim asleep——

She said slowly:

"You haven't any right to say that. You don't know. No one knows now—but myself. Anyhow," she added thoughtfully, "it filled a time that might have been filled more harmfully elsewhere."

"'Elsewhere,'" Bret said bitterly, "he'd have gone without illusions."

She looked straight at him.

"If he had illusions about me," she said, "it wasn't my doing. I never promised him, or led him to hope for more than I could give."

"You couldn't give much, could you?"

She flushed.

"Not to him."

"Although he gave everything to you."

She'd grown a little angry then, nervous, edgy with strain and grief.

"Haven't you any justice? Could I help it if he did? I gave him the best I had——"

She stopped abruptly, forcing back tears, a threatening wave of hysteria.

"This is becoming an argument. There isn't any need for that. I'm going now——"

He said more quietly:

"No, not yet. I'm sorry I—as you say there's no point in arguing about it. There's something I have to say, though. He told me about the child."

He'd waited for a moment but when she didn't speak he went on, "I didn't mean to be unfair. I can't help—" he'd stumbled a little there so she'd helped him out:

"Disliking me——?"

And he'd answered quite naturally, "Yes," and then looked rather staggered as if he felt some other self than the one he knew had made that curious admission. She'd prompted him:

"He told you about the child. Well?"

He looked at her helplessly.

"I don't know. What are you going to do about it?"

She was suddenly fiercely resentful. She said sharply, scornfully:

"I'm going to bear it and then I'm going to look after it. What did you expect?"

He said grimly:

"You're game, anyhow," and she answered with weary exasperation:

"It isn't a question of gameness. It's only common honesty to accept the results of your actions without kicking. If only—it doesn't seem fair that the baby should have to suffer too——"

It was then that he'd said rather contemptuously:

"You're young enough to feel surprised when things aren't fair."

And after a long pause he'd sat down abruptly on the other end of the couch and gone on talking without looking at her.

"When I was looking out the window just now I—it occurred to me that there's a way out of all this. Jim asked me to see you through and look after the child. Well—I—of course I said 'Yes,' as one does to a sick—to a dying person—— You don't boggle over requests like that at such a time. You don't say, 'How?' or ask questions. You just promise—and then afterwards when it's over——"

She'd interrupted passionately:

"I'm not asking you to help me! I——"

He said:

"Wait a minute. I'm not suggesting that I help you. I don't want to help you. I don't," he continued with deliberate sincerity, "care a damn what happens to you. But I do want to help the child. Jim's child. And the only way I can see is that you should marry me——"

Well, Susan thought, moving restlessly as the first drops of rain spattered against the side curtains, when you'd got through a moment like that you could get through anything. That's what Bret had said to her. "I don't care a damn what happens to you," and in the same breath he'd gone on to suggest marriage——

And the most dreadful thing had been the way she'd seen right through it all to the end—that there was no way out. She'd have to do it. And yet, with a blind instinct of panic she'd fought and fought with arguments that he broke like sticks and tossed away——

"No—— No!"

"Why not?"

"I—you don't love me."

He shrugged his shoulders.

"You didn't love Jim but you were going to marry him."

"For the baby's sake."

"This would be for the baby's sake too."

He'd added after a moment, dispassionately:

"As a matter of fact you have no right to refuse."

She knew that was true, but she went on struggling.

"I have the right to spoil my own life, but I haven't the right to spoil yours."

"We aren't considering your life or mine. We're considering the child—who interests me only as Jim's child."

She'd cried despairingly.

"It—it wouldn't be—honest."

He was puzzled by that.

"Why not?"

Then she'd collapsed. There simply hadn't been strength left in her for any more conflict. She said putting her hands to her face:

"All right."

He nodded.

"I think it will be best. And as soon as possible. To-night?"

She said dully:

"You'll have to get Dad's consent."

He looked, for a swift second, rather amused.

"You aren't as modern as I thought," and she retorted irritably:

"Evidently I'm *more* modern than you thought. I'm not of age."

After that he'd seemed gentler.

"Shall we go and see him at once, then?"

"I'd rather go alone. Will you come later?"

"Very well."

They'd left the flat together, silently, and gone, still silent, down in the lift. Outside the sky was greenish, and the air heavy. In the taxi she'd heard a few heavy drops of rain begin to come down on the roof; hard, heavy like blows, faster and faster, like the agonising thunder of native drums——

4

Bret said sharply:

"Susan, what's the matter?"

She came back to reality with a gasp and a pounding heart. She seemed to hear, still echoing, a faint sound that had been half sob and half cry. Bret was leaning towards her anxiously and she was clutching his hand. She released it and laughed nervously:

"Nothing–I must have been half asleep–I–the rain–it startled me, coming down on the hood so suddenly——"

CHAPTER ELEVEN

I

DREW hadn't heard. He was peering through the little fan-shaped patch of clear glass which his windscreen wiper allowed him, and through a silver-grey sheet of rain, at the road. With the defeat of the sun a nip in the air which had seemed only a pleasant stimulation became a bleak and insidious cold. Millicent turned, said:

"My coat, please, Susan," and saw her daughter sitting with her eyes half shut—not sleepily but painfully, as though her head were aching; and Bret looking at her with a queer expression—pity, puzzlement——

She sighed, struggling in the cramped space into the coat he handed her. It was just as well that she knew Bret! How she might have hated him otherwise! Just as well that she'd known him as a baby, heard of him as a small child from Agatha, known him again as a schoolboy, Colin's idol, a silent youth with his mother's sudden smile and a god-like proficiency at football and rowing. And later, going off with Colin to that unspeakable shambles——

Well, anyhow, he was all right. And it was strange how she seemed always to be thinking of him with relief, with a grateful sense of reliance. She'd thought when Colin went to school: "Oh, well, Bret Maclean is there—Colin will be all right with him." And that hideous morning when they were all marching down to the troopships—her one glimmer of comfort: "Oh, Tom, look, there's Bret." And again years later when he had helped them so much to settle Colin on Kalangadoo. There wasn't any one who could do so much with Colin as Bret—until Margery appeared——

And now Susan. All through this last dreadful year it had been her one cry—her one selfish maternal thought: "Thank goodness it's Bret!"

She could even wonder now if she'd spared enough of her concern for Bret himself. He'd done a strange, quixotic, characteristic thing, swept off his feet emotionally, as she supposed they'd all been, by the suddenness of tragedy. But she wondered sometimes if she would have allowed it if it hadn't been for Tom. Tom, bless his heart, had very simple views. He probably, she reflected, had thought of his daughter as being "in trouble," and of Bret as "making an honest woman of her!" He hadn't felt and feared, as she had, dark undercurrents swirling beneath the surface calmness of Bret's and Susan's rational discussion. He hadn't looked ahead as she had to this time which they were now facing, when a strange situation was to become quite abruptly a normal one, and they were to have no normal feelings with which to meet it. There was so much more to it, she'd felt apprehensively, than a few words in a registrar's office, a signature or two, a wedding ring. Those things didn't change you. Bret was still Bret, fighting an inner hostility: Susan was still Susan, her love stinging itself brutally, scorpion-wise, into strange frenzies.

She hadn't told Tom that first day. So that the second day, when, watching from her bedroom window she'd seen Susan get out of the taxi and come into the house, she'd felt a little shiver of pity for him invade the more overwhelming compassion she was feeling for her daughter. And regret, too, a quite simple feeling of regret that her son-in-law was to be Jim, not Bret. Yes, she'd thought, going quickly down the stairs, it was a muddle the poor child had got herself into, falling in love, at such a time, with Bret——

And then she'd seen Susan standing just inside the front door, her face wet and streaked with rain, her eyes shut. She'd said quickly and softly, because Tom was in the library and she didn't want him—just yet: "Darling! Susan! What is it?"

For she'd seen suddenly that the wet streaks were tears, not rain. Tears pouring out steadily from under closed lids, down a face so utterly still it might have been carved——

Upstairs, half an hour later, Susan had looked at her with a queer apathy. It was from the order in which she gave, unemotionally, her two stark bits of news that Millicent found the full realisation of her tragedy. For she didn't say, "Jim's dead and I'm going to marry Bret," but first, "I'm going to marry Bret," and then, exhaustedly, seeing her mother's face blankly uncomprehending, she'd explained dully: "Jim's dead."

From that hour there had begun to beat in the background of Millicent's mind the refrain which it was still repeating, "Thank goodness it's Bret."

She'd put Susan to bed. The child was just about finished. And Tom, looking as if his world had crumbled about his ears, had tramped the house muttering to himself, storming at her, but somehow even in his first anger, she liked to remember, not saying hard things of Susan.

"Well, Milly, it's a nasty business, but if this chap offers a way out——"

"As long as it *is* a way out, Tom, and not a way into worse unhappiness for her."

"Don't be absurd, Milly; it means—well, you know what it means. Disgrace for her—for the child——"

Dear Tom! He hadn't said, "For us." She doubted whether he'd thought it. She suggested:

"There might be even worse things than disgrace. She could be with us, couldn't she?" And she'd added with a wintry little smile, "You wouldn't turn her out?"

He'd snorted ferociously:

"This isn't a time for joking, Milly," and she'd answered meekly, hugging his arm: "No, dear."

"I always said," he cried out, beginning to walk about again, "that I didn't want her to go. I said so at the time. And look what's come of it. But you would have your own way. I was most definitely against it. Wasn't I?"

"Yes, darling."

"When's this fellow coming?"

"Bret?"

"Yes."

"Any time now, Tom."

"What sort of a chap is he?"

"A very good chap indeed."

"How long since you've seen him?"

"Oh, a long time—years—when he came back from the war."

"Well, I'm going to the library. You can send him in there."

He'd stamped away. "Send him in there!" She'd hoped, smiling after him ruefully, that he wouldn't try to be too school-masterish with Bret——

And she'd gone to the window to watch for him——

As he got out of the taxi she caught a glimpse beneath his hat of a profile she didn't know she had remembered so clearly. All his movements as he banged the door shut, paid the driver and turned to the house, were so brisk, so business-like that she'd felt a fleeting sense of resentment; but at the foot of the steps he'd paused, so brief a hesitation in his movement that it was scarcely perceptible, but it turned her swiftly from the window to get the front door open before he rang.

They'd looked at each other blankly for a moment across the threshold. She thought he looked tired—more than tired, ill——

And she'd remembered that he had probably been doing miserable and distressing things—arranging for a funeral, telling Kathleen and Ken—collecting Jim's belongings from wherever they were——

And she'd held out both her hands to him suddenly, forgetting all about Susan——

"Come in, Bret."

"Thank you." He followed her into the drawing-room.

There seated opposite to her, he had begun at once:

"Susan has told you, Mrs. Drew——? About Jim——"

"Yes, Bret. I——" And she'd discovered that you can't look at some one just bereaved and say, "I'm sorry," because those are words which you use if you bump into him or hit him accidentally with a tennis ball—and there are no others but phrases of stilted formality. So she'd just waited, looking at him unhappily, and he'd ploughed on:

"And about us? That we want—that we think it best——" And she'd interrupted him quickly:

"She's told me everything, Bret. I don't know yet

what to think. I can't feel sure what's best. It's a difficult—a dangerous way out, a marriage of this sort."

He'd shrugged his shoulders.

"Can you suggest a better?"

She'd admitted, "No," watching the rain beating against the window she had left uncurtained. And she'd said at last, "The only alternative I can see is for her not to attempt a 'way out' at all."

"Which is rough," Bret had said shortly, "on the child."

2

The child. Millicent, huddled in her fur coat, seeing the road dimly through a blur of rain, thought that it seemed ironical that the child for whose welfare they had all thought and acted, should have slipped casually out of a life so carefully prepared for him. There'd been, somewhere, for all of them, a snub, a jeer in that death of something which had hardly been a life at all. As though a guest of honour should come at last to a reception most laboriously arranged for him, and, after the briefest glance, cynical, faun-like, turn his back and walk out——

Leaving them all——

Well, rather foolishly stranded. Rather absurdly committed to something whose essential reason simply didn't exist any longer——

It *would* have been rough on the child. Bret, from first to last, had talked plain facts. It was, indeed, his magnificent nonawareness of any other aspect which had frightened her most. What did he think a marriage was? A wedding-ring and a double bed? It almost sounded as if he did not really conceive it as anything more——

So she'd said slowly:

"Yes, possibly in some ways it would be rough on the child. Legally and socially——"

And he'd asked, quite seriously:

"Are there other ways?"

She stared at him.

"Happiness? A child born by a happy mother—brought up in a—harmonious home——? You don't think that important?"

He'd moved restlessly, spoken politely:

"You know best, of course, how much such things count. In any case I—I don't see why marriage with me should necessarily make Susan irretrievably miserable. I know there isn't—she doesn't care for me, but——"

She'd spoken swiftly then, almost anxious that a persistent glimmer of what she knew to be quite unreasonable hope should be sharply and finally quenched, leaving her with a clearer if a harder problem to tackle:

"And you don't care for her?"

He made a desperate movement with his hand.

"How could I? I hardly know her. What I do know is not——"

He stopped. Her, "Yes? What were you going to say?" was not less a challenge for being so softly spoken. He met it at once, his face curiously hard.

"Is not to her credit, was what I was going to say, Mrs. Drew. I stopped because—I'm not quite sure. I haven't had time to think about it—to make up my mind if she has any justification for what seems to be a very definite point of view——" And then he'd said suddenly, wearily: "Anyhow, it isn't relevant."

Not relevant! She'd only felt able to stare at him. He protested:

"You must take my word for it that I'll treat her decently——"

She smiled a little.

"I wasn't questioning your good intentions, Bret. I was only wondering if they're enough to save Susan from the misery of an unhappy marriage——"

Then suddenly he was on his feet, furious, speaking fast and bitterly.

"Susan's welfare! Susan's happiness! I tell you quite plainly they don't concern me. Jim was worth a thousand of her, and he's dead—not able to help the child. I want to take over his responsibility—but not for Susan's sake. Legally because she's not of age, the decision rests with you and her father. Please let me have it, Mrs. Drew. I can't talk any more——"

So she'd gone away to find Tom, leaving him standing at the window, his hands in his pockets, his mind wrestling, she felt sure now, with a doubt, a torment, which a few days afterwards he had confessed to her——

Not that he need ever have felt it. She had told him so strenuously at the time, feeling sorry for him in his sudden lapses into silence, the brief abstractions of his gaze. Later on, she had promised him, he would be able to feel what even now he must know, that he could not reasonably blame himself for what had happened. What influence he had with them all—Jim, Kathleen, Ken—he had won less by holding than by letting go.

"Jim wasn't a child, Bret——"

"No—but I knew. I might have done something. I might have told you—I just stood back and let it go on——"

And she'd said, sighing:

"Well, you're doing your best now."

And it was only that conviction which had remained with her, the conviction that he was always doing and would always continue to do his best, which had saved her from utter despair in the last few months. She should have realised, she saw now, that Susan married was Susan most terribly isolated. Whatever new miseries and problems had come to her as Bret's wife, she had to deal with them alone. Millicent would have bitten her tongue out rather than imply a doubt of Bret by questioning; Susan would have died rather than portray him to her family by words or manner, as anything less than perfect. So they'd all found themselves playing parts. It wasn't easy between herself and Tom——

She remembered now, before the wedding, behind all their fears for Susan, their grief for her in this bitter-tasting one-sided love of hers, they had surprised sometimes in each other's eyes the glimmer of a smile, born of some deep, unshakeable parental pride! "Ah, but it's Susan! Our Susan! Just wait—of course he'll fall in love with her. Who could help it?"

And how only this morning, walking back up the path which she had so mendaciously proclaimed too steep, their eyes had met again with a vague bewilderment, an unacknowledged fear——

To Tom, she knew, it had been a year of incessant irritation. It was all so indefinable, the very kind of trouble he most detested. What was there to do with a problem but grab it and wring its neck? But when you weren't quite sure where its neck was, or even if it had a neck at all, you were being most intolerably victimised by Life—— He had rumbled and grumbled his disapproval, he had picked and brushed at his doubts as at persistent cobwebs, but still they were there——

So that at last, finding it all quite unsupportable without a definite theory in which, like a pigeon-hole, he could place the whole bothersome affair, he'd fallen back gratefully on that invaluable fable of feminine cantankerousness! Because, when two people didn't agree it was obviously and inevitably the "fault" of one or the other. To Tom, every question had a "right" and a "wrong"; Bret, with his imperturbable face, his irreproachable behaviour in what Tom saw as an excruciatingly delicate situation, could not possibly be wrong. Susan, therefore, passing from a glitter of high spirits to heavy eyes and long silences; Susan goading her husband, sobbing stormily in her room, behaving, in short, with all the capriciousness of the eternal feminine, must be the culprit. It had helped him, Millicent knew, to have the matter so clearly and satisfactorily decided. So that when he said, sometimes, "She's spoilt—that's her trouble. I hope he brings her to her senses," she only smiled at him, knowing his love for his daughter quite unaffected by his disapproval——

But that little cry of Susan's just now. What were they doing to her—the three of them—what was in her mind to force from her lips such a dreadful little sound? Had she suffered more than any of them knew? Had she damned it all back too successfully for a time, and was it now——?

Bret called from behind:

"I'd take this hill very slowly, Mr. Drew. It's liable to be greasy after rain."

Her eyes focused on the road again. It was hewn out of a mountain-side, high walls of rock rising on one side of it, unknown depths falling away on the other.

She saw Tom's foot go down cautiously on the brake, and felt, at the same moment, the back wheels of the car begin to slide. They slid to one side and then to the other in widening sweeps. Never before had she known a car to feel so alive, so malignantly and powerfully destructive, like a jungle beast long caged and free at last. She felt her heart turn over and a queer feeling of tightness in her head, and she had a second's glimpse of Tom's face looking greyish. The car, then, seemed to lose its independent character. It became a toy-car swung on the end of a string by some peevish child. It whirled round. They were facing for a fraction of a second the high rock wall, then the slope down which they had just come, with the crazy wheel marks of their passage standing out like part of a too-long continued nightmare. Then there was nothing in front of them but a distant glimpse of tree-tops and a white-painted railing which didn't look strong enough——

The front wheels, Millicent thought with calmness which amazed herself, must be very near the edge. Poor Tom! She could feel, though she wasn't touching him, the strain of his intense muscular effort. And suddenly, like a skittish horse, the car sidled back crab-like to the middle of the road, beyond the middle, and came to rest gently, conclusively, with its back wheels in a gutter full of soft mud.

CHAPTER TWELVE

1

DREW wiped the sweat from his face, and put one hand down to clutch Millicent's in a grip that nearly crushed her fingers. He asked without turning his head:

"All right behind?"

Two voices reassured him. He sat still looking straight in front of him over the bonnet of the car. He knew now that he was old. He knew it because his resilience was gone, because his nerves, his brain, his muscles, reacting from the violence of the strain which had been on them, had sagged into a kind of helpless apathy from which he felt at the moment no desire to rouse them. Something, he couldn't remember what, was stirring in his memory. A fleeting second in the middle of it all when he had noticed something quite extraneous——

Never mind—it didn't matter. For the present it was enough to rest his tired body and feel Milly's hand, warm and steady, in his own——

2

Bret, too, was content to sit still. He was wondering vaguely what happened to your mind in moments of great danger. He supposed that just as your body releases, instinctively, all its stored up energy, giving you for your moment of need a surprising strength and agility, so your brain might make one last frantic effort to release into the daylight its many unsuspected prisoners——

For while he'd watched the bonnet of the car swing nearer and nearer to that cliff-edge he'd been conscious of only one sensation, the agonising knowledge of something which he could have grasped and hadn't—of some opportunity missed, of some transcendent beauty left untasted, and when it was all over he'd found himself staring dazedly at Susan——

Susan, who was sitting in her corner with her hands in her lap very much as she had been before it happened several hundred years ago! Time, he thought, still rather ramblingly, what the devil was it? Absurd to contend that the minute or less during which they had all been so close to death was the same as any minute during which they travelled uneventfully over an unremarkable half-mile! He said helplessly to Susan:

"Cigarette?"

"Thanks."

She took one and he held a match for her. Millicent was smiling at them over her shoulder.

"All right, darling?"

"Rather. Are you?"

"Of course."

"Cigarette, Daddy?"

Drew roused himself with a sigh. He pulled himself round heavily in his seat and accepted one from the case Bret was offering. Bret said, lighting it:

"Best skid I've ever been in. You did well to hold her on the road at all."

Drew grunted between puffs:

"Precious little you *can* do in a skid. I was just going to yell to you all to jump when she slithered away from the edge." He glanced at the wall behind them. "And now we've got to get out of *this*——"

Bret peered through the back window and said, "H'm!" rather doubtfully. There had been a kind of grim finality in the way the back wheels had settled into the mud. He opened a door and climbed out. As he did so he looked up the hill at their meandering tracks, and felt a brief catch in his breathing. They'd been as near as that, had they? He turned back thoughtfully to the car.

He found himself mentally continuing the day as it would have been continued if those wheels had slid a foot farther; and beyond the inevitable momentary glimpse of them all lying in a tangle of twisted metal and broken scrub he saw suddenly, blotting out everything else, Coolami.

He seemed to hear distantly, like a far-away voice speaking over a telephone, some one regretting to be the bearer of bad news to Ken; being really very sorry indeed to have to inform him that his brother had been killed in a car accident—— He seemed to hear Ken's two thoughts falling neatly into place like two pennies in a slot, "Good Lord, poor old Bret!" And then, "Now what the deuce are we to do with Coolami?"

Not much doubt, thought Bret grimly, what they'd do with Coolami. And you couldn't blame them. What else could they do with it but sell it—a lawyer and an artist? He was so blackly lost in this realisation that he looked up startled when his father-in-law demanded:

"Well, what do you think of it?"

He was getting out, sliding his big body beneath the wheel stiffly as though he were not sure of it. Bret shook his head.

"I wouldn't bother to move," he said, "I think it's

quite hopeless—there's nothing for the wheels to grip on at all. We aren't more than two miles from Kerrajellanbong, though. I'll walk down and rout out something to tow us."

Millicent protested:

"Bret, what a bore for you. Won't," she suggested happily, "something come along soon? Surely?"

He laughed.

"Well, it might or it mightn't. If it does I can pick it up lower down." He turned away and then turned back on a sudden impulse:

"Like to come, Susan?"

Then he swore at himself, and settled the muscles of his face into an expressionless calm against the coming of her cool, "No, thanks."

But she said, after a brief pause:

"Yes, I'll come."

He felt his mouth twitch as he watched her climb out, pulling her coat off, her cigarette still dangling between her lips. Really she was a funny little cuss! More than half, he thought, of the charm he'd never failed to acknowledge was in her gift for being, for looking, rather endearingly quaint!

And he marvelled as they set off down the road that until she was beside you, with the top of her head somewhere between your shoulder and your elbow, you didn't realise how absurdly small she was——

She said presently:

"If we'd gone over then—what would have happened to Coolami?"

He looked down at her sharply, but he couldn't see anything except her hair and the tip of her nose and a drift of blue smoke. He said shortly:

"Ken and Kathleen would have sold it, I should think."

She didn't answer that and they walked silently for a half-mile before he asked suddenly:

"What was it really that made you cry out in the car?"

"It *was* the rain."

"Do you expect me to believe that?"

She gave him one of her swift smiles.

"It wouldn't be the first true thing you've refused to believe."

"If I've got to believe that," he said, "I've got to believe you're on the verge of a nervous breakdown–" He glanced at a curve of cheek brilliantly coloured by mountain air and exercise and finished dryly, "Which is absurd."

Again she didn't answer for a long time. When she did her voice was quick and low.

"I suppose it is. But there must be something wrong with you when you see death coming at you and feel glad——"

He said sharply:

"*Glad*? Just now–when the car——?"

She said helplessly:

"That's what I felt."

He snapped:

"Take that damned thing out of your mouth before it burns you."

She threw her cigarette butt away with absent-minded obedience. He said more gently:

"I'm sorry, Susan. I'd do anything I could."

She acknowledged this wearily with a little wave of her hand.

"Oh, yes, I know you would. You do. We both do. It's pathetic how well-intentioned we are! Let's talk about the scenery."

He said at once, rapidly:

"The Blue Mountains offer panoramic views of unparalleled magnificence. Nowhere else in the world are to be found scenes of more majestic splendour, while the bracing atmosphere, sparkling water, exquisite flora and intriguing fauna provide endless attractions for the tourist. In addition to these natural advantages many improvements have been effected; unrivalled opportunities exist for golf, tennis, swimming, dancing, petting, necking and suicide. All beauty spots are lavishly provided with seats, railings, fences, arches, rubbish bins and other conveniences—"

She said:

"Oh, Bret, you are a fool. Bless you."

Arm in arm, basking in a brief patch of contentment as one basks in stray gleams of winter sunlight, they came down the hill into Kerrajellanbong.

3

It was nearly midday when at last, roaring and protesting, flinging mud from her back wheels and blue smoke from her exhaust, the Madison was hauled out by a lorry into the road. Splashes from passing cars and from her own elephantine plungings had dried into blotches on her once gleaming paint. Her back wheels were caked, hardly recognisable as wheels at all, and one mudguard had been crushed against the wall of rock.

Bret, in his shirtsleeves, very hot, and trying with one overworked handkerchief to scrub the grime from his face, saw Susan studying this ruination with a wicked glee. She looked, he thought, smiling involuntarily, pretty grubby herself. She had stood for a moment, unwarily, in the spatter of mud flung up from the helplessly turning wheels, and she'd carried wet branches with him to place beneath them. He watched her get into the car and climbed in beside her feeling irrationally light-hearted.

Drew, following the lorry cautiously down the hill, asked Bret:

"How far did you say to this Kerra—what's-its-name?"

"A couple of miles or less."

"Level going then?"

"Well, for a while. We climb up pretty high again near Capertee." And he wondered for a moment if the old chap was feeling a bit shaken by their mishap? Nasty to be at the wheel in a skid like that. He opened his mouth to offer to drive, caught a glimpse of the arrogant nose and closed it again. Millicent suggested:

"We'll buy lemonade or something in Kerrajellanbong and then we needn't boil the billy when we stop for lunch."

Drew said testily:

"Upon my word these idiotic names get on my nerves. Why the deuce can't they name their towns after—well, after explorers or—or Governors—or—give them descriptive names or something——"

"Well," Bret pointed out mildly, "Kerrajellanbong means 'the place in the shadow of the mountain'—you couldn't very well have anything more descriptive than that."

Drew said, "Humph!" and then demanded:

"And what does Coolami mean—if anything?"

Bret said modestly, with a twinkle in his eye:

"Without wanting to appear conceited, it means 'birthplace of heroes.'" And then suddenly, with his grin frozen on his face, he found himself staring hard at Susan.

Funny that he hadn't thought of that before—the appeal—the demand, even, which was in the name of his home. What would he have done about that, he wondered, if all this hadn't happened? Just gone on in comfortable hard-working bachelorhood trusting to Ken and Jim and Kathleen to produce heirs for Coolami? And what, anyhow, was he going to do about it now, with this strange small wife shut away from him by indefinable barriers——? His trouble was, he told himself irritably, that he wasn't quite perceptive enough or quite obtuse enough! Not perceptive enough to be able to feel in more than passing glimmers any comprehension of this mysterious affliction called love—not obtuse enough to be able to consider without a sharp distaste and dissatisfaction an unwilling wife—an unhappy, driven wife submitting because she must——

It occurred to him suddenly that if he couldn't manage to love her she might manage some day to stop loving him. Wouldn't things be better then? A certain comradeship would be left, respect and a definite liking—good plain emotions which one could understand——

And then inwardly, helplessly, he began to laugh. Because after all what did you do to make a woman stop loving you? He'd behaved badly enough to her once or twice——

And he suddenly brought out an envelope and a pencil and scribbled:

"Don't you think you could manage to hate me?"

She looked at it, at him, smiled uncertainly and wrote beneath:

"No."

His pencil jerked wildly as the car came on to a bad patch of road. The words were hardly legible: "Why not?"

She scrawled quickly:

"I can't imagine."

He grinned at this Susan-like dig, and managed laboriously:

"Would it be better if you did?"

She answered aloud, rather sharply:

"Don't be absurd!" and Millicent asked, turning her head:

"Did you speak to me, Susan?"

"No, Mother."

The car lumbered into Kerrajellanbong and stopped austerely in front of a tiny shop with a notice which said, "Fruit, Confectionery, Soft Drinks."

4

While Bret was buying ginger-beer, Drew was staring absently at his dashboard. The clock and the speedometer, the oil-gauge, the petrol indicator. Just there above his eyes the little windscreen-wiper which worked briskly, fussily, like a busy housewife. Here to his left hand a knob which moved intricate gears. Under his left foot something that bewitched the world into a streak of ribbon whirling past, and under his right something that made it secure and stationary again——

What a waste, he thought, awed, what a frightful

sinful waste if she'd been smashed up on her first trip! All that complicated and beautiful mechanism, all that shining paint and nickel——! Not that it was so shining now. He got out of the car and stood back, frowning, to examine it. He thought that he was angry, exasperated, but he found suddenly that he was smiling, and remembering Colin as he'd come home one day, bloodily victorious from some schoolboy scrap. The poor old bus looked just like that! She was transformed now, by her dilapidation, from an opulent new model of a costly car into something as intimately and personally concerned with his journeyings as the war-horse of any mediæval knight riding forth to forays and ambushments! Surprising, the character it gave her, the air of having travelled far and gallantly, and of being ready, standing there, powerful and solid and begrimed, for any amount more——

Any amount——

How far were they from Sydney now? A hundred miles or so? Well, it was a fair bit, but a fleabite compared with what lay ahead. What exactly, anyhow, *did* lie ahead? He realised, watching Bret come out of the store with his arms full of bottles and brown paper bags, that apart from a mental picture of its coast and boundary lines, of a vague impression of Mudgee somewhere west, and Orange somewhere west of that again, he knew very little indeed of his native state——

Something stirred in him restlessly. Old? Fifty-eight? Good Lord, no! The prime of life! But all the same, back there on the hill——

Queer how your life vanished, flickered past you, a succession of scenes like the lights that waver across your ceiling at night from passing trams or cars. And you don't notice them any more than that, either; not when you're busy. Climbing towards something, watching it come nearer. Time doesn't count then, as time. It's just one of your weapons. But then when you've got what you were after, when you've won your victory, you're left standing—with your weapon still in your hand. And nothing to use it on——

Well, not exactly nothing. You go on working, of course, but the fight's over. And you're fifty-eight, so time has become, mysteriously, rather precious, rather terrible. You can't—you don't want to use it just—just *fiddling* with things. Like opening an egg with a battle-axe——

Time. Fifty-eight to sixty-eight. Ten years, say, of *active* life. Ten years when you're still not quite an old gentleman. God, how short, how horribly short, how sickeningly, mercilessly inadequate! Milly, what the devil have I been doing? Thirty-seven years we've been married, and I've spent them getting ready to settle down and live with you!

Funk! Yes, that's it, pure funk! Why? Reaction from that near-tragedy up there? Well, that would have been a sell, to go out like that with these ten years now ahead of you, these ten priceless years unlived! Would you care less about death if you'd always lived widely, colourfully, adventurously——?

And suddenly he remembered what it was he had noticed when there was nothing in front of him but space and tree-tops very far below—his little silver absurdity on the radiator still straining towards the final mystery, still pointing them victoriously forward. . . .

CHAPTER THIRTEEN

ONLY blue sky was to be seen ahead of them when they took the road again. It was still greasy, and they made slow enough progress for a time. Nobody minded. The sudden transition from mountain to plain country was intriguing, Millicent thought, watching green, wet paddocks where for the past few hours she'd been seeing the bush and the blue depth and distance of far-away gullies. She found too, that she was feeling a bit slack, tired, glad to relax into her well-upholstered corner of the seat and watch the landscape absently from eyes half focused, seeing it only as a strip of moving, slightly hypnotising colour. She'd had a fright, she thought, a fright which had been psychological rather than physical, when they had hung for a second or two so near to death. Her feeling, she realised had been one of amazed incredulous protest. "Oh, *no*!" her whole being had cried. "Not yet! It can't be—I haven't *nearly* finished!" And her fear had been for something in the unguessable future which could not—*must* not thus be cheated of its day! She smiled ruefully to herself, thinking of her future. It was clear enough—had always been clear enough if one wanted (which one didn't) to think of it. But there must have been some hope, some feeling, some entirely irrational conviction at the back of her mind that some day before she died life would take on the flavour of adventure again! Rather alarming, the revelations one had now and then of unsuspected dwellers in oneself! No paltry dweller either! No vaguely fluttering hope, no half-baked impression, but a lusty and ravening desire lifting its voice in frantic protest against extinction unfulfilled! Well, poor dear, now that I know about you, what are your chances? Poor—very poor!

And yet after all, what does one want, at fifty-seven, with extraneous adventures when one has just discovered inexhaustible unexplored territory in one's own mind?

Fascinating thought! But not, she admitted regretfully, of much practical use. You can't dig and delve for those intriguing buried things. They'd hide away deeper and more darkly. You can only surprise them as it were in flashes, by accident, as you might put your hand in the dark on a sleeping animal and not know which of you had the greater scare!

Well, one had still the children. But she sighed. Adventures meant dangers, of course, and it was one of the penalties of motherhood that you couldn't, however hard you tried, enjoy your children's dangers. Your instinct was to hustle them willy-nilly to the smooth, the safe, the easy, the everything which you so hated for yourself. And when you found you couldn't do that because one simply didn't interfere in other people's lives and you hadn't ever been able to think of your children except as people, individuals, you had to watch their adventures with a sinking of the heart, a sickness of dread and a shrinking of fear which no dangers of your own had ever roused in you.

And she had to confess to herself now that for years, ever since Colin came back from the war, her pity for him, her dread for him, had been draining something out of her as though she were bleeding incessantly from some tiny wound. There had been the makings of something so very good in Colin. He'd been like a lusty young plant thrusting upward to its maturity, and shrivelled overnight by frost. Some plants will stand it, and others won't——

Bret had come through all right—as far as one knew. But then, as he had written illuminatingly once to her after their return, "I had the luck to be wounded." How many men, she wondered now, owed their continued mental stability to a shattered limb or a sightless eye or a damaged lung? Something which had released them for a little from the incessant nervous strain of danger, discomfort, boredom. Something which had meant respite, turning the taut brain to new preoccupations—the walls of a ward in place of mud-bespattered dug-outs; cleanliness, silence, instead of dirt and nerve shattering noise; uniforms of nurses instead of endless khaki—the queer wonder of watching them, their movements, their voices so blessedly different——

Colin, and his "charmed life"! Colin who couldn't get hit! Colin, eighteen, who went too long without his respite——

Returned to her, after four years, sound in wind and limb! She remembered how meeting him at the troopship she'd actually grieved for other mothers walking beside sons on crutches, sons armless, eyeless; felt an almost awed gratitude for the straight and unharmed Colin at her side!

For you don't see them quickly, those other hidden injuries, those wounds which strike deeper than the body. You don't see at a glance a mind once gay and vital, distorted into an ugly contempt for life, an ugly disgust at itself, a still uglier fear——

Once when he was quite small, she remembered, he'd won an egg and spoon race at school. Red and flustered, the others had wobbled, glanced round, hurried too much, clutched at their spoons with their hands, failed one way or another. She had watched Colin with surprise. He had moved with a machine-like steadiness and precision, his face slightly pink but immovable, his spoon rock-steady between his teeth. He had never lifted his eyes, turned his head, altered his pace. But she had seen with faint dismay after he reached the winning post, that he had stood for a second or two with shaking hands and brimming eyes, his small face queerly distorted——

Well, here it was again. There in front of him, stretched like the tape across the course, was the end of a different, an unspeakable contest. Beyond it he hadn't looked, hadn't thought. "*Get* there!" he'd said to himself, moving through it with machine-like efficiency. "*Get* there! *Get* there!" And then when he'd got there—what——?

Again the unbearable cessation of strain, the unendurable leisure to think. The cracking of a control too heavily weighted, too long sustained——

If she were built that way, thought Millicent, she should be thanking God that much as she loved her son and daughter she loved her son-in-law and her daughter-in-law hardly less! For just as she always thought with relief of Bret, she thought too with hope and confidence of Margery.

She began to think about her grandchildren. Richard would be three now; she hadn't seen him for eighteen months. And quite soon, now, there'd be the new one. Her suitcases bulged with clothes and playthings for them both, a bear for Richard and a set of ingenious toys which you fitted together into shapes of animals so deliciously ludicrous that even Tom had stopped to fiddle with them and roar with laughter at the absurdities he fashioned. And picture-books, and a clockwork train and a petrol-lorry. Not soldiers; she had looked at them for a moment, wondering. There had been a cannon too, and a machine-gun, very elaborate, with a kneeling soldier beside it—— And she'd turned away with a sudden revulsion, thinking "If he must, he must—but not from me!"

It had been foolish, perhaps, to buy so much. Margery would put some of them away, perhaps, for rainy days and Christmas. But the clothes she would be glad of—strong overalls, brown and blue, and little linen shirts and trousers, and a blue linen hat. And for the baby——

But here again a little prick of worry obtruded. While she was packing Susan had come in with her arms full of baby clothes, fine woollens, flannels furry soft and smooth, heavy silks. She'd said, "You might as well give these to Margery, Mother." And put them down on the bed. What could one say? Nothing, without tearing that charming veil of perfection which they had all, by common consent, laid over the tragedy of her marriage to Bret. Nothing to do but murmur. "Thank you, dear, I expect she'd love them," and pack them away beside the other little pile——

All the same, girls have queer feelings sometimes. It mightn't mean—Oh, well, what did it matter after all? They'd looked very happy once or twice to-day, grinning together like a pair of naughty children as they came up the hill to the rescue on a coal-lorry; carrying their soaked branches to put under the car wheels!

It wasn't any good remembering with too deep an apprehension sounds of stifled sobbing through a closed door, the lines of a figure crouching over a picnic fire—lines that a sculptor might have striven for, the listless grief strangely and movingly mature, of youth——

No good remembering Bret's bent head against the blue valley, Bret's face closed, defensive, against the goad of a stinging tongue. All that was near its end—surely? Surely? This journey was an interlude—a little isthmus of time connecting a difficult and stormy past to a new life at Coolami.

Who wouldn't be happy at Coolami?

Who wouldn't find difficulties fading in that lovely place? And she reflected that, confronted by the joyous and uncaring fecundity of the earth, one would probably, sooner or later, begin to feel that until one had shed, somehow, one's unhealthful complexities, one was something less than any ripening ear of wheat!

Wheat. The mere thought of it made her feel homesick! She looked out with an impatience that was vaguely apologetic at a road climbing again into bushland. On the eastern slopes to the left there were huge orchards; apple-trees with buds just breaking misted away as far as you could see, a pinkish film against the dark earth. Pear-trees reared old trunks, blackly vigorous through the white foam of their blossoming. An elusive fragrance came from them borne up by the sun out of wet earth and leaves and petals.

Drew said:

"By jove, Milly, that's lovely!" and she said: "Yes, isn't it?" feeling guilty and strangely sad because in her present mood her hunger was all for a pathway cut through wheat lands where you walked shoulder-high and the tops looked like acres of green lawn, so smooth and even with the kurrajong trees rising out of them.

That kurrajong in the far paddock at Wondabyne—it was supposed to be the biggest in the district—amazing how clearly she still remembered it. She could shut her eyes now and see the very movement in its leaves and its pale bell-shaped flowers, see a ewe with its lamb as she must have seen them one hot day sheltering beneath it. And not far away the wilga which, as children, they had imagined to be in some way bewitched or accursed because the sheep wouldn't eat it; not till she was very nearly grown up had she seen others in other places which lay beneath the same incomprehensible ban, and she had never quite lost her childish awe of that one outcast, standing shaggily among its brethren whose lower branches were trimmed by the stock to such a perfection of horizontal neatness.

Oh, was it wise to come back to it again like this? Fleetingly, for a day or two as a stranger, a visitor from what a different life! If a memory could do this to you what would the sight of it mean, the very breath and being of it again——

So close to Wondabyne. Why hadn't she ever gone back? While she could have gone; when Agatha was still there, when it might still have seemed with only a little effort of imagination, home. Why hadn't she gone with Susan? How different then, things might have been——!

But she realised with a faint comfort that those differences might not all have been improvements. Susan mightn't, possibly, have singed her wings, but in that case she wouldn't have been going back now with Bret to Coolami. That, Millicent insisted on believing, was a good thing. And she wouldn't be here herself, nor would Tom; nor would they have had that quiet, drowsily happy hour together this morning while the young people went off down the hill leaving them to confess silently to each other that they were glad they were still alive even if they were getting old. To admit without words that in the rather unfriendly vastness which life became when you had just missed losing it by a hairsbreadth, it was comforting to be together, and still more comforting to be aware of that comfort as something mellow and full of virtue like old wine——

No, it had all been for the best. It wouldn't have done to let Tom see her craving for the country. It would have baulked him in his steady onward rush; it would have made him uncertain of his goal, and uncertain therefore of those qualities in himself which were fighting towards it. That would have been a dreadful thing—a Tom not sure of himself, disgruntled, feeling all the time an indefinable sense of failure! Inconceivable! She glanced at him sideways, alarmed at the vivid mental image she'd had for one dreadful moment of Tom with a stoop to his shoulders and a flickering doubt in his eyes! Tom robbed of his endearing arrogance which was so like the arrogance of a little boy with more marbles than his schoolmates! Tom without his hearty confidence, his dominance, the slight rotundity beneath his waistcoat, the whole satisfying aroma of his success!

A little fear gripped her. Perhaps she hadn't thought hard enough about this trip? Perhaps, in her first surge of almost incredulous joy when he'd suggested it, she'd dismissed too hastily the mystery of his seeming capitulation?

Was it a challenge? Was he, like a poker-player, flinging down his hand on the table and saying, "There! That's my little lot! Let's see yours! Beat it if you can!" And of course she could. What could she do about it, this devastating Royal Flush that she held? No good putting it down and trying to pretend it was threes! Tom wasn't to be bluffed that way. For the first time she was a little afraid of that swift perception of his, that rarely-flashing quality which made him so much more than the owner of two cars and a house at Ballool and a cottage at the seaside——

And to be bound for Coolami, of all places! Wondabyne, with its weatherboard homestead, its scattered, tin-roofed outhouses, its general air of rather happy-go-lucky comfort, might not have impressed him much. But the Tom who liked things sound and solid, who insisted on efficiency, who craved rather pathetically a beauty he didn't quite know how to create, would only need to look once at Coolami——

And of course when she'd known it it had been new; now from photographs, from Susan's descriptions she could see it hungrily in all the perfection Bret's mother had planned and Bret's father worked for. She could see its stone, weathered to subdued greys, almost windowless so that it seemed like some vast rock flung there in prehistoric ages, all its life turned inward to the cool garden in its centre. She could see the trees round it, Wilga and Currawong and Silver Wattle. Even the little crooked Coolabah which Bret's mother had so stubbornly insisted on planting though every one protested because it suckered so, and which, Susan said, had grown with the years not as big as it should because it wasn't near enough to the river to be really happy, but more gnarled, more macabre, so that it threw a shadow incredibly wild and distorted across the ground. Bret's mother had seen, Millicent thought, better than any one, the strange loveliness of an ancient land. She more than most of her countrymen had been able to escape a gospel of beauty handed down from generations which had dwelt on a milder and gentler soil. She had abandoned, somehow, an ancestral reverence for landscapes softly painted in lush greens for sappy, fragile flowers and the smooth charm of an unfailing fruitfulness. She'd seen new and more difficult beauty; beauty that rioted opulently in a frothing mass of honey-scented gold, and then a step farther on, in a vast tree, dead, skeleton-white, lifting naked branches to the sky, took on a wild and tragic aloofness.

So she'd planted the trees of the country, the flowers of the country and fought them into living. That was how she had described it herself in one of her letters to Millicent: "I'm still at war with my garden." For they hadn't easily capitulated, the wild flowers, defensive behind their sharp hard leaves, their prickles; they resented their captivity as a nervous animal might; bitter, mistrustful, they had died to elude her. But by degrees she'd persuaded them; she'd told of boronia with feathery leaves won round at last to life and a profusion of fragrant blossoming; of a geebung, prim, old-maidish, with its stiff leaves and its green, astringent fruit; of tea-tree and pink melaleuca and white star-flowered eriostemon——

And then she'd died. The trees grew and the flowers went on. "Well, we keep it in order more or less," Bret had said once to Millicent's questioning, "but of course we can't look after it as she used to—there's always so much else to do."

Millicent thought with a strange and restful conviction:

"Now, of course, Susan can take it over."

CHAPTER FOURTEEN

I

SUSAN was nodding in her corner. Now that the sun was out again and the hood and side-curtains kept the wind from her face she felt warm and tired and increasingly sleepy. That wasn't really to be wondered at because there hadn't been much sleep for herself or for Bret last night and they'd had to be up again at the crack of dawn——

Why had they argued, talked, torn themselves and each other to shreds with words that got them nowhere——

Poor Bret——!

And there was another emotion! Compassion! Heavens! why couldn't you be made so that you could only have one feeling at a time? Was it any wonder that people did crazy things when their whole nervous make-up was being lashed this way and that by a dozen conflicting cross-currents of emotion? There she'd stood in front of Bret last night and felt—what? Well, first and last, of course, love for him, a small, steady-burning flame. From that came all the torture—and all the joy. Dread of an embrace without meaning, dread of what it might do to her, of a flame extinguished and a sudden darkness. Pity for him, caught with her in hopeless tangle of good intentions, pity for his desire and the long effort of his self-denial. And a longing of her own that came chokingly from untold depths, pushing up for a second or two through her love and her dread, clutching at her pity for him as at an ally, sinking again, wavering down out of sight and knowledge.

There had been a moon. Lying in bed with eyes hot and swollen from soundless weeping she'd been able to see his reflection in the swinging mirror of her wardrobe. How long he'd sat there on the edge of his bed, smoking one cigarette after another, thinking probably, as she was thinking, long profitless, weary thoughts! There'd been moments then when, if he had come, some part of her would have welcomed him, bartered everything else feverishly for a mutual bodily assuagement, for an illusion of easing even for so brief a time the loneliness in which they were both engulfed.

Now she was glad. Now she felt, dimly and unreasonably, fighting her sagging eyelids, that some better, some almost bearable way out might present itself. Now that he didn't have to see her all the time as the mother of Jim's baby, he might by degrees begin to think of her as a separate human being. Not Jim's mistress nor his own wife, nor the daughter of her parents, but just Susan. He might begin to like her then. Like her–like–love her——

Oh, wake up! Stupid to fall asleep like a kid or an old lady! And you might snore or leave your mouth open and you don't look your best——

Not that that matters much–now! He's seen you looking worse than that, with your body clumsy and spoiled, the yellow pallor of exhaustion on your face.

There are the locusts beginning now that the sun's out again. A nice noise, whirry, hot, drowsy; a nice movement of the car, rocking gently, a rhythmic vibration——

2

Bret had hardly seen the road for miles. Following his thoughts idly as one might follow some meandering bushland track, he had come slowly into a dark and bitter anger that roused him at last to consciousness of himself and of the way he'd come. He'd been thinking of Wondabyne, and from there he'd got on to some friends of Adela's who had wanted to be shown his stud sheep. And from that he'd remembered riding down with them towards the home paddock just when the three o'clock whistle was sounding and seeing in the distance Ken and Susan walk up from the windmill paddock by the creek. Just a glimpse, instantly forgotten except for a faint momentary worry that Ken, confound him, with his caustic, unguarded tongue, might upset her again as he had once or twice before——

So he'd seen his visitors off and gone back to the wool-shed to speak to Curtis. It was hot in there, he remembered, humid, familiarly-smelling of hessian and newly-shorn wool; quiet now that the machinery had stopped and the men's voices in scraps of conversation made the only sound. Bars of sunlight alive with floating specks of gold lay across the floor and there was a faint smell of ammonia that mingled now and then with the other smells. He turned towards the press to look for Curtis, threading his way between the tumbled bales of wool that surrounded it, and behind a stack of them he came suddenly on Ken with his arm round Susan, and Susan laughing.

His anger had been almost purely for their colossal indiscretion. The realisation afterwards of his total lack of any sensation of jealousy or even of personal injury, had, in fact, disturbed him rather. He'd thought, at first, of nothing at all but the undeniable fact that it might just as well have been any casual shearer who had seen them.

Ken's eyebrows had gone up; he'd made a comical gesture of dismay. Nothing, Bret reflected grimly, had ever been known to upset Ken's attitude of airy cynicism! And Susan, her colour higher and her eyes brighter than ever, had gone on laughing. There, of course, nothing could be said, or done. He'd simply turned and left them, and it was that night when he and Susan had talked and explained and gibed and protested themselves into a semi-exhaustion of nervous strain, that her arm had been scratched so badly by his watch-buckle——

And, when it came to the point he'd found there was nothing, really, that he could say to Ken. Lacking a natural resentment he was left without a case. Unless, indeed, he said, in effect, "If you want to make love to my wife, do it more discreetly." He couldn't even feel that Ken was particularly to blame. Susan had deliberately vamped him (she'd said as much herself) and he'd always been inflammable. And he'd protested, shrugging:

"I'm sorry it happened. But for the Lord's sake don't do the injured husband—under the circumstances it's a bit absurd."

And Bret himself had actually said:

"It's not absurd when you do it under the eyes of every shearer on the place——"

And then stopped, facing the implication of his sentence, seeing the sharp amused appreciation of it lurking wickedly in Ken's faunish grin——

And on that memory he'd wakened to a veritable drum of anger beating in his pulses, the same torturing impotent rage which he felt so often now. Not anger at Ken for making love to his wife, not at Susan for encouraging it, nor at himself for an attitude which could only be put into words that stuck in your throat if you even tried to say them; but at the something behind it all, driving them into unnatural actions, false to each other and themselves.

And what was it but this confounded love business, mischievous, incomprehensible! Jim's love first, tangling and enmeshing them all. Then Susan's, building barriers about her. And he remembered the first time he had felt it, that wall of something invisible and intangible about her, when he'd first suggested marriage and she'd looked at him as she might have looked if he'd stabbed her and she'd been trying to understand before she died why he should harm her so.

And again in the garden at Ballool—the vegetable garden! He remembered that even then, when he was so worried and exasperated, so wretched about Jim's death and so irritable with want of sleep, he'd had a moment or two of pure amusement that they should be talking this thing out with cabbages on one side of them and spinach on the other!

Millicent had said she was in the garden and he'd gone out to look for her. She wasn't on any of the beautifully built "rustic" seats in their rose-smothered arbours, nor in the fern-house, moist and abundantly green with its pool of goldfish and its tiny artificial waterfall. He'd looked beneath the row of camphor laurels and even up into the branches of a couple of the larger ones, and then he'd followed the path round to the back and stood for a moment at a loss. He mightn't have found her then only that he wanted to look at the passion-vine, and there on the other side of its trellis he'd come on her sitting with her back against the chopping-block, and her arms clasped round her knees. He'd realised presently that it was the only spot in the garden with the exception of that dank and depressing fernery which was not visible either from the house or the road. When he did his amusement faded; it did not seem any longer particularly funny to conduct what was after all, in a sense, a romantic interview, with the wood-pile and the vegetables and a heap of garden rubbish for a setting—— She must want pretty badly to be alone—must feel, he thought, fresh from his 70,000 acres, rottenly cramped and restricted in this bit of a suburban garden——

She'd glanced up as she heard his step, and waited without moving. She looked rather alarmingly young with her curly hair brushed back behind her ears and swinging just clear of her shoulders, and the skirt of her pale blue frock spreading round her like a pool of moonlight. He said:

"Hallo. I've been searching the garden for you." And she explained with a note that made him feel he had sounded complaining:

"I didn't know you were here."

There was a wheelbarrow near by so he turned it upside down and sat on it facing her and wondering how to begin.

"May I smoke?"

"Yes."

"Will you?"

"Thanks."

Still, by the time their cigarettes were lighted, he had

no words ready. She didn't seem to be disposed to help, either, and that had annoyed him rather. So he said presently, politely:

"Noble cabbages."

She looked at them and answered indifferently, "Yes."

"Do you like spinach?"

She met his eyes then, and a little glint crept into her own.

"Very much indeed. Do you?"

"Not at all."

"What a pity. They say it's full of vitamins."

"What are vitamins?"

"I haven't the least idea."

There was a pause then. For the first time, born out of their swift exchange of absurdities, he had felt a faint liking for her. He remembered thinking, poor fool that he'd been, that if, to her undeniable though wrong-headed honesty she could add a spark of humour they ought to get along all right. So he said:

"Let's begin again. About this—well, about our wedding. When is it to be?"

"Whenever you like."

"I should think the sooner the better. I—we're busy at Coolami—I don't want to be away too long."

"Is there any need for you to be away at all? I mean, as far as I'm concerned we can be married this afternoon and leave for Coolami to-night."

He looked at her doubtfully. It was so impossible to know what she was feeling. He could only trust to Millicent who had said, "Don't take her straight back to Coolami, Bret. So short a time—just give her a breathing space somewhere else." So he said:

"Well, we want to be—or to seem—as orthodox as

possible. What about a week or a fortnight at the sea-side—I'd like some surfing—haven't had any for years."

He did think that for a second he saw a flicker of relief pass over her face. But she only said:

"Just as you like."

Her complete acquiescence chilled him. He said quickly:

"I want to be agreeable, Susan. If we're to be married we may as well be as nearly friends as possible." A suspicion of the grin which occasionally made him look so like Ken passing fleetingly over his face, he added, "After all, I'm fifteen years older than you, so you can look forward to a happy widowhood."

She'd cried furiously:

"Don't! Don't say such—stupid things!"

Then he felt it again. Something elusive and disturbing. Some factor in his problem which he was failing to take into account. Something incomplete in his knowledge of her. He shrugged.

"Sorry."

She said still flushed, still angry:

"You haven't got to do this. You know very well that I must take an escape for the baby when it's offered to me. But you needn't offer it. There's no reason why you should. I—I wish you'd never thought of it——!"

He'd answered her coldly, remembering again, suddenly and vividly, Jim's bandaged face and head and his difficult words.

"We've had all this out before. It's settled. But I feel that to begin with—with resentment and hostility, is asking for more trouble than we need necessarily have."

She said slowly, playing with a little pile of chips which she had heaped beside her:

"I don't feel hostile—and if I have any resentment it isn't against you."

He said sharply:

"Not against Jim?"

"Oh, no—no!"

His anger, ready to flare in Jim's defence, sank into contrition when he saw her eyes wet with tears. And he felt again a vague uneasiness which had been nagging at him these past few days; a feeling that perhaps his present to Jim's child of the name it should have borne was not, after all, the beginning and end of the fulfilment of his promise. Not much use, he admitted, giving marriage with one hand and years of misery with the other——

He said:

"Look here, Susan, I suppose I've said some pretty rotten things to you since—since this happened. You can't exactly blame me—I don't blame myself altogether. After all, you go in for honesty, don't you?"

She gave him a queer glance.

"I did."

He said ironically:

"Well, it's a bit too late to reform now. It seems to me that all we can do is to—to forget this—— All right," he burst out, answering her expression, "——pretend to forget it, if you like, but we've got to have a—a truce of sorts. One can't spend one's life fighting, even in a marriage of convenience."

She didn't move or answer. Her eyes were dry again, but the stillness of her face gave it a look of hopelessness, of unquestioning abandonment to grief. Bret dropped his cigarette butt at his feet and trod it into the ground. It must have been because he was pretty well exhausted both physically and mentally that he'd lost his temper so easily during those few days. He didn't remember ever feeling before what he'd felt then, and what, even now though more faintly, he felt sometimes when they were quarrelling—a definite desire to hurt her. Watching her sitting there on the ground, so motionless, so utterly unresponsive to his well-meant efforts, it had overwhelmed him alarmingly, a bewildering dark tide, unfamiliar and strangely exciting. He beat it down disgustedly and said:

"You needn't even live at Coolami unless you want to. Just now and then for the sake of appearances."

She looked up, and he thought it was queer how an expression could wipe the youth from her face. She asked:

"And what would you get out of that?"

His control broke away from him in sudden mad exasperation. He answered smoothly:

"I don't expect to get much out of it, anyhow."

Her face flamed. He waited for the return thrust which would make him feel that his blow had been part of a battle. Instead she said nothing, and he found himself in the position of one who has attacked an unresisting foe. That had made him angrier still. He heard his voice adding:

"No more than I can get any day for a few pounds."

There in the back seat of the Madison he put his hand up to his head for a moment as if, after all this time, such a memory were still almost unendurable. A black rage, whipped up from God knows where, and over in a moment. But while it lasts you can say such things——

He glanced sideways at Susan. She was asleep in her corner with her hair tumbled across her cheeks and her mouth slightly open. It had been slightly open that day, too, when she'd sat with the flare of colour draining out of her face and her eyes, which looked as if they could hardly believe her own hurt, fixed on him. He'd got up and gone away nearly to the house and then come back again to find her still sitting there with her head bent, arranging her chips elaborately in a star-shaped pattern. He'd apologised briefly, not daring to say more for fear it should lead to another tangle of words, another treacherous morass of emotion.

She said listlessly:

"It's all right," and then added, "We haven't decided yet when the wedding is to be. If you still want to go on with it."

"Of course."

"To-morrow, then?"

"Very well."

She stood up, brushing and smoothing her skirt mechanically. He noticed that there was a faint vertical line between her brows—as though she had a headache. She said slowly:

"Talking of honesty—you said it was too late to reform. This isn't a marriage of convenience for me. I've been in love with you for months."

She'd gone away then, though he hardly saw her go, standing there with a slow, ridiculous flush burning his face and the back of his neck—dumbfounded, aghast.

CHAPTER FIFTEEN

I

DREW stopped the car on a downward slope because all his life he would never outgrow the economical habit of saving his self-starter, and asked expansively:

"How about a spot of food?"

Bret glanced up from his rueful contemplation of Susan's sleeping face, and Millicent from her memories. "Where are we?"

Drew shrugged.

"How should I know—a poor City mug? We passed a town of sorts a while back."

Bret said:

"That would be Cudgegong. We aren't very far from Mudgee now."

Susan woke up with a yawn and a shiver. She looked out straight at a willow-fringed creek where she'd lunched once with Jim, at a fence she'd clambered over to fall, laughing, into his eager arms, at a whole remembered scene flung back at her with such brutal vividness that she seemed to feel suddenly on her lips the kisses he'd taken, hear his very voice, ghost-like, say, "*Susan, Susan darling, you'll feel differently some day*——!"

She said shakily:

"Is it worth while stopping, do you think?" And bent down to do something unnecessary to her shoe because she felt Bret's quick eyes on her. Drew said:

"Well, I'm *hungry*. And you said the last bit was slow

going, didn't you, Bret? After we turn off the main road?"

"Rough surface," Bret answered with his eyes still on Susan, "and gates galore."

He wondered if she'd been dreaming. Her hands, still fiddling with her shoe-buckle, weren't quite steady, but her face was hidden by her forward-falling hair. Millicent decided:

"Oh, well, there's heaps of time. And Margery doesn't expect us till latish afternoon. So let's stop for a little while if you're hungry, Tom." And she added, to Susan, "Did you have a nice sleep, darling?"

Susan sat up. Well, this was just one more of the little twistings of the knife in the wound. She should be used to them by now. So she answered, "Yes, thanks." And climbed out of the door Bret had opened for her. She was still tired, and now she felt hot and grubby as well, and she wondered, glancing at her watch, what time they'd get to Kalangadoo where she could have a wash and put on something cooler than this beastly flannel frock.

Drew was looking round for a place to spread his rug. She watched him with a dull determined indifference. There was so obviously only one place to picnic, there where the smooth grass sloped down to the water, and two trees gave a sparse but grateful shade. He squeezed, grunting, through the wire of the fence, and called:

"Come on, this is the spot," and spread his rug triumphantly where, through an abrupt, involuntary film of tears she still seemed to see Jim's long figure stretched out on its back, his hands clasped under his head, his brown laughing face turned towards a ghostly Susan——

Bret, just beside her, said, "Susan?" And she glanced at him, startled. He asked in a low voice, desperately, helplessly, "What is it?" But she whisked a handkerchief, and blew her nose, and said quickly, "Nothing. Why?" So he shrugged and held the wire of the fence up for her, and she climbed through and walked slowly down to the trees.

Bret went back to the car and returned laden with bottles which he handed through the fence to Drew. Millicent, rummaging in the hamper, called out:

"Is any one else really hungry? Because I'm just bringing one packet of sandwiches."

Susan, settling herself very deliberately against a tree-trunk, answered, briskly cheerful:

"I want one sandwich and three or four, or possibly five long, cold drinks."

Bret asked, at her elbow:

"Ginger-beer, lemonade, orange-crush, palato, or something without a label which looks like slightly diluted blood?"

She took a mug from her father and held it out.

"Anything. Here's room, Mother; sit down and have some blood."

Drew grumbled:

"What *is* that stuff? You know what we should have done was to go on to a hotel in Mudgee and get a decent lunch and some iced lager. I'll have plain ginger-beer, thanks."

And then, between sips he asked Bret carelessly:

"You heard anything of Colin lately?"

Bret felt Susan's quick anxious glance at him. She'd been there one day at Coolami when a shearer, working westward, had said, not knowing who she was, that it was a sin for a fine little property like Kalangadoo to be left to go to pieces under a drunken swine like Drew. He knew she was wondering what else he might have heard through the strange gossip of the country which travels so fast——

He'd written once a few months ago to Margery offering to go to Kalangadoo at any time if she and Colin needed help. He remembered now the very words of her answer, "Don't come, Bret. He's so touchy, so easily hurt and made suspicious, and then he gets defiant. He'd think his father had sent you to watch him or something like that. He's getting better–he really is——"

So he answered now with equal carelessness:

"No. Why, haven't you?"

Drew muttered hurriedly:

"Oh, yes, yes–we–Margery writes regularly, you know. Colin never was much good at letters——"

His florid handsome face clouded. He stared away across the paddocks, sipping his ginger-beer, and Bret, leaning over to get a sandwich, saw Millicent's hand go out swiftly and cover her husband's——

He got up feeling suddenly restless, depressed–lonely. He walked down to the creek and stood there with his hands in his pockets pretending to be interested in the slowly flowing water.

There wasn't any getting away from it. A few years ago when he read, or when people talked of love he'd shrugged and thought of it cynically as the giraffe among emotions–impossible, incredible! Then, almost like the old tales of mythology when the gods heard your boastings or your doubtings or whatever they might be, and resolved to punish you, he'd had this impossible, this incredible thing flung at him from all sides! Jim, Susan, driven by it; Margery and

Colin using it like a lifebelt in a stormy sea; Drew and Millicent after God knew how many years, still——

He remembered talking to Margery about it just after she and Colin had married and settled down at Kalangadoo. He'd gone down to stay for a week-end and give Colin a few tips—a Colin marvellously well, just then, marvellously buoyant and eager and determined—Margery had said in her downright way.

"Why don't you get married, Bret?"

He laughed.

"Why should I?"

"Why shouldn't you?"

"Because I don't feel like it."

"Haven't you ever been in love?"

He parried that, thinking grimly of Lilian.

"What is love?"

She'd said, "Good God, will you listen to that! What's love, Colin?"

Colin had grinned and suggested "a bio-chemical reaction between two persons of opposite sex," and then he and Margery had gone off into peals of laughter——

Well, Bret thought, that description seemed to him as—as comprehensible as any other—— He began to feel for his cigarettes. A bio-chemical reaction. Whatever that might mean. But it opened up again a train of thought which never failed to disturb him, because its logic, its essential reasonableness was always upset before very long by unspecified emotions whose vagueness he most bitterly resented——

Ken, blast him, had no doubts about it at all. They'd come nearer to quarrelling in these last few months than ever before. Ken, descending on Coolami from time to time was always blandly and infuriatingly amused.

"Susan not home yet?"

Or,

"Where's your wife?"

Or,

"Lord, Bret, why didn't you wire me to come back and marry her for you? My name's Maclean too."

That idiotic sentence had stuck in his memory. It had a sting in it. It had the true Ken-like flavour, malicious, satirical. It said very plainly, "If I had a wife I'd *have* a wife!"

And, Bret admitted, his every coherent thought, his every logical bit of reasoning told him that Ken was right. Artificial, all this. Nothing in the world needed but the opening of that closed door between their rooms—a baby—a wholesome adjustment of natural, bodily needs! Easy enough!

And yet impossible.

There, by your smooth road of logic and common sense, you came to it again. Nothing you could see, nothing you could get hold of—just something that made you as helpless as if you were struggling and writhing in the invisible grip of an electric current. Some kind of mental, moral or spiritual recoil——

Damn! No cigarettes left! He put his empty case back in his pocket and turned to rejoin the others. Susan was coming down the bank towards him with a packet of Capstans in her hand.

"You haven't any left, have you?"

"No. I'd forgotten. Thanks."

Holding a match for her he found himself asking.

"What *was* it just now, Susan? I—it—oh, hell!"

She said coolly, blowing an eddy of smoke away from her eyes:

"Jim and I picnicked here one day. I—woke up to it too suddenly. That's all."

He said, "Oh," rather flatly. Something froze up inside him. He had nothing to say, and silence became like something heavy and almost tangible, so that he felt he couldn't stand there any longer beside her where Jim had probably stood once, watching the same willows trailing eastward in the water, the same reeds, the same fallen log across the creek——

He turned away. She said in the low, malicious tone of the mood which always infuriated him, "Bret?"

"Well?"

"Are you jealous?"

He dropped his hardly-smoked cigarette in the water; his words and his short laugh sounded like some stranger's heard from a distance.

"Jealous? Of you? Good God!"

2

He went back up the bank and began to collect the unopened bottles. He didn't know how plainly his face betrayed him; didn't realise the contraction of his brows, the suddenly expressionless opaqueness of his eyes, the ugly jutting of his underlip. He said briefly:

"Shall I take these back to the car? Would you like any more, Mrs. Drew?"

She shook her head, wondering miserably what had happened now. Drew with his back against one of the tree-trunks was pleasantly comatose. She jumped up on an impulse and ran after Bret. But when at the fence she caught up with him, her old dread of interference overwhelmed her again, and she was glad of the excuse which stooping under the wire gave her not to look at him while she said:

"There's a devil in Susan sometimes, Bret."

He said dryly:

"I've met it."

She stood erect again and looked at him.

"It's nothing on earth but unhappiness."

He answered that with an inflection of conventional politeness which made his words sound, she thought, rather grotesque.

"I'm sorry she's unhappy."

She answered:

"Well, naturally so am I. But I'm also concerned for you. Don't think my maternal prejudices are blinding me to the fact that you're finding it unpleasant as well."

He opened the car door, and began stowing the bottles away methodically. He said something indistinctly and she asked:

"What did you say?"

He straightened up and repeated:

"She suggested a divorce."

Millicent's heart gave a little lurch.

"And you?"

"I don't want it."

She felt a gleam of comfort, instantly destroyed by his belated addition of, "At least I don't think I do."

She asked:

"Are you sorry you did it, Bret?"

He shrugged.

"We couldn't know the child wasn't going to live."

She turned away, chilled, despondent, and yet at the

same time, faintly amused. Dear Bret, how tenaciously he stuck to his point! Even now in the thick of the obscure difficulties of his marriage, he wouldn't forget the unblemished logic of his original reason for it! She said sadly:

"I'm afraid I'm rather to blame. I knew in my heart that logic and rectitude and a handful of good intentions don't make a marriage!

He looked at her with a queer intentness. She thought that his expression was that of a man amused by his own earnestness. He asked:

"Well, what does? You of all people should be able to tell me that."

But suddenly she knew she couldn't. The inhibitions of her temperament, her training, her age, descended on her. Stand there in cold blood, aged fifty-seven, and expound to a politely uncomprehending young man the ultimate mystery of the human race? Absurd! Impossible! She shook her head.

3

They stood without speaking after that, watching the others come up the hill. Drew walked ponderously, his breath coming rather short by the time he reached the fence. Susan, until she saw her father waiting for her with one foot on the lower wire, her mother and her husband watching her from beside the car, had her eyes on the ground and a little drag in her walk. Something in Bret's attitude annoyed her; he looked appraising, speculative, standing there beside her mother with his hands in his pockets and his hat pulled down over eyes which she knew held nothing for her but an intent, detached curiosity, an impersonal and equally detached regret——

She began suddenly to glitter. The blue flare of her skirt swung out as she ran; her whole body, from a slack despondency, became alert and vital; she laughed and flung her head back so that her hair flamed back from her face like fire in a changing wind. She was through the fence, across the road with a movement rather, Millicent thought, like the dart of a blue dragon-fly across a pool, and as she passed Bret she fairly hurled at him the contemptuous, arrogant gaiety of her defiant youth.

Bret, without moving a muscle, said casually to Drew:

"Perhaps I'd better sit in front to show you the way. We turn off the main road pretty soon."

CHAPTER SIXTEEN

I

WHEN they did turn off at last they faced a range of hills, a narrow road that twisted and turned, following a creek fringed with she-oaks and flanked by tall rung timber. The grassy bank near the water seemed, as the car passed, alive with sudden movement; a flicker in the shade of a darker shadow, and a whisk of white that vanished swiftly; as though the earth, after drawing into itself some secret life, lay there still and passive, with nothing to tell of the vanished movement but its surface, pitted and scarred with holes——

Susan said from behind, ruefully:

"I'll never be a proper country woman till I've learnt to hate rabbits, will I?"

Bret wondered, getting out to open the second gate, whether that remark had been addressed to him. And whether there had been intended the suggestion of an olive branch which he imagined he detected in it. He thought, wrestling irritably with the ramshackle fastenings of the gate, that he was possibly too anxious to read into Susan's more casual remarks meanings which she never meant them to have. All the same he maintained, climbing back into his seat, the words had had a pleasant ring. They'd suggested that she wanted—that she hoped—that she thought it possible——

Oh, well—why try to analyse these things? Why not simply be thankful that into the disheartened apathy of your mood a sentence had come refreshingly, with an indefinable promise of an unspecified happiness! And he said to her over his shoulder as he banged the door shut:

"They're disarming little devils if you let yourself look at them."

Drew, driving slowly, asked:

"Pretty bad, aren't they?"

They were. Up the hill-slope to their left among an outcrop of grey-green granite boulders they moved like an army. Every now and then with a flash of its white bobbing tail one scampered across the road in front of the car. Bret, looking worried, grunted something non-committal, opening the car door as another gate came into view. He was wondering now how sharp the older man's eyes were; whether he noticed the dilapidation of the gates and the disrepair of the fences.

He looked at the hills as the car drove through the gate he held open. He'd always rather envied Colin that granite mountain of his, barren land as it was. There was something about its shape that made it look, for all the massive solidity of its naked rock, airy and aspiring; in this light with purple shadow round its base and its distant peak in sunlight it had an almost insubstantial look as though it were something you were dreaming about rather than seeing. No wonder, he thought, the natives had called it Jungaburra—"a spirit place"——

All the same, Colin would come to grief on it some day, scrambling round alone as he so often did——

Drew asked him as he got back into the car:

"That's the mountain Colin's so keen on?"

"That's it."

"You been up it? To the top?"

"Yes, once, with Colin."

"Pretty stiff climb, eh?"

"In patches. One in particular. Colin has a sort of cave about half-way up. You can——"

His hand was half raised to point. Up there, looking like a tiny black spot on the cliff face, his far-sighted eyes could see the cave, and faintly, almost indiscernible in the sunlight, something that looked like a wisp of blue smoke. Bret didn't know what made him stop. He only felt abruptly some deep-rooted instinct to camouflage his barely begun sentence, to mark time, to wait and see——

So he finished quickly: "——see it from the other side of the mountain." And then asked, though he knew quite well, "Is this the third gate or the fourth?"

"Third," Drew said, stopping the car again. "How many more?"

"Only three. You can see the house when we get over that next rise."

Bret, holding the gate, stole another glance at the cliff face as the car went through. It was smoke, sure enough, which meant——

Well, not necessarily. It was conceivable though not likely, that some one else might be there. But Colin didn't encourage visitors to his mountain. Even before he owned it, so the local people said, only one or two parties had ever reached the top. Bret didn't wonder. His memory of the one ascent he'd made with Colin was still very vividly with him, and his eyes, as they came over the crest of the hill, went towards the distant homestead with an anxiety he couldn't quite explain or subdue.

By the time they reached the last gate he had seen

that the car shed was empty, and that there were no fresh wheel marks on the road they themselves were travelling. He heard Millicent say eagerly:

"Look, there's Margery on the veranda."

2

Margery, with Richard beside her, sat on the veranda seat and watched for the car to appear. Only now, the feverish activity of the day behind her, her anger and her feeling of reckless bitterness were beginning to wane. All through the day she'd been telling herself savagely that when they came and asked, "Where's Colin?" She'd just say, "He's been drinking, and he's taken the car and gone." That would break up the cheery family gathering all right, and if Colin did come back before they left he could pick up the pieces for himself as best he might! She was sick of lying for him, acting for him, hiding his lapses behind a barricade of her own weary and half-nauseated loyalty.

To-day, cooking and sweeping and making up beds for her four guests, trying through the sick desperation which had followed the scene with Colin to answer patiently Richard's incessant questions, she had decided that for the sake of the coming child she must snatch an interval of quietness and peace.

Go away somewhere with Richard. Be quiet and relaxed, and learn to hear footsteps without listening, heart in mouth, for fear they should go unsteadily.

Somewhere noisy and alive with people, where there'd be no time for dwelling with one's thoughts. Where there were no days such as this had been, crammed with the drudgeries of a household, every movement of a heavy reluctant body going to an accompaniment of despair and shame and goading anxiety——

While the work had lasted, and physical weariness had kept her anger burning fiercely, she'd answered a hundred times the pricking question, "Where is he?" with a defiant, "I don't know and I don't care!" Now in the late afternoon coolness of the veranda she began to feel rested and the turmoil in her mind smoothed out to quieter thoughts.

She knew now, her hand absently caressing Richard's cheek, that she had acted stupidly, cruelly. You can't marry a man possessed of a devil and hold him responsible for the devil's actions. Was that the right attitude, or was it to excuse too easily those things in him which made him so poor a father? She looked down at Richard's smooth dark head wondering how soon he would realise that the "sickness" for which he gave his father the awed sympathy of healthy childhood had another, harder name——

And yet, she thought, pressing the child's head against her, feeling the soft curve of his cheek and chin with loving fingers, he was right, and the harder name, with all the attitude that it implied, was surely and definitely wrong. For it *was* a sickness. You don't rail at a man for having asthma. You don't pour scorn and condemnation upon him because he's tubercular——

You blame with futile fierceness the unknown powers which sent boys of eighteen to war. You blame those horrors which stayed always fiercely photographed on their memories so that a spot of whisky now and then to bring sleep, oblivion, became by degrees to seem like a friend—an only friend, merciful and saving——

She sighed and stood up. She thought she couldn't really be a very maternal kind of person or the coming of her children wouldn't make her so nervous and irritable. She'd been sometimes vaguely ashamed of the sensations she had felt in the months before Richard's birth and again now—not as if she shared her life, her body, gladly with the newcomer, but as though some deeply resented interloper were annexing something that was sacredly her own——

It wasn't as if she didn't want the children. It was only that she longed to feel sometimes more alone than was possible when she was conscious all the time of new life within herself, insistent and demanding.

So that really, she thought, when Colin's sickness and her own nervousness happened to clash on the day when four visitors were arriving for the night, it wasn't to be wondered at if sparks flew a bit. And perhaps she was rather silly to feel, every time, such black disappointment. By now, surely she should be prepared, resigned even, to its happening every now and then; content if only the intervals between grew—as they had been growing—longer and more blessedly, peacefully happy. Why, after more than five years, did it still strike her every time afresh with such a torturing sense of disillusionment?

Perhaps, she thought rather fearfully, it was only the faith which had so far always renewed itself in her which had made those intervals as long and as happy as they had been. A hint in her of doubt, of scepticism, a suggestion that her thought was "Till next time!" might have broken down his resistance far more often, far more ignominiously. Just as to-day if she'd managed to hold her tongue, keep him quiet, give him black coffee and make him lie down, she might have got him into some sort of shape before his people arrived.

Whereas——

If he hadn't pushed Richard——

That was the spark which had lit her smouldering resentment to a bonfire, a conflagration of uncontrollable fury. For the child, round-eyed with sympathy, had been trying to help him—trying to guide his clumsy feet up the two steps into the room where his mother was making beds, saying anxiously, reassuringly, "There's one n'other step, Daddy—only one n'other step——"

She'd looked up from her work with the giddy feeling of disaster which always overwhelmed her when she saw her husband like this.

"Colin! Oh—*Colin*!"

He'd asked her thickly, resentfully, what was the matter, and Richard's voice had said over and over again excited, admonishing in the heavy silence, "No, not any more, Daddy—you've come up all the steps, Daddy, now it's just floor—look, Daddy, it's just floor——"

She'd said with an effort, holding out a hand:

"Richard——"

And then Colin, exasperated by the pulling hand, the small insistent voice, had given the child a clumsy push. Not enough to hurt him, not even enough to make him lose his balance. That would have been better, his mother thought, her bitterness stirring up again at the memory, than the sudden revelation she had seen written on his face that his help, so eagerly and lovingly given, was being rejected.

She had snatched him up and run with him to the back where Bill, the wood and water joey, was stacking kindling by the kitchen door. She'd said, "Watch him for a few minutes, Bill." And then she'd gone back, storming, to Colin.

Well, it had been ugly and unnecessary—and futile. An hour later, face downward on the half-made bed, she'd heard the roar of the car engine and thought wildly, "I hope he never comes back!" And she'd dragged herself to her feet and gone on with her work because somewhere between her and Sydney there was a car making for Kalangadoo——

Not easy in a small house and with one indifferent country-girl for a servant, to prepare for four additions to one's household. Not easy either in the confusion of one's mind, the slack weariness of one's body, to know whether one dreaded or looked forward to their coming. How fond she could have been, she thought wryly, of her parents-in-law if she hadn't been forced into the position of incessantly acting to them! "But never again!" she'd sworn vigorously, unfolding two stretcher-beds on the veranda. This time they could see and judge for themselves. This time they could know that Colin had chosen the day of their coming for a drinking bout—— All through the sultry morning, the din and flash and battering rain of the brief thunderstorm, she'd felt her anger and her bitter disappointment bearing down like a weight between her shoulders. It was only with the house swept and garnished behind her, and the long purple shadows coming down from the hills to the creek, that she could feel them cracking, falling away from a truer emotion, as a hard shell from the sound and wholesome fruit inside.

They were completely gone, and with them she realised had gone most of the nervous strength that had sustained her through the day. She felt anxious and remorseful and unbelievably tired. She wondered for a moment, drearily, if she should go inside and ring people up to try to find out where Colin was. Menzies' store perhaps; or the bakers might have seen him go by and noticed which road he took. Or—the hotels in Mudgee——

But she didn't move. It wouldn't really help. If he was sober he'd come home by himself, and if he wasn't—well, as things were the longer he stayed away the better. They wouldn't let him drive the car if he wasn't fit to. He'd be dumped down somewhere to sleep it off and the men would glance at him and look at each other and shrug and say, "Colin on the bust again?"

She put her hand to her cheek and found it hot, but not with anger. Her pity and love for her husband expanded achingly, so that they seemed like some other living thing within her, and she knew that drunk or sober, her only wish was to have him home——

Richard, rushing up from the corner of the veranda, called excitedly:

"Car, Mummy! Look, Mummy—car!"

Her heart leapt. The shock of disappointment when she saw the Madison told her how intensely her mind, her whole desire had been centred on another car, small and brown and dilapidated, with Colin at the wheel——

She had actually, for the moment, forgotten her guests. Now she knew, her practical common sense succeeding the warm and irrational emotions of a moment ago, that it was better—far better that he should be absent—remain absent—while she lied for him. She'd have to chance his not returning till late—or even till to-morrow morning. She'd have to keep awake somehow and listen for the car and smuggle him in and coach him, and feed him, and tidy him up for his parent's eyes——

She'd have to take her luck.

There was Bret getting out to open the last gate. She remembered almost for the first time in that troubled and unhappy day, Susan and her matrimonial impasse. Her hand went down again to Richard's thick hair and the warmth of his cheek. Something of contrition was in the instinctive caress, and gratitude; relief mingled with it for the difficult husband who yet remained a lover, and for the living child and the other who was so soon to live.

CHAPTER SEVENTEEN

I

NOT that Susan didn't seem jolly enough when she jumped out of the car. Not that Bret, waving a hand towards the veranda while he helped with the luggage, didn't look his usual imperturbable self. Margery felt, as she went down the steps to meet them, a sudden genuine gladness that they were here. Loneliness, she thought, was not unlike physical weariness—you hardly realised how bad it was till the respite came. But warily through her pleasure in seeing them a kind of defensiveness waited alertly at the back of her mind. She kissed Millicent, thinking, "Will she ask it?" She said to herself, an arm round Susan and a hand in Bret's, "Now, surely?" She felt Drew's hearty paternal kiss on her cheek and heard it come at last:

"Where's Colin?"

Amazing how glibly one learned to lie! The fluent sentences of excuse slid off her tongue like lines spoken automatically for the hundredth time in some stage success! She marvelled even as she spoke that her fabrication sounded so convincing! It wouldn't be difficult, perhaps, to believe it herself! They, at all events——

Over Millicent's shoulder she saw Bret looking at her. The expression, whatever it was, which had been in his eyes was so quickly gone that she could not analyse it. She only knew that in a second, from a feeling of half-excited relief, she was plunged into a vague uneasiness.

Drew, having carried a couple of suitcases to the top of the steps, was at the wheel again. Margery said:

"There's plenty of room in the shed for the car. Bret, would you show the way?"

She watched the big car go lurching round the side of the house over the uneven ground. Something about it made her see her home suddenly as a place rather depressingly crude and comfortless, and when she turned back to her two remaining guests she looked at them for a moment absently. Millicent, sitting on the bottom step, had Richard at her knee. She was showing him the zip fastener of her handbag, and he was wrestling to open it with fat, hurried fingers. And Susan, too, was looking after the car. Susan, too, when it had vanished round the corner, remained standing with her hat in her hand, her thoughts quite obviously not on the shadow streaked hillside where her dark eyes were fixed.

Margery said quickly:

"Come along inside. You must want a wash. Susan, I've had to camp you and Bret on the veranda. There's a dressing-room for you but it's not big enough for beds. Richard, give Gran back her bag, darling. We'll go through this way. I'll have some tea made for you."

Millicent protested:

"Not tea, Margery—really. We had a picnic only an hour or so ago. Come and watch me unpack my suitcase, Richard."

Margery opened the door of the room she had prepared for her husband's parents. It was, she always thought, the pleasantest room in the house, large and cool, its creamy coloured walls flickering with the greenish light from a window half masked by the frondy leaves of a giant pepper-tree. But now, as she said,

"There are two steps up from the door," she felt its whole atmosphere weighted, oppressed by a memory of Colin lurching across it to that bed now so smooth and unrevealing——

And the steps, too, had wakened some such memory in Richard. She saw him look back at them and from them to his grandmother with the look in his eyes of the child with news to tell.

"Gran–Daddy——"

Margery slipped between them. On her knees in front of him she said swiftly:

"Darling, Gran's tired and she wants to have a rest now. You come along and——"

But Millicent urged:

"I'd love him to stay, Margery. There's a parcel for him in my suitcase——"

Margery looked at her son. She searched his small face intently. There were no memories there now–only excitement, only visions of unspecified glories in brown paper and string——

She sighed.

"Well, be good then. Come on, Susan."

2

In the tiny dressing-room they faced each other, Susan and Margery, questions and answers in their eyes.

Margery said:

"Well?"

And Susan, with a little shrug, answered:

"Not so very."

She pulled her frock over her head and sat down on the window seat fanning herself with her hat. She asked:

"And what about you?"

It wasn't very hard now, she thought, looking at her sister-in-law, to guess what about Margery! There was a sudden abandonment of effort in every line of her burdened body as she sat down wearily, her hands dropping like lead into her lap. She said:

"Oh, much as usual."

"Colin?"

"Mostly he's all right."

"To-day?"

"No, I haven't seen him since this morning. We must try not to let them know, Susan."

"I don't see why you mind so much about their knowing."

"He does. And when he knows they think—your mother thinks—he's all right, he—it seems to help——"

Susan stood up restlessly. Something in the sight of Richard, in the knowledge of Margery's pregnancy had stirred a never wholly buried grief for her own short-lived baby. She said shortly:

"Are you all right?"

Margery looked surprised. She was surprised. Beyond the weariness and the nervous stress it had never occurred to her to question her own health in child-bearing.

"Oh, yes—quite!"

"I got Mother to pack my baby-clothes for you. You might find them useful."

"Rotten luck, Susan."

"Maybe."

Margery looked at her. A few years ago when she'd first met Susan she had said to Colin with a faint superciliousness which, she now admitted, had had its roots in envy, "That young sister of yours gives herself a good time, doesn't she?"

She hadn't ever had that kind of good time herself. She hadn't been rich enough or pretty enough, and she'd always been too serious. Sometimes, now that life had really become such a difficult business, she often found herself smiling at the extreme seriousness of her university days; wondering what in the world she had found to be serious about in that incredibly far away and care-free existence——

She found herself thinking now that apparently Susan's frivolity had been quite as good a school for subsequent endurance as her own more austere youth. Not that Susan's trouble——

Her idle thoughts, the very movement of her hand to brush her hair away from her forehead, stopped abruptly. She realised with Susan sitting there before her that she had, so far, given her young sister-in-law's romance and tragedy only the scantiest and most superficial attention. Certainly last year when she had been playing the fool with Jim—when they'd come dashing in on their way from Coolami to Sydney, or from Sydney to Coolami, demanding lunch, demanding tea, demanding shelter for the night, laughing, teasing each other, filling the house with a very tempest of youth and vitality, she'd warned Susan several times to watch her step. Susan had laughed and hugged her, at first. Later she'd grown more subdued, and Jim had followed her with hungry, resentful eyes. And one day—on their last trip down from Coolami, Margery had stumbled on the reason. She'd gone to her room where Susan was having a wash and found her standing before the dressing-table with a brush in one hand and a framed enlargement of a snap of Colin and Bret taken on their troopship in the other. Margery had seen, as she entered, an expression on Susan's mirrored face that surprised her. Not one that she could analyse—not one that gave her any clue to the amazing truth which Susan later confessed to her, but just an expression that struck her instantly as being queer, of lying unfamiliarly, like a mask, over the girl's usually merry face.

She'd said, looking over Susan's shoulder:

"Colin's changed a good deal, hasn't he?"

"Yes."

As the expression on Susan's face, so the tone of her voice gave Margery an instant sensation of strangeness. And then, putting the photograph down and turning away from the mirror she had added:

"Bret hasn't, though."

Almost as though she realised herself that her face, her voice, were betraying something she wished to hide, she had bent her head down suddenly so that her flame of hair swung downwards round it, and she had brushed and brushed with her face hidden——

And later, after lunch she had vanished. Jim, sitting on the veranda with Colin and herself, was moody and restless. His eyes were always on the door into the house, his conversation scrappy and disconnected. Margery at last, taking pity on him, had gone to look for Susan and found her face downward across the foot of the double bed, quite still, her hands clasped over the back of her head. She'd sat beside her, anxiously:

"Susan, what's the matter?"

Susan rolled over and looked at her. She hadn't been crying, evidently, but she looked so despairingly miserable that Margery found herself wishing for the sight of a tear or two, as for a sign of alleviation. She asked desperately:

"Look here, Marge, how *do* you stop a man caring for you?"

Margery had asked, puzzled:

"Jim, do you mean?"

"Yes. I've tried–I–he——"

"I thought you–don't you care for him?"

"I like him–I'm really awfully fond of him. But I don't want to marry him."

"Have you still got that flat?"

"Yes–in a way. I—— Oh, that's where all the trouble is, Marge. I won't go there any more and he–sometimes he seems nearly mad with unhappiness–I can't bear to see it. I told him I wouldn't see him at all last time I was down, but he just followed and followed and hung round and wrote letters begging me to marry him so that I *had* to——"

"Well, why on earth did you go back to Wondabyne this time?"

"It was getting simply impossible at home. You know what Dad is–he was beginning to wonder what Jim was at with his precious daughter. And Mother–I was afraid–you know how people talk–lots of people knew about the flat apparently and I was afraid Mother and Dad would hear of it. It seemed safer to get him back to the country and leave him there——

"Leave him there——!"

She had finished with a little shrug and a wave of her hand towards the veranda. Margery had asked slowly:

"Are you sure you don't care for him enough to marry him? He's a nice boy—I'm fond of Jim."

Susan had nodded soberly:

"That's just it. He *is* a nice boy. I'm fond of him too."

Margery had asked at random:

"You're not in love with anybody else?"

And then sat staring at the sudden flood of colour over Susan's cheeks, the painful twist of her face as though from some sudden inward agony. She said awkwardly:

"I'm sorry, darling—I had no idea. But if Jim knew that—if you told him——"

Susan rolled over on her face again. Her voice came from the eiderdown, muffled and despairing:

"I can't tell him—I can't—it's the one thing I can't do——!"

Margery asked, mystified:

"Why not?"

The voice this time was so smothered that Margery could not believe that she had heard it properly.

"*What* did you say?"

"It's Bret."

Well! She'd sat there helplessly looking down at the tumbled red hair on the eiderdown and wondering why the news should be so staggering, so impossible, grotesque. Just because, she supposed, Bret had always seemed so very much a bachelor, so intensely occupied with and satisfied by his work——

She'd asked doubtfully:

"Does he—is he—well——"

Susan sat up, smoothing her hair. She said crisply:

"He can't bear the sight of me. Marge, it's been getting late while I've been having emotion-trouble all over your best eiderdown. We won't get home till morning at this rate. Don't tell any one, darling. I'll get over it—maybe."

Maybe.

It was perhaps that echo of the word Susan had just spoken which had taken her thoughts back to a day so long past. And she saw now that since that day she had never really thought much about Susan except for a brief time after she had had the letter from her brother. That had been a nasty shock! Although, of course, it had crossed her mind several times that Susan, even armed as she was with knowledge, was living very dangerously indeed!

"*That young sister-in-law of yours has got herself into a mess. She said I could tell you. She came to see me yesterday. I'm writing to you because you may be able to do something—help her in some way—you probaby know who the man is? She looked a bit queer when she left——*"

For a week or so after that she'd thought hard. She'd written to Susan and waited anxiously for a reply. Before it came there'd been that brief, staggering paragraph in the paper—"Mr. James Maclean of Coolami station——" "injuries to the head and back——" "taken to the hospital where he survived only a few hours." And almost, it seemed, on the top of that bald announcement had come Susan's amazing letter. She and Bret were going to be married. Almost at once. Because of the baby. Short sentences like that, giving, Margery remembered thinking, in their bare statement of fact, a dreadful impression of despair hidden and beaten down——

But somehow, from the moment of reading that letter she hadn't worried any more about Susan.

Bret was taking it on. She'd be all right with Bret. She'd got out of a tight corner very well, and even if Bret didn't really care for her he'd always be decent, and probably Susan was too young anyhow to know anything about love. As for her infatuation for Bret it was probably a good thing. Given that and the dreadful jolt, poor kid, that Jim's death must have been to her, she'd be a good deal more amenable, a good deal less wilful and mercurial and red-headedly impetuous than she'd been in the past——

That was how her thoughts had run—skimming, as she now saw, the surface of Susan's troubles. It was only the sight of the girl sitting there before her, limp and listless, only the flat sound of her voice saying that one word, "Maybe," which made Margery see with the swiftness of revelation that her young sister-in-law had come through a year of varied sufferings, and was now facing what was, she could not help thinking, a queer fate, for the fascinating and much-coveted Susan! She remembered talking very glibly to Colin about it just after the marriage had taken place. "Oh, it'll right itself—Susan's a dear kid but she's a bit superficial, isn't she? I mean her reactions would be rather shallow —ephemeral—— She'll be miserable for a while and then she'll settle down and forget all about Jim and be as happy as a cricket——"

Something like that. Funny that it hadn't seemed to occur to her that Bret would have "reactions" too! She saw now, shocked and amazed by her former denseness, that Bret's reactions, which would naturally be anything but shallow, were the key to a situation far less simple than she had so carelessly imagined.

Susan was roaming about the little room, still using her hat as a fan. Margery thought, watching her, that there was a Peter Pan-ish look about her—slender and small and with an intriguing air of having just alighted on the ground. That was something she got from her mother—there was that about Millicent, too, which always made you feel that her presence at any given spot was accidental, temporary, even illusory! That you wouldn't be surprised altogether if the spot were suddenly vacant and you were left half-wondering if it had ever been occupied at all!

And then, as Susan turned from the veranda door, she had to admit that that impression of her belonged almost entirely to her back view. You couldn't, seeing her face, feel that she was anything but a blend, endearing to others, but painful no doubt to herself, of too many very human qualities.

She swooped suddenly to perch on the arm of Margery's chair. She flung a cool bare arm round Margery's neck. She said:

"Cheer up, darling. Colin will be all right. I'll change my dress and then I'm coming out to do a chore or two for you. Have you still got Simple Sarah the Idiot Child?"

Margery laughed, and stood up.

"No, Richard started imitating her—roaming round with his jaw dropped and a vacant expression. I really couldn't stand it. I've got a lass called Annie. She's strong and willing to such an extent that she's broken all my best china, but she's fond of Richard and she's clean, so what's a plate or two——?"

Susan said brightly:

"What, indeed?" And began to sob with her head down on the back of the chair. Margery stroked it silently. She thought:

"Oh, hell! What a houseful of misery!"

But Susan was sitting up again in a moment smearing the tears out of her eyes with the back of her hand like a child. She said calmly:

"Don't take any notice of me, Marge—I'm liable to burst into heartrending sobs at any moment. All I need is a hanky and a cold bath."

Margery said, giving her a handkerchief:

"Well, that's easy. You know your way to the bathroom. Don't hurry—there's nothing you can do. Everything's cold and Annie is quite equal to it."

But she thought, closing the door behind her, that a hanky and a cold bath would not go far towards the easing of Susan's unhappy heart.

CHAPTER EIGHTEEN

I

BRET, following his father-in-law in from the shed where the Madison had just been lovingly bestowed, paused for a moment to speak to Bill, who was pottering aimlessly about the wood-pile.

"Good rain last week, Bill." But he was watching Drew out of sight round the corner of the house as he spoke and he only half listened to the man's rambling answer.

"——an' they do say that over by Malibar they never got a drop. Real good fall out your way, Mr. Maclean."

"Yes—fine——"

There hadn't been any wheel marks on the road——

"Did you have much rain this morning?"

"Too right. Came down 'ard for an hour or so."

Well, that was that. There wouldn't be. Bret put down the two suitcases and lit a cigarette.

"Mr. Drew been doing any more climbing lately?"

The sun was gone now behind the hills. Jungaburra when they both glanced up instinctively at its peak stood out menacingly, a blackish-purple mass against the fading sky. Bill scowled at it and spat into the middle of the wood-pile.

He muttered:

"Break 'is neck up there some day, that's what 'e'll do——" And Bret who, held by some queer fascination, had not taken his eyes from the forbidding summit, felt a sudden chill, a moment of shock almost as if, with some other sight than the physical, he'd seen Colin's body like a black speck hurtling down into the silent darkness of the trees below——

He picked up the suitcases abruptly, and said with a laugh:

"Let's hope not! Good-night!"

But on the veranda he paused again for a moment and stared at the mountain. It was possible, of course, that Margery's excuses had been genuine, but he doubted it. Too damned glib, he thought, blowing the smoke of his cigarette away from his eyes and frowning still, though unseeingly now, at the darkening skyline.

And if they had been, as he suspected, fabrications, where was Colin? And if he was—well, in a state that called for fabrications, he was certainly not in a state to be where that drift of smoke had shown this afternoon, blue and wraith-like against the bare cliff face——

Strange how quickly the light died in these hill-enclosed hollows. He half turned to go inside and then suddenly in a black wave of weariness and depression put his suitcases down again and leaned his elbows on the veranda rail. Not much to go in to! A houseful of unsolved problems! And yet what could look more peaceful than this place sinking into twilight, the last afterglow fading out of the sky, the frogs beginning to croak down there near the creek-bed, and the mosquitoes, blast them, to buzz!

And to sting! He slapped viciously at his ankle, and a path of light wavered out across the veranda from an open door. He looked up and saw Susan come to the french windows to draw the curtains across them. What little she had on was made negligible by the soft lamplight behind her and he had before the curtains hid her a momentary impression of strangely arresting beauty. He stood now with his back to the night still looking at the curtained doorway, wondering a little that he should be so stirred. Wondering too, gropingly, because he was not used to introspection, why that stirring of his heart had seemed in some vague way to be at once for the intimate and human beauty of Susan silhouetted against the light and for the dark majestic, and rather intimidating beauty of Jungaburra, black against the sky? Why, too, he did not feel obscurely exasperated with himself because he had had no instant reaction of a righteous, husbandly desire, but rather a more nebulous, queerly satisfying emotion which utterly defied his powers of analysis——

Well, whatever it was it had made him feel good! Good, as one feels after a close game won, or a hard trip ended, or early in the morning for no particular reason at all! So good that surely in such a mood one could really do something about this bothering difficult marriage which had in it somewhere, if one could only find and cherish it, the germ of a beautiful simplicity——!

He knocked at the curtained door.

2

Susan snatched at her blue frock and then with a faint shrug threw it down again across the bed. She said:

"Come in."

She turned back to the mirror and went on combing her hair, the light from the lamp standing beside her showed him only vaguely in the glass as he entered, but she saw the red tip of his cigarette swing out and down as he took it out of his mouth to throw away.

She said casually, still combing:

"I'd go on smoking if I were you. The mosquitoes are fierce."

The glowing tip described a swift arc in the air and vanished. He came in and closed the door behind him.

"It was finished, anyhow."

She asked:

"Did you bring the suitcases in?"

He said:

"Lord, I'd forgotten them – they're just out here on the veranda."

He was out and back with them. She turned with the comb in her hand.

"Would you open mine, please? I want a cool frock. Here's the key." And as she held it towards him he took her hand and said awkwardly:

"Susan——"

But he found no other words. He had realised with a sudden feeling of helpless and rather crestfallen surprise that a mood is not transferable.

She said:

"Yes?" And he could feel the faint pull of her hand against his grasp. He released it and said, unlocking the suitcase:

"I hardly know. I – well, when I was out there on the veranda I had a sudden feeling that there must be some—— Things can't be quite so hopeless——"

He put the open case on the chair and she bent over it. She asked non-committally:

"What made you feel that?"

He frowned, tangled in a genuine and misguided effort to express the inexpressible. He said:

"I saw you just now—you came to the window——"

She straightened up and looked him over with a slow, contemptuous smile. She said, "I see." And shook out a frock like a primrose, pale and star-yellow in the soft light. He said angrily:

"You don't see at all—I——"

She bent over the suitcase again, yielding him no more attention than a fleeting glance such as one might give to the protestations of some jam-besmeared small child. He looked down at her bent head flickering with filaments of fiery gold, at her bare arms and shoulders, and he felt a heat and a throbbing behind his eyelids, and a wave of energy almost nauseating in its mixture of anger and desire. He knew, obscurely, that the fury which possessed him was more than half grief for the death of that elusive happiness which had so briefly warmed his heart. He was hurt in a way in which he had never been hurt before, by the discovery that any mood so full of the promise of beauty could be so abruptly and ruthlessly destroyed. He knew even at the moment when he caught her in his arms that he was succumbing to an emotion as primitive and illogical as the temper of a child who smashes a whole toy because one part of it has been damaged. But it was an emotion which, once started, fed on other emotions roused to violence by his senses; the feel of her, and the faint scent of her hair, swept him forward on a tide of reckless and sadistic passion, till he felt her resistance cease suddenly and her arms go round his neck.

He stood quite still, almost as though he were listening. He didn't know why that sudden response had chilled instead of further inflaming him, but he was, instinctively, giving his body a chance to find out for him, as one might for a second or two hold some flavour on the tongue to test its palatableness.

In those moments of immobility he realised that although they stood there in each other's arms, his head bent over her, his face against the smooth skin of her neck and shoulder, there was about them an atmosphere of incredible and rather terrifying solitude. She, too, seemed to be listening. There was a sense of aloofness, remoteness, as though they were suspended in some timeless gulf of silence——

Something had arrested in him a passion which no logic had been strong enough to subdue. Turned it off, he thought wonderingly, like a tap or an electric light—flick! Something had made of him, in an instant, a creature as instinctively aware of danger as a wild forest animal, held him as motionless as a stag sniffing the air to find where danger lay!

His arms fell away from her. They stood facing each other warily. A glimmer of understanding came to him and with it a passing moment of exultation. He said:

"Was that the beginning of your play-acting?"

She nodded.

"It didn't work, did it?"

He said slowly:

"Perhaps—I'm not quite so dense as you thought me?" And they looked at each other intently, consideringly, until her face wavered into a smile, and involuntarily he felt his own responding.

She took a long white slip from the suitcase and dropped it over her head. She said, emerging:

"Evidently not. Or possibly my acting might be improved."

"I wouldn't try if I were you."

"Why not?"

"I find that I have a keen nose for it."

"And you don't like it?"

"I certainly don't like it."

Her frock was descending like the petals of a gigantic flower. It stopped suddenly and hung suspended, twisting and swinging with the movements of her hidden arms. She said in a muffled and exasperated voice, "Well, I don't know what else to try. This damn thing's hooked in my hair. It might be better to get a divorce now while we're still comparatively decent than later when we'll probably be anything but. For goodness' sake see if you can find where this hook is caught."

He said, fumbling with a handful of bright hair and flimsy muslin:

"Give me time, Susan. There you are."

"Thanks." She pushed her hair back from a face flushed by her struggle with the hook and asked, "Time for what?"

He looked at her for a moment without answering. What he wanted though he did not know how to express it was time for that vagrant and miracle-working sense of beauty to descend on him again. A chance to learn, less impetuously this time, whatever it was that it had to teach; to see more clearly the distant horizon of the land it promised. All that, in his mind, was confused, a shapeless and amorphous loveliness, tantalising, useless.

He said, turning away:

"To think, I suppose."

Her voice said evenly from behind him:

"That isn't very wise. Your thoughts will take you straight back to Jim."

He winced but found himself admitting:

"Well, even that might be—salutary."

She sat down suddenly on the arm of the chair and her hands dropped limply into her lap. She said drearily:

"It's awfully exhausting talking to you. I can't follow your thoughts. What do you mean by salutary?"

He said shortly:

"One makes mistakes."

She couldn't resist that. She asked, softly and maliciously, innocent-eyed:

"Not *you*, Bret?"

He moved restlessly and said, "Don't be ridiculous." And then there was a long, empty and disheartened pause. Susan broke it with a sigh and a not altogether contrite, "Sorry!" but the meagre springs of Bret's self-expression had dried up and he only shrugged, waiting with poised hand for a hovering mosquito to settle on his arm.

Susan said flatly:

"You did get splashed to-day. Do you want a brush?"

He turned and twisted, trying half absently to see the back of his coat and trouser-legs. He was thinking that this journey, with its succession of rather brutal associations, its clinging, pricking memories lying in wait by the roadside like so many Bathurst burrs, was probably being a pretty fair purgatory for her. He said, "I thought I'd got most of it off," and went on to the realisation that she was going back to a whole lifetime of relentless reminders that she had once made a mistake which had set her off on an endless path of futility——

Well, after all there it was. She'd made her mistake and she'd chosen her road and he couldn't——

Unless something should happen which could make her feel that the roughest journey had been worth——

She was brushing at his coat with a small ivory-backed brush from her dressing-case. She said in the same flat voice:

"It shows so on this light grey stuff."

He stood still with his hands jingling money and keys in his trouser pockets till she had finished. He was so deeply tangled in his thoughts that he was not properly aware of them, as one might be, in fighting through some almost impenetrable undergrowth, unaware of the actual nature of the shrubs and creepers in one's way. From one clear painfully acute desire, his thoughts had leapt irrationally into varied and panic-stricken flight. He'd felt suddenly with his whole heart that he wanted her to be happy, and from that wish he'd plunged into a tumult of mad plans and wild surmises. There'd been a kaleidoscopic vision which showed him a kind of toy-shop of the adult female's heart's desire—clothes, and jewels, and cars and trips abroad——

The cessation of her rhythmic brushing woke him up, irritated and ashamed of what he instantly recognised as a collection of ridiculous compromises with an uncompromising situation.

He even realised between chagrin and amusement that among the tinsel and candles of the imagined Christmas-tree delights with which he had proposed to soothe her hurts, he'd actually had a glimpse of a couple of be-ribboned babies—toys of some vague immaculate conception—to assuage an equally vague and uncomprehended "maternal instinct."

She said:

"That's all right, I think. I can't really tell in this light. But it's better anyhow."

He answered without moving:

"Thanks. Is there anything you want, Susan?"

She asked doubtfully:

"Want? How—in what way?"

"Well—in any way."

He saw the glimmer of a smile in her eyes and said hurriedly:

"You can make your joke in a minute if you like. But for the Lord's sake stay serious just long enough to answer that. Is there anything you want?"

She said slowly:

"You know what I want. If you mean things one buys—no, there isn't anything—thank you."

He felt his mouth twitch. Susan was, in between her fits of malice and impudence, so carefully and sedately polite! She asked now, picking up a powder puff from the dressing-table and dabbing it rather cavalierly over her flushed cheeks:

"Do you want to give me something?"

He admitted:

"I did feel an urge that way." And she said deliberately, still intent on her reflection:

"An interesting psychological manifestation of your remorse at feeling yourself unable to reciprocate my affections. Poor Bret! You could buy me some chocolates in Mudgee when we go through to-morrow! That would make you feel better, wouldn't it?"

He said, smiling at her:

"Stop daubing that stuff on your face, and stop talking rot and come out on the veranda. This room's as hot as hell."

She threw her powder-puff down and gave his arm a squeeze as she went past him to the door. She said:

"You'd have been quite fond of me if I'd been your sister, wouldn't you?"

She was gone along the veranda like a moth in the darkness, without waiting for the answer he didn't attempt to give.

CHAPTER NINETEEN

I

MARGERY was putting Richard to bed. He was telling her, while he struggled with his braces, a long rambling tale about a mythical country of his own invention, and she was saying absently, "Yes, darling," and "Was it?" and "Did it really?" And thinking sadly as she watched him how vulnerable he was in spite of his sturdy body and his rosy brown face. Always in this world of crude violences and brutalities he would remain vulnerable, and yet she could not bring herself to believe that it was other than desirable that a child should grow with a horror of bloodshed, of killing so deeply rooted in him. Some day, she thought, all children will feel like that and it'll be a better world—perhaps—than it is now. But in the meantime, poor Richard!

She winced, remembering a day when he'd rushed into the kitchen where she was preparing breakfast, his face greenish-white, his eyes mad with some violent and inescapable horror. He'd clutched her round the knees, his hard little head boring against her as a panic-stricken animal beats and plunges against a wall in futile attempts at escape. She'd gone down on her knees to hold him, her own distracted brain alert, her eyes busy, her ears listening to try to find what had so shocked him. There was no sound from outside but the clatter of the mowing-machine where Bill was mowing the square of grass beneath the clothes-lines. Holding Richard in her arms she'd moved towards the door, and felt instantly his whole body contract, resist, strain away from it. She went back into the cool dimness of the kitchen, sat down with him, soothed and stroked him, murmured reassurances. And after some minutes he'd stared up at her with a strange look of incredulity on his face, as though he felt, as a last hope, that she might be able utterly to deny the reality of what he'd seen.

"Mummy—there was a snail—in the grass—and Bill *mowed it—he mowed it all in pieces*——!"

He'd been violently ill then, and when she had changed and bathed and put him down in his cot he'd slept long but restlessly, his hot hand twitching in her own.

She put out an arm for him to steady himself by as he stepped out of his small blue trousers. She thought with a wave of pity and tenderness that he was really very tiny to be made to look after himself so much. But she knew that when the other baby came she'd have less time for him—he must learn to manage some at least of his daily needs for himself——

He was explaining earnestly:

"In Riverburra there's snakes and they live in the ground and they poisonous the ground——"

"Do they, darling?"

"Yes, and they poisonous the water too, but the people in Riverburra only drink milk so they don't get dead from the snakes."

"I see. Those buttons don't do up, Richard—don't you remember mother put press-fasteners so they'd be easier for you?"

"I forgot—I only have to go *woosh*! and they all undo theirselves——"

"Yes, only don't woosh too hard."

She thought wearily that right or wrong Richard would have lived a far happier life if he had been like that small hearty Goth his cousin, her brother's son, who went about the lawns of their Sydney home trampling on snails with a rich and expansive gusto; who upon one occasion she remembered, had opened a sardine sandwich to inspect it and, remarking cheerfully, "H'm! Dead fish!" consumed it with Gargantuan relish. Well, she thought bitterly, how far had the world gone on? Would he some day be glorified as a fine soldier, while Richard was being scorned and pilloried for a conscientious objector?

He was standing still looking down at himself consideringly, trying to remember how she had told him to go about the removal of this tiresome shirt. She clutched him to her as though the menacing years had taken shape before her very eyes and were reaching out hungry hands for him.

He said wheedlingly:

"*You* take off my shirt, Mummy."

She answered, with wet eyes, "Yes, darling."

"*And* put on my pajompers?"

"Yes."

"*And* read me?"

"Yes, one story, sweetheart."

"Two?"

She laughed, carrying him to his cot.

"*One.* Mother must go back to the Grans, and Aunt Susan and Uncle Bert."

He was silent while she put on his pyjamas and tucked him into his cot. She asked:

"Did you bring in all the friends-and-relations?"

"Yes—want them to sleep with me."

"Where are they?"

"They're looking out the window; they're watching for Daddy."

They were arranged along the window-sill, a teddy-bear and a golliwog, a wooden camel called Tripps, and Wingo the china frog. She brought them to him and watched his careful disposal of them beneath his sheet and blanket. He asked:

"Is Daddy coming home soon?"

"Yes, soon."

"Is he better now?"

"Yes, darling, quite better."

"In Riverburra when people get sick the doctor makes them come well again."

"That's very nice of him, isn't it? What shall I read, darling?"

While she went to fetch the book she began to wonder whether a world of peace-loving men would really be the Utopia of the future. Often when she was worried, hemmed in by the difficulties of daily life, her mind escaped in this way to some restful tangle of impersonal problems. She unravelled them as many people work out crossword puzzles, for a mental relaxation, separating thread from thread till she had achieved in her own mind some kind of neatness, some approximate conclusion.

She came now from her original doubt to a feeling that the differences between the sexes had been enormously and unjustifiably exaggerated. What were they, after all, beyond a few physical variations biologically necessary? And as those differences were complementary so, she realised, feeling a knot in the tangle give, and a long thread come cleanly away from it, the one fundamental psychological difference between them was complementary too, rather than, as she had always thought it, antagonistic.

She stood in front of the small bookshelf in her bedroom running a finger absently along the top row. If then, you took away from him man's primeval urge to kill, to destroy, you might possibly be doing just as harmful a thing as if you took away from him his power to propagate? For as woman's creative urge implies peace, toil, construction, stability, surely man's destructive instinct must imply strife and friction; change—mobility——

You could argue then, that a civilisation reared on the feminine ideal would remain entirely static, while one reared on the masculine ideal could not endure at all?

Where *was* the thing? Orange, with gold lettering.

In that case the old Adam must remain? They must continue to have, from time to time, these increasingly frightful orgies of killing? But why should they, after all? Men still like to smash and women still like to create, but surely, surely, it was no longer necessary that man should expend his destructive force, every year more diabolically ingenious, on the life which woman was still faithfully renewing after the fashion of uncountable ages ago? If they must do that, she thought, there could not come too soon the brave new world peopled by artificially produced babies, food for their vile and artificial slaughters!

She sighed, abandoning her search of the bookshelf and looking wearily round the room. Centuries ago, her brain went on arguing, there hadn't really been anything for man to smash except his neighbour's head, so of course he had smashed that. But now——! She saw the whole world suddenly as a gigantic nursery full of delights for the half of humanity which has never grown up. Not only the weapons that his own ingenuity had conceived, but there to his hand an inexhaustible supply of enemies and victims to annihilate! What was the matter with him? Did he really think it more interesting to pick a quarrel with his fellow man than to pursue his quite reasonable argument with, say, a typhus germ to its victorious conclusion? Did he really prefer sinking under the ocean for the purpose of ambushing and drowning some hundreds of human beings, to cruising about in a new world of smothered light and sound, still virtually unexplored—the last remaining mystery—land of his globe? Did he really need to make enemies of his own kind? Why not war on sharks and rats and blow-flies?

Hasn't he, her heart cried despairingly, enough to do? The most magnificent collection of toys, the most lavish supply of playgrounds—the air to turn somersaults in, the bed of the ocean to explore, the vast unknown forces of electricity, atomic energy to harness, the whole universe of suns to conquer——

She lamented over him as any mother laments over the besmudged copybook of her schoolboy son.

"He's so clever! It isn't that he can't do well! If only he'd apply himself!"

There it was, on the bed half hidden by the eider-down! She remembered now through the veil of her other continuing thoughts that Richard had been "reading" it to Wingo——

Richard. The memory of him stirred the impersonal grief of her thoughts to a sudden savage personal resentment. Let them take care, these irresponsible child-mates of womankind! Let them not hold too cheaply the life which she is growing tired of producing for such a senseless purpose! Let them not forget that of the fundamental differences between the sexes a difference of mentality is not one—that the feminine brain starved and hampered through the ages is fighting at last into its own. So that a day may come when she will say, "No. I bear no more children into a world not fit to receive them——" And then what? Not safe for very many centuries longer to talk too confidently of the unfailing maternal instinct, when even now, she herself and how many thousands of others like her felt revolt flame in them, cried, as she was crying now, "After this one—no more!"

She picked up the book and went back to Richard's room. He was half asleep, his heavy eyes opening with an effort to watch the door. She sat down beside his cot and began to read softly the first story she came to:

"*One day Rabbit and Piglet were sitting outside Pooh's front door listening to Rabbit and Pooh was sitting with them——*"

If Colin didn't get home to-night she'd have to think up some new excuses. But he would—he'd come back as he'd come so often before, silent and vanquished to the comfort she had always been able to give him——

"*Piglet said that Tigger was very bouncy, and that if they could think of a way of unbouncing him it would be a Very Good Idea——*"

Richard was nearly asleep already. He must have been very tired. All the same she'd been glad she had let him stay up to dinner for a treat—his questions and breathless infectious laughter had helped her through what might have been many conversational difficulties.

"There's a thing called Twy-stymes," he said—"Christopher Robin tried to teach it to me once, but it didn't—"

How soundly children slept! Soundly and suddenly. The book lay open on her lap; she watched Richard's face, closed, still, the tides of his life welling in a warm flood of colour beneath his petal-soft skin. She saw abruptly with a shock between fear and joy, that it was his father's face.

2

She went out slowly on the veranda where she had left them to put Richard to bed. Susan was lying back in a deck chair, half in shadow, puffing cigarette smoke about her to discourage the mosquitoes. Drew, on his knees, had a huge map of Colin's spread out on the floor with the lamp beside it, and Bret, squatting on his heels as bushmen do, was pointing out something to him with the stem of his pipe. Millicent, dim and still, outside the circle of lamplight, said:

"Here's a chair, Margery. You must be tired."

Margery, sinking back against its comfortably yielding canvas back, realised anew that she was. Drew was saying:

"Now where are we? Here, put this cigarette-case on that corner. This is how we came—Sydney, Parramatta, over the mountains—this would be about where we were stuck, because here's that place Kerrajellanbong. Now there was a turn-off somewhere—— Hallo,

Marge, young man in bed?—— Yes, here it is—now where does that go? Bathurst, eh?"

"That's right." Bret's hand dived down into the lamplight, his forefinger sketching a route roughly on the map. Drew went on:

"Lithgow—now where are we? We went through there, didn't we?"

"Not exactly through. We skirted it—here."

"By jove, we're going more north than I thought. Capertee, Tabrabucca, Cudgegong—you know, those names don't sound so bad when you say them in a string like that! Now where's Kalangadoo. And here we are!"

He stared at the map. He said slowly:

"You know—I'd had a sort of feeling that we'd come a goodish way!"

Bret, puffing at his pipe, remarked that there was still a good deal ahead of them, and Drew, absorbed, began to trace slowly with the point of a pencil the continuation of the road they had travelled. There stirred in him a sudden faint excitement such as one feels, before one's mind has begun to work, on the moment of awakening to some long hoped-for day. He glanced for a half-startled second in the direction of his wife as if he thought that she might have seen in his face some hint of the ridiculous sense of revelation which had so disconcertingly assailed him. She had not, but in that abrupt lifting of his face, its lower half lit brightly by the upward glow of the lamp, and its eyes looking for her, strangely disturbed, out of a half-shadow, she did become aware of a change in him, and because of it, a change in herself——

Drew frowned down at the map again. A thought, very clear and definite like a notice in block capitals seemed to hang itself up before his consciousness, as if defying him to ignore it.

No wonder, really, if she missed all this——

He seemed to see, rather horrified, a circle draw itself on the map enclosing the life she'd lived with him since their marriage—from one suburb of Sydney to another—school-holiday trips with Colin to the mountains, summer cottages at Bowral, summer cottages at Cronulla, at Terrigal, at Wollongong—and it was, on that vast and adventurous expanse, a very little circle indeed!

But he hadn't known—hadn't realised——

When a man's busy earning a living——

Funny how school lessons took the glamour out of a thing! Why hadn't it ever shown to him somehow that every miserably bethumbed page of his atlas was the picture of a story—a thousand stories——? He could see now that page upon which the long coastline of his native state wavered down the right-hand side, and the countries, bewilderingly indicated in colours whose ugliness he even now remembered and resented, stretched away to its western boundary. And all it had ever meant to him had been a few parrot phrases, a few lists of names learnt rebelliously by heart. Even now he could say the rivers—"Tweed, Richmond, Clarence, Hastings, Manning, Hunter, Hawkesbury, Shoalhaven"—and much good it did him!

Why hadn't any one ever told him about this road, for instance? Oh, yes, of course he'd scrawled laboriously in examination papers that, "In the year such-and-such a party of explorers led by so-and-so set out to discover this-and-that——" But why hadn't they told him, somehow, things about it that only to-day, at fifty-eight, he'd begun to realise—that it was a road of inconceivable glamour and romance and that it went on—and on——

He said to Bret:

"Who made the Western Road?"

Bret answered between puffs:

"Chap called Cox. In six months from Penrith to Bathurst."

"*Six months!*"

"Six months with a gang of thirty. Mostly convicts, I think they were."

Drew stared down at the map. Perhaps because he'd had a long day and was beginning to feel tired, the black line of the road faded by some optical illusion into the moving winding strip that his eyes had been watching since early morning. The darkly shaded valleys, stretching out like talons towards it, became blue and luminous, incredibly deep, dreadfully remote, so that he had a brief sensation of vertigo, and a ridiculous momentary feeling that he, Tom Drew, in clothes with arrows on them, and chains about his ankles, was toiling perilously on a moving road that stretched like a tightrope with blue death on either side——

His finger moved slowly westward. Names shone up at him out of the golden lamplight, tantalising mysteries hidden from him behind the soft syllables of an alien tongue; Gulgong, Dunedoo, Merrygoen, Tooraweenah——

No, they weren't bad, those names. There was a sort of music in them, difficult, elusive, like the difficult and elusive beauty he'd discovered that morning in the bush; and still the road went on.

Jove, what a fleabite was the distance they'd come compared with what separated them still from the western boundary of this eastern state! Amazing to think you could still go on, right out of this map into another and right out of that other into a third before you reached the sea!

Not that one would, of course. Desert. Waterless. Hundreds and hundreds of miles—— The sort of mad journey you tackled when you were young——

Fifty-eight——

His eyes came up rather forlornly from the beguiling map. Fifty-eight—and feeling it! He climbed heavily to his feet and the map, released, rolled itself up with a little rattle to the cigarette-case which Bret took and handed up to him.

He said:

"Well, I'm off to bed, Milly. We've had a long day. Don't suppose I'll sleep for a while, so if Colin comes in——"

Margery cut in a little too quickly.

"I don't think he'll be back till to-morrow morning now——"

And Millicent, who from the dark had been watching her husband and feeling a faint ache that was half excitement and half apprehension, stood up as he passed and put a hand on his arm.

"I'll come too, Tom. It's ridiculously early, but I am tired. You don't mind, Margery?"

Margery said, "No, of course not!" Squeezing the hand that her mother-in-law put out to her. She wished very much that they'd all go to bed. And as if answering that wish Susan stood up. Bret, re-rolling the map on the floor, saw her skirts pass him faintly golden, diaphanous. She was saying something softly to Margery and then she was gone through the open door into the house following her parents.

Bret, snapping an elastic hand over the map came slowly over to Margery. He sat down in the chair Millicent had just left, and took his pipe out of his mouth.

He said deliberately:

"Marge, where *is* Colin—really?"

CHAPTER TWENTY

I

SHE turned to him in the darkness, and with the startled movement came a small startled sound as if not till that moment had she allowed herself to know how afraid she was.

He prompted her:

"Drinking again?"

"Yes."

"When?"

"This morning——"

For a moment as she said it she wondered. Only this morning? It seemed a hundred years ago that she'd lain, her face downward, on a half-made bed and heard the sound of the car fade in the distance, and let her anger overwhelm her fear. Bret asked:

"Did he say where he was going?"

"No. He just went. I didn't ask him. I didn't care."

Bret went over to the veranda rail and knocked his pipe out on it. He reflected as he did so that it was strange how some sounds were, of their very nature, sinister; how that mild and innocent knocking of his pipe should break the quietness so forebodingly—"Didn't care," eh? He thought, with a sudden wave of surprising bitterness, "Love!" and asked her, without turning:

"Was he in a fit state to drive?"

She came and stood beside him, put her elbows on the

rail and her face with a sudden distraught movement in her hands.

"I think so. He's often driven home much worse. I–I've been nearly mad–I didn't know what to do–well, there *wasn't* anything to do. Some one in Mudgee will find him——"

Bret asked:

"You–think he's in Mudgee?"

She lifted her face from her hands to look at him. He saw uneasily that though she had made no sound of weeping her cheeks in the dim light glistened with tears, and instead of waiting for her reply he found himself asking another question:

"Why did you say you didn't care?"

"I didn't–then. Sometimes you go–past caring about anything at all. I suppose," she added half to herself on a breath like a sigh, "it's to give you a rest. Before you give way altogether–so that you can go on afterwards caring harder than ever——"

And then she said sharply:

"Where else would he go?"

Bret didn't answer. He was wondering whether it was not perhaps rather a mad thing to do, to alarm her because of a suspicion, a feeling, a wisp of blue smoke——? Whether it wasn't, after all, far more likely that Colin was somewhere in Mudgee, poor kid, sleeping off another failure, another capitulation——?

Margery's voice startled him–a whisper with an edge to it.

"You don't think–he's up there?"

He found that he'd been staring at Jungaburra, and hearing the terror in her voice his first instinct was to deny and comfort. He realised, too, that he needed reassurance himself; absent-mindedly as he'd been staring at the mountain, something in its vast black mass, its spire-point soaring into the sky, must have chilled him—— He said hastily:

"No, no. Why should he be? He—he didn't go in that direction, did he?"

She shook her head miserably.

"I don't know. The turn-off is down the hill—you've stopped hearing a car by the time it gets there, anyhow."

"Did he ever—say——?"

"No!"

Bret looked at the mountain again. He found himself remembering in rather terrifying detail his one ascent of it with Colin. There'd been one damn place—— He realised that he was in a state of acute and agonising funk, and instantly he said:

"When we drove down this evening there was smoke up there—in his cave."

2

As he followed her down to the garage ten minutes later he was feeling faintly amused. It was all, he told himself, rather ludicrous. Colin, probably, was safely asleep somewhere in Mudgee, and he himself was off on a ridiculous wild-goose chase. He followed Margery into the darkness of the shed where her electric torch made for a moment a moving pool of light across the mud-splashed glories of the Madison. It passed on then, found a wall, travelled up it and paused, and with its pausing Bret was aware of a little shock, a tension, a hair-thin crack in his self-possession—the same sensation which he had felt when he heard the knocking of his pipe on the veranda rail.

What was there, in heaven's name, about a coil of rope hanging on a nail? He wondered, staring at it, if its quality of drama—or one might almost say, of melodrama, came from the suddenness with which it had leapt out of the surrounding darkness and now hung there in a circle of light which invested it somehow with a wholly disproportionate significance.

Queer. He reached over Margery's shoulder and took it down from its hook. He asked:

"How long is it?"

"Fifty feet. But you won't climb alone, Bret?"

"I probably won't need to climb at all. If the car isn't there I suppose we can take it Colin isn't either."

"But if it is——"

"Well, I'll just find out where he is and do what seems best."

"You won't take this car?"

He grinned, thinking of the crazy and precipitous track which led up the foothills of the mountain. He said, slinging the rope across his shoulder:

"She's had enough adventures for her maiden journey. Besides if Colin—I might have to drive the other car back."

She said in a low voice:

"Yes." And then, with an effort, "You won't take me, Bret? I'm all right. I could do it."

"And supposing he turned up from Mudgee in the meantime?"

She nodded.

"Yes. What about Susan?"

But he said very finally and abruptly, "Not Susan," and she sighed, switching off her torch and following him out into the night, already faintly silvered by the rising moon. She said wearily:

"If you want help you can signal with the torch from that flat rock at the top of the first hill. It's pretty powerful. I'll see it all right. I'll watch for it."

"Right. You go in now and rest. It'll be at least an hour before I could do any signalling even if I want to."

But she went after him quickly as he turned away.

"Bret?"

"Well?"

"You—you—I'm not quite blind because I—happen to love Colin. You mustn't do anything—risky. I know your life's worth more than his to every one but me."

He said, "Nonsense!" rather uneasily, and then felt an unspoken answer to that remark of hers flood him with a wave, a torrent of black and bitter depression. "Worth more than Colin's!" Something in him cried out at her savagely, silently, that he was worth nothing at all to any one, not even to a wife who inexplicably and uselessly happened to be in love with him. Least of all her! Dead, he thought, adjusting the rope so that its knot came comfortably clear of his shoulder, he would at least mean a name; an income; and, perhaps, a well-meaning memory——

He said rather shortly:

"I haven't the slightest intention of breaking my neck. I'll watch the house when I can and you'll signal with flashes from the window if he comes home. Right?"

"Yes."

She watched him go off across the paddocks, his

white shirt glimmering more and more dimly, till it faded altogether out of sight. Then her eyes went to the peak of Jungaburra and stayed there.

3

Bret walked fast in the moonlight. When he came down the hill to the flat grassy bank of the creek he stopped for a moment, looking up and down for the crossing. That pause, brief as it was, had been enough to impress upon his mind a gurgle of running water, a croaking of frogs and a dry faint rustling of leaves. Sounds which, by way of memory and association, took him back to another creek, not unlike this one, where on a grassy flat behind just such another fringe of she-oaks he'd camped once, three years ago with Jim. A good camp, that one had been – a holiday camp, a week's poking about, and exploring among the Warrumbungles, coming back each evening, tired and scratched and dirty, and bathing at dusk in a pool paved with smoothly rounded pebbles.

Like these——

Stepping from one boulder to another, he paused midway across the stream looking down into the limpid moonlit shallows. So strongly that he did not even try for a few seconds to resist it, came a feeling that all the time between then and now was an illusion; that he would see, if he looked up from these familiar seeming pebbles, a long familiar figure on the opposite bank, a tent pitched on the grass between a she-oak and a gum, its white sides flickeringly painted with the rosy light of the camp fire——

Then, sharply, his head did come up. No long figure, no tent, but——

But certainly, somewhere, a fire.

He sniffed. The breath of wind, which was stirring the leaves of the taller gums, barely touched him here; a vagrant breath of it had, all the same, carried from somewhere a scent which, always unmistakable, seemed too, coming in the wake of his thoughts, disturbing. Not a bush fire after this morning's rain. Possibly a log still smouldering up there in the paddock where they were ring-barking. Possibly——

He began to walk up the hill on the other side of the creek. A little farther on he thought he'd strike the crazy track which connected, after a fashion, the road with the mountain, and he'd be able to tell, then, if a car had used it that day. And in the meantime, walking steadily, there persisted in him an unrest, a bitterness, a grief roused up anew by his moment of immobility down there by the creek. No matter how long he lived, he supposed, he'd never really get used to the thought of Jim's death. It would always return to his memory with the jar of an idea not properly assimilated, a fact never wholly believed——

Perhaps because there had always been at the back of his mind a devout thanksgiving that Jim had been too young for service in the war. "*He's* safe, anyhow." War made you think like that when you'd got used to seeing youth butchered; made you feel that nothing else could conceivably touch it. If somehow it escaped *that* it was safe. But it wasn't. Not safe from a wet street, a skidding car, a——

Susan. That was *Susan*. He had to tell himself so clearly and insistently before his mind would recognise that the ugly words which had been in it applied to the girl who was now his wife. And upon coming to it again, that tangle, that unmanageable knot of complicated emotions to which, inexorably, his every thread of thought must lead him, he uttered half aloud an exclamation of helplessness, despair.

He wished suddenly, angrily, that he'd been, after all, as obtuse as she'd expected him to be. That he'd felt only their satiny warmth in that tightening of her arms round his neck; in her recklessly offered beauty nothing of that obscure and inexplicable peril.

As it was——

Things became worse and worse. More and more impossible. Ludicrous——

As he walked his anger mounted. He saw furiously two alternatives ahead of him, each menacing, poisoning, what he had always valued most, the orderly contentment of his life at Coolami. Making of it, whichever road he took, a life of dingy frustration, of furtive compromises, of endless situations in which one's self-respect must shrivel and fade like young corn in drought——

He saw, sharp and clear and miniature, hanging brightly in the dark confusion of his thoughts, like a tiny illuminated symbol, the door between their rooms at Coolami. Saw it shut, hiding loneliness and bitterness, all the unwholesome maladies of normality tortured and denied. Saw it open revealing subtler but no less poignant misery; things he couldn't analyse, but from which instinctively he recoiled; efforts at decency failing and failing and failing again, till at last they renewed themselves no longer; friendship, admiration, fading into hatred and contempt; children, perhaps, conceived in secret, unadmitted loathing——

All that—at Coolami! There, really, was the root

of his resentment. Born there, brought up there, the perfection of his parent's happiness reflected all round him, he had felt sometimes before, as he felt more strongly now, that this marriage of his to Susan was little short of sacrilege. And he remembered again what he'd told old Drew this morning—"*Coolami, birthplace of heroes!*"

Well, what was the heroic line now? Take her, leave her alone, let her go? Not very——

He stumbled in a rabbit burrow and came down heavily on his knees. The jar of it, breaking into the midst of his mental turbulence, a hardly realised physical fatigue, and a certain nameless foreboding of which, till that moment, he hadn't been fully aware, shook out of him a brief blistering spasm of profanity. Still on his knees he looked up, and a cold nausea hit him suddenly like a blow in the pit of the stomach.

Good God, what a thing it looked in the moonlight! Its base still hidden from him, its soaring spire framed in a gap between the trees, it had, a million times magnified, that same breath-taking, nerve-shocking touch of drama which he had already felt twice that night. The moon was on its right now. That side of it gleamed, falling abruptly here and there into the darkness of shadowed chasms; the other side, impenetrably black, was menacing and magnificent in the fierceness of its triumphantly ascending outline.

He didn't know how long he knelt there staring at it, wondering vaguely how something whose very essence was its immense, its overpowering immobility, could convey so clearly an impression of energy, force, a sinister and latent power. And, rather paradoxically, could capture, too, in the formidable masses of its naked rock so elusive a suggestion of the delicate, the insubstantial fabric of a dream.

He was suddenly deadly tired. He put his finger-tips on the ground and pushed himself wearily to his feet. Life, he thought, soberly enough and without any of the turmoil of his recent reflections, was really a silly business. It took such a moment as that one he'd spent on his knees gaping like a fool at the mountain to make you abruptly rather sick of yourself and your frenzied worm-like wrigglings on the barbed hook of your existence. Rather disgusted with what was shown to you as your own incredible transience, your altogether galling unimportance——

"*Worth more than Colin's!*"

How was it worth more than Colin's, this futile life of his? Well, he was a better farmer, a better judge of sheep, and he happened to dislike whisky. Apart from that——

He was aware, painfully, of solitude. Not only, he realised gropingly, of the physical and mental solitude of his immediate environment, but another more alarming aloneness in the whole of space and time, so that he felt, ridiculously, an overwhelming desire such as a child might feel in the dark, for the comfort of some human companionship. His, he thought, was the one solitude against which all nature cries aloud—a biological solitude that made one outcast, contemptible, of less importance, finally, than the smallest ant dragging its egg to the friendly shelter of a stone.

He stopped. At night, in this transforming silver light, it would have been easy enough, he thought, to miss this track altogether—a track which had never been made, but worn after a fashion by the cars of infrequent sightseers and picnic parties. Just here the earth was too hard, too thickly sprinkled with fallen gum leaves and twigs for him to find wheelmarks. He began to follow it, staring at the ground. It doubled and twisted, skirting vast outcrops of granite, squeezing between tall trees, climbing in zigzag fashion, obstinately, laboriously; finishing, as he remembered, in one steep pinch, just wide enough for a car, which swept it up in triumph to the very foot of the first great wall of rock.

There, Bret thought, shifting his rope to an easier position, even if not before, there would be wheelmarks, or, better still, the car itself. He didn't like, very much, the thought of Colin, desperate and drink-bemused, climbing that last little bit of the track. Might very well be risky after last week's rains – washed out, narrowed——

He began to walk faster, feeling in his pockets for a cigarette, lighting it as he went, trying by such small and everyday actions to repel the sudden savage assaults which his imagination was making upon his habitual imperturbability. He'd seen, years ago, too many mangled human bodies not to feel now a prickling of the skin at the thought of Colin lying at the foot of that steeply ascending bank in the wreckage of his car——

And now at his feet, in a patch of softer ground, were unmistakable wheelmarks——

That steep incline, when at last he came to it, rather breathless, and rubbing his hot forehead with his handkerchief, was undoubtedly in worse repair than when he'd seen it last. It was corrugated with deep gutters whose water had swept away down the hill large sections of the earth bank which was the only made part of the track; but he saw with relief that the wheelmarks went up it steadily enough, keeping well in to the side of the mountain——

And he reasoned, slackening a little with a mixture of heat, weariness and relief, that if Colin was sober enough to drive his car up there without mishap he was probably sober enough to climb——

He came to the top of the incline and stopped dead. There on that open and rather steeply sloping place where the car should have been, the moonlight came flooding down brilliantly on to a few stunted shrubs, a little grove of wattle, ash-gold in the moonlight, breathing out the scent of honey; and wavering wheel-tracks that went out of sight over the opposite cliff.

CHAPTER TWENTY-ONE

I

WHEN Bret stood back at last from the shattered car and drew his shirt sleeve slowly across his forehead, he could feel his whole body prickling with sweat, limp with abrupt release from nervous strain. For Colin wasn't there. Quite methodically and thoroughly he'd searched, forcing up the crumpled hood, peering and feeling into the car where it was shadowed by the vast tree-trunk into which it had crashed, poking about in thick undergrowth, streaked and dappled with moonlight, for a still body flung there by a terrific impact.

But he hadn't found it, and now with a sudden violent reaction he was aware of exuberance. An energy that was half defiance sent him scrambling up the steep slope to the plateau, and held him there for a moment or two, his head craned backward, staring up at the menacing black bulk above him. Step by step his eyes picked out the different stages of the climb, and he surprised in himself a faint half unwilling exhilaration at the thought of tackling it again. Rather a sheer bit at first—about fifteen feet of it very nearly perpendicular but with quite fair foot and handholds. The sort of thing you did gaily enough with good earth so close below you, but which, a few hundred feet higher, made your stomach feel queer and your knees wavery——

Then twenty or thirty feet of scrambling up a sloping face of rock to a chimney. Bret, peering, thought he could place it, but it was hard to tell from here just how much of it there was. He remembered it as strenuous but not particularly difficult, and moved farther back to try to refresh his memory of the next pitch. With his final backward step it leapt into view and with it memories he didn't know he had preserved, of his first encounter with it. That vile ledge! He could see it as a dark line edged with silver, disappearing round a corner into the great cleft in which nearly half the ascent was made. Well, it was broad enough—nearly two feet six in some places and never less than one, and it wasn't more than sixty feet from the ground. If it hadn't had that gap in it. Not, Bret acknowledged, admitting all the excellent qualities which Colin, like any collector exhibiting his favourite specimen, had claimed for it, that it was a wide gap. Not that it hadn't two splendid handholds, one on each side. Not that the ledge itself didn't obligingly almost double its width at that particular spot——

All the same you did have to step across it. There did come a moment when, with one handhold released and the other not yet achieved, with one foot on the point of leaving its solid rock and the other already in mid-air, you realised acutely with every cell in your body that you were far enough from the ground to get quite nastily messed up if you fell——

After that, he remembered, once you got into that cleft there was nothing to it but exertion for a least a couple of hundred feet. A steep slope full of stunted growth and great wedged boulders——

He looked up sharply at the moon. Now, and for perhaps an hour longer, it would be shining straight into that cleft. It would be lighting every foot of the way and you'd take it almost as confidently as if it were a staircase. But later when the moon was higher, that great buttress on the northern face would shadow it. It would be black night in there, and if you stumbled—— Well, you'd roll and bounce and bump till you brought up against a rock or became jammed behind some clump of bushes, and you mightn't be actually dead, but you'd be lucky if you hadn't broken a bone or two somewhere——

He looked at his watch, and realised with no more than a feeling of fatalistic resignation that if he went back as he had intended to signal for help, and then waited till his helpers arrived, they'd be lucky if they got into that cleft before the moonlight left it; and luckier still, he thought grimly, if they got out of it intact.

He threw his head back suddenly, cupped his hands round his mouth and shouted. He didn't know quite why he was so dumbfounded when there came, faintly, but clearly from far above him, an answer. He must, he supposed, have considered it possible that Colin would hear him or he wouldn't have coo-eed, but nevertheless he stood for a moment or two with his hands still at his mouth, petrified with astonishment and relief.

The whole thing became, suddenly, a lark. The anxiety and depression of his mood vanished so abruptly that he almost imagined he felt them flowing upward from him like a vapour, like ectoplasm—— The word chimed in his mind with the name of the mountain, and he found himself thinking with ridiculous amusement, "spirit place"!

He shouted again:

"Hallo there! Colin!"

But although the answering call was repeated he

couldn't distinguish words. He went over to the wall of rock and tried, tentatively, the first few feet. Funny stuff this trachite. Too smooth—didn't give your feet much to grip on. Not like sandstone. He jumped down, pulled off his shoes. He tied them together by the laces, then fastened them behind him to his belt and tried again.

Easy enough. His toes slipped once from a foothold not quite as good as it had looked, and he barked his knee, but so near the ground, he thought, you don't lose your breath over trifles like that! Later on, when you're up a thousand feet or so, your heart turns over if your little finger slips so much as a hairbreadth——

He pulled himself up over the top of that first small pitch and sat for a moment readjusting the rope across his shoulders. Then he went on up the slope, clambering, touching the ground before him with his fingers, to the black cleft of the chimney.

It looked, he thought, squeezing himself into it and peering up, a deuce of a long way, and there was no moonlight here. He took out his torch and flashed it above him, trying to memorise roughly the footholds and handholds available. But anyhow, he thought, vaguely surprised at his own cheerful unconcern, in so narrow a chimney you could do a lot by just bracing your feet against one wall and your back against the other——

He began to try it, first running his shoes round his belt till they hung in front of him. For quite a long way he went up fast and easily, feeling with his hands, feeling with his feet, his legs, even cautiously with the back of his head. In this funnel of darkness all the strength of his temporarily useless sight went into his other senses. He even realised that his first awareness of the opening above him came to him in a faintly different fragrance, an elusive scent of freshness in the air that he was smelling. He looked up; there wasn't any moonlight to be seen. He put one hand warily above his head and touched rock. Then he remembered, for the first time, the chock-stone, and in the same instant his body began a veritable clamour of protestations. Wedged there in the darkness, half his weight on one foot whose leg had suddenly begun to shake violently and uncontrollably with strain, and the other half on his shoulders braced against the opposite wall, he felt as if his muscles were melting and flowing through his limbs like a warm fluid. He groped for his torch and got it out of his pocket with difficulty, but its yellow light showed him instantly a respite. Just opposite and above him in the broadening chimney, a ledge quite nine inches wide ran along the wall, and he gripped it, pulled himself up, rested his arms on it and found another foothold. There he stayed for a moment, wriggling his bruised and aching shoulders a little and cursing the rope which had constantly impeded him.

When at last he had clambered on to the ledge he used his torch again and considered the chock-stone doubtfully. A child, he thought, or a small person could squeeze behind it possibly, but he remembered now that he'd tried it last time and Colin had called out something about the camel and the eye of a needle. So there was nothing for it but to stand up on the ledge where he was, for the moment, so securely seated, and launch himself out, spread-eagled, over the rounded surface of the stone. Once you're on top of it, he told himself kindly, you just walk off on to the outside ledge. So he put his torch away, hoisted himself on to his knees, and then, carefully on to one foot. It was the rope which upset his balance. He hadn't realised how accurately, in the dark, his body was aware of its surrounding objects. He'd touched the wall behind him with his hand to make sure of its exact position, and the rest of his body, now, was acting on the information of that reconnoitring hand. It hadn't allowed for the two extra inches that the rope added to his back, and as he came up on to his other foot he felt himself pushed out sickeningly just beyond the limit of his precarious balance. It didn't, of course, take his brain one second to reassure him that an outstretched hand would bring him safely against the opposite wall, but he died, all the same, in that second of falling forward into darkness, a thousand atavistic deaths. His whole body when, with a foot braced against the wall which his outstretched hands had met, he pushed himself back again to his ledge, was soaked and clammy with sweat, and his throat closed up queerly——

And he was angry. Swearing under his breath, and reckless with sudden temper he flung himself at the chock-stone as though it were a mortal enemy. Some of his anger died with his easy conquest of it; it wasn't more than a minute later that he was sitting astride it with the moonlight on his face.

The ledge led straight away from him like a silver path along the cliff face, vanishing round a corner. Here at its beginning it was a substantial platform; as he stepped out on to it the mere thought of being able to see his way ahead of him gave him a sense of relief and confidence. He began to move along it slowly, his left shoulder brushing the wall, and was surprised to find how easy, how entirely without terrors it was. When he turned the corner his shadow, which had kept pace beside him along the cliff wall, ran out suddenly in front of him, and he stopped, vaguely disturbed. Ridiculous, he thought, beginning rather more warily to go forward again, how a little thing like that could, for a moment, be so disconcerting. It just showed how very finely balanced your sense of equilibrium must be, how narrow a margin of safety you were allowing to your usually careless body, when a dark, wavering blot of shadow, obliterating, for a few paces ahead, the clear junction of wall and ledge could check you so suddenly. Demanding readjustments; your movements slower, your left foot feeling along the wall below your left hand, your eyes focused a yard or so farther on——

And now the gap. Well, yes, it was pretty providential that the ledge widened just here. He lifted the coil of rope over his head and threw it carefully across well beyond where his feet would land when he stepped——

His whole widely roving consciousness suddenly narrowed, contracted like the lens of a camera, focused itself with a tremendous, an agonising intentness on that one stride ahead of him. It was as though not only his eyes but every cell in his body was joined in an overwhelming co-operation of awareness. Awareness of depth, awareness of distance, of the quality of the rock, the small unevennesses of its surface; awareness of himself, the exact length of his legs, the exact strength of his arms, the steady but rather heavy pounding of his heart. Nothing at all, for the moment, existed outside a radius of three yards around him. Not Colin or Susan, or even Coolami. The world had become two points of silvered rock with a black chasm between them; he himself a nameless, emotionless, brain-driven organism whose sole function was to cross that chasm.

It was suddenly behind him, and with a click the lens of his consciousness was wide open again, collecting from everywhere, avidly, a medley of sensations, thoughts, emotions. He thought, "Hurrah, I'm over!" and, "Damn that shadow!" seeing it again in his memory as he'd seen it in the second when he had, between heaven and earth, no support but the vanishing balance of his right foot—a black blotch leaping clumsily ahead of him——

And he thought with a strange feeling of exultation, "By jove, there's something *in* this game of Colin's!" He stood up, lifting the rope and readjusting carefully a disordered coil before he slung it again over his left shoulder. The ledge here made a slight turn to the right, so that his shadow retreated again to the wall, and he went on, feeling rather above himself, and trying to remember exactly what happened after you'd gone up the cleft and climbed out on to the wide ledge where he and Colin had eaten their lunch that day, looking out over vast undulating miles of plain and bush——

Was that where you skirted round——

No, it was the straight climb. Thirty feet or more, and only one place on it where you could stop for a moment, crouching, resting the ache, subduing the weakness of your arms. And when you got up that you were practically in Colin's cave.

The ledge turned, narrowed. Bret stood still, looking into an ascending cavern of tumbled rocks and dark, moon-silvered shrubs. He shouted again.

The nearness of the voice that answered startled him so much that he actually retreated a step before he realised with a violent heart-thud, that he was standing on a two-foot ledge. The voice answered, hoarse, not very loud, but with a strange, echoing sound, from about half-way up the cleft;

"Here! Who's that?"

Bret called:

"That you, Colin? Where are you?"

"Bret, is it? I'm up here in the cleft. Had a spill."

Bret moved forward cautiously. The ledge ran out on a steep slope. The softness of earth and decaying leaves felt strange to his feet after the rock and he sat down, untying his shoes from his belt. He called:

"Hurt?" and began mentally to curse himself that, moonlight or no moonlight, he'd been fool enough to come up alone to rescue a possibly badly injured man. But Colin answered:

"No. Only a few cuts and bruises. Knocked myself out for a little while. But I can get back all right if you've got a rope."

Bret tying his shoelaces in a double knot said, "I've got a rope. Give me a call now and then. I can't see you," and began slowly to clamber up the slope. He was thinking now that what they wanted was a car. The prospect of setting out, when they got down again, to walk the two miles or so back to the house, filled him with an enormous despair, and he began to realise acutely in every bone of his body that he was tired.

He became so exhausted at last that Colin's voice seemed disembodied, now coming from beside him, now receding to such a distance that it was almost inaudible. The sound of his heart thudding high in his chest seemed to overwhelm it, to overwhelm everything, and his thighs ached with a pain that was like fire. He knew in a dim, irritated way that the unfamiliar and violent contrasts of light and shadow were making him spend, on what was really no more than a strenuous scramble, a vast superfluity of nervous and physical effort; so that suddenly, when a small stone rolled under his foot and brought him forward on to his knees, the sting of a prickly bush brushing his cheek made him gasp out an exasperated, "Blast the thing——!"

Colin, a few feet higher and a little to the right, said: "Here. Can you see me now?"

2

The relief of stretching out, flat on his back, with the rope for a pillow and a cigarette between his lips, returned Bret to his disturbed equanimity. Colin, propped against a boulder, smoked too, a streak of dried blood down one cheek sharply visible in the moonlight. He asked:

"What made you think I was here?"

"Smoke in your cave. Wasn't there?"

"Yes. It poured this morning when I was coming up, but I always keep wood in the cave. I lit a fire to dry off."

Bret, frowning, wanted very badly to ask why he'd left it till night time to make his descent. Colin, though, was a queer bird; you had to go warily——

But Colin said suddenly, quite without expression:

"I was shot—of course. Lord knows how I got up without crashing. After I'd lit the fire I fell asleep. It was nearly dark when I woke but——"

Bret grumbled:

"Why didn't you stay put till morning?"

Colin said:

"I remembered the family. Thought I might get back before you all arrived. Thought you might have been delayed or something. But then I had to wait for the moon——"

He asked suddenly:

"How's Mother?"

"She's well."

"Susan?"

Bret felt his forehead contract. That one word with its question mark was, he thought, so very much the sum total of all his own problems. But Colin without waiting for his answer went on peevishly:

"I know that handhold as I know the doorknob of my bedroom—or the gears of the car. I don't see how I missed it. Things look different somehow by moonlight——"

Bret asked:

"How—what happened to the car?" And Colin, taking his cigarette butt from his lips, repeated:

"Car? My car? Why, what *did* happen to it?"

Bret sat up wearily:

"Didn't you know it had gone over the edge down there?"

He was sorry then, in a resigned and nebulous way, that he'd spoken of the car. Colin sat quite still and said nothing at all about it except, "That hand-brake wasn't any good. I—it wanted a couple of stones under the wheels."

There followed then a long silence. Bret was thinking between the last puffs at his cigarette that Colin sober enough to get the car through that crazy bush track was not, surely, Colin too drunk to remember his faulty hand-brake? What other kind of nervous stress must have been added, what other mental suffering and shame? What dreadful purpose, even, had there been, perhaps, behind that desperate climb——?

He turned sharply on the thought. Colin's face in the white light looked ghastly and his eyes were shut, but as if answering Bret's sudden movement he opened them and said:

"We'd better be moving. There are two good trees I know for belays. We'll go down on a double rope. It'll be quicker and easier. What's that?"

Across the shadowed side of the tree-tops far below them a light had passed, gleaming, fading. There came then, faintly, smothered by the intervening buttress of the mountain, the sound of a car engine. Bret threw away his cigarette butt and stood up.

"Marge must have sent some one. Just as well. You're about done."

But it wasn't till they had looped the rope and were about to descend that Colin answered suddenly, with violence:

"Far from it!"

3

It was slower work than they had hoped. Before they had reached the bottom, the moonlight had gone from the cleft, and even with the rope they moved awkwardly. Once it became entangled in the undergrowth and Bret had to climb twenty feet to release it. When at last, with it re-coiled on his shoulder, he came round the corner of the ledge before the gap, he saw Susan standing on the other side considering it, her bent head amber coloured in the moonlight.

CHAPTER TWENTY-TWO

I

THE moonlight filtering through the leaves of the tree outside the window dappled the opposite wall with faintly moving spots of brilliance. Drew watched them unwillingly, his brain heavy, his eyes weighted by a weariness which brought no sleep. When he closed them he had an illusion of still seeing the road; it curled and twisted, it shot up hills and sank away into hollows, and always, with a jerk that brought him back violently from the edge of unconsciousness, it ended in a white railing over unfathomable depths——

So he kept them open and watched the pattern of moonlight, and wondered about Colin. What the devil did they all think he was, telling him a cock-and-bull story like that? What did you do about it when your son, your only son, drank, and played the fool with his property? What? He stirred restlessly but with caution because Milly was lying so still beside him. Nothing. That was the answer all right; just plain nothing.

Colin was a grown man and the mere detail of your paternal anxieties meant nothing any more. But years ago——

"What is it, Tom?"

Milly's hand felt for his; he grumbled:

"I thought you were asleep."

"No. What made you jump like that?"

He burst out in a ferocious undertone:

"*That's* when I should have put my foot down! That was the time! Eighteen! Good God, were we all crazy——?"

She said, rubbing one of his fingers:

"He'd have hated us," and he replied with a scornful snort of unmirthful laughter:

"What odds? He was nearly grown up anyhow. We were almost at the end of our job. We could have finished it decently. Instead, we let him—— What's that?"

"I didn't hear anything."

"Thought I heard voices outside." And then he added, "Perhaps it's——" And she at the same instant began eagerly, "It might be——"

They lay still, listening. Over and about them like a breath of wind, through them like a strange elixir ran something which was the essence of their long life together. In that moment of anxiety for their firstborn their lives which in the inexorable now were always so unrelentingly two lives, ran backward through time beautifully and mysteriously united. One life so surely that the thoughts, the memories, the emotions which now beset them seemed to come with a blessed alleviation of spiritual solitude, to him through her, and to her through him.

Colin, in that brief interlude of their abandonment to their love for him became less a human being than a medley of remembered joys and sorrows. They lay silently, their present anxieties dimmed as a narcotic will dim physical pain until the mere absence of suffering becomes, by contrast, a drowsy pleasure.

Drew said presently:

"I don't think it was Colin. Sounded like Bret's voice. Go to sleep, Milly."

But she said with sudden violence:

"I can't sleep. I—I don't want to sleep."

He was silent for a few seconds, in sheer astonishment. It was not so much her tone that amazed him, taut though it was with strain; it was the realisation that he had not for many, many years heard it other than cool and controlled, measured, amused, faintly ironic. This, he thought, feeling rather stirred, and turning his head slowly on the pillow to peer at her, was a voice not missed but very clearly remembered, the voice of his young wife.

He patted her hand.

"What's the matter? Worried about Colin?"

"Colin—yes. And Bret. And Susan. And us."

He repeated, bewildered:

"Us?"

She began to laugh a little; laughter which did not, he thought, trying uneasily to see her face, ring quite true. He was more perturbed than he cared to own by his own failure instantly to demand, "Us? What's wrong with Us?" As he would undoubtedly have done yesterday. Or even this morning.

He had to admit, though it irked him, that during this day's drive, behind and beneath the comfortable commonplaces of the journey, and without any words at all, something had happened to his thirty-seven year old relationship with his wife. No use, he told himself rather irritably, trying to put your finger on the disturbing factor. It might have been anything from the fanciful geegaw on the radiator, to that only just eluded death which had waited hundreds of feet beneath the front wheels of your skidding car. Things had happened to you. A great deal of new and disturbing beauty. An illuminating if painful moment when you'd seen your house at Ballool through other eyes. You'd caught for the first time a hint of music in outlandish names, felt a stirring of excitement in the mere thought of distance, an urge, vague and ill-defined, for some sense of spaciousness which you had never yet enjoyed——

All of which, he pondered, brought him—where? To this journey which had been, in his heart, a kind of challenge. There in Ballool he'd taken stock of his life and decided that he'd done pretty well. No need, he'd felt complacently, to be afraid of the country any more. Now that he'd finished, now that he could honestly say that there was, almost literally, nothing he couldn't buy for her, it wouldn't do any harm to take Milly for a brief while back into this life she had forsaken to share his climb with him. He even confessed to himself, perturbed by a new perceptiveness which suddenly illuminated motives hitherto comfortably obscured, that it hadn't been altogether accidental, his having so costly and magnificent a car brand new for this momentous occasion!

Where, he wondered ruefully, was the victorious mood which had so elated him this morning? Was it only this morning? Looking at the luminous dial of his watch, he curbed severely with accurate calculations an absurd conviction that this morning was separated from him not only by a hundred and fifty odd miles, but by an immeasurable gulf of time. Nearly eleven o'clock. About fifteen hours ago they'd set out, and all the way, he told himself grimly, he'd been shedding imperceptibly little pieces of complacency! Until now, lying wakeful on a queer old-fashioned iron bedstead in a big room whose walls were vertical weatherboards, through whose window, wide upon sloping paddocks, came strange scents and drowsy sounds, he felt less secure, more spiritually astray than he had ever felt before.

Now he was ready to begin living. Now he was ready to play. And he had ten years left. Nonsense, he was as strong as an ox! Twenty years! And yet, what was twenty years? Twenty years ago Susan had been born—and it was yesterday! Time—what a strange thing; what a mysterious and disturbing thing! Twenty years of your life were like a short step, and fifteen hours like a journey so long that you had almost forgotten its beginning!

His involuntary sigh merged wearily into a yawn. He turned over towards Millicent and threw one arm across her as he had done for thirty-seven years. He said indistinctly into the pillow:

"We'll be all right. Don't worry. Go to sleep."

2

Something wakened him. He was sitting up in bed listening with strained attention to the sound of a car—the *fading* sound of a car——

What, he wondered, peering at the luminous dial of his watch, could that mean? A car arriving might have meant Colin's return, but what car was this, setting out mysteriously after midnight——?

Hang it all, there *was* no car except his own!

Unless——

And on that thought he was out of bed and across the room fumbling with the unfamiliar catch of the door.

If some one had brought Colin home it must mean, surely, an accident? If it were—anything else—they'd bring him, wouldn't they, in his own car?

Millicent asked, sleepy, startled:

"Tom! Where are you? What is it?"

He answered over his shoulder as he went out that it was nothing, that he'd thought he heard something, that he'd be back presently and that she was to lie down and go to sleep again.

So she sighed, got out of bed, threw her fur coat over her shoulders and followed him down the hall to the back veranda.

Something in his attitude, the unbelieving forward thrust of his head, the hands frozen in mid-movement by sheer astonishment, made her realise before she reached him that she was to see something very strange indeed. But her mind was so full of Colin, her expectations unconsciously fixed so firmly upon some news or sight of him, that even when she joined her husband, stood beside him, stared where he was staring, she could not, at first, see anything amiss.

Her touch on his arm released him from his stupefied immobility. He cried, pointing:

"The car—it's gone! Some one's taken the car!" He turned furiously to the house. "Where's Margery? Where's the telephone? I'll have to——"

But Millicent, looking beyond the shed whose open doors revealed moonlit emptiness within, had seen a dark shape turn suddenly at the sound of Drew's voice, and become Margery walking slowly towards them. Walking so wearily, looking so solitary and so strangely tragic that even Drew, plunging round to Millicent's pull on his sleeve, damned back the thundering flood of his wrath enough to make his question merely a question, shorn of profane embellishments.

"Who was that went off with my car?"

Margery, at the foot of the steps looking up at them, said flatly:

"Susan."

They stared at her. Susan? Drew, momentarily speechless, struggled with a mind whose utter blankness refused to be filled by any reasonable and coherent thought. But Millicent's, frightened, leapt like a startled animal straight back to that dreadful little sobbing cry of Susan's just before the accident. Plunged on from there, terrified, through dark woods of imaginary horrors. Why should Susan, in the middle of the night, drive away in a car? Escape? Flight? From what? From——?

But there they stopped, quivering, confronted by a darkness, a tangle too impenetrable even for thought. Not that—not that——

Her lips said, unwillingly:

"Where—where's Bret?"

Margery put her hand up in front of her eyes, and sat down suddenly on the bottom step. She said:

"He went to look for Colin. On the mountain. I didn't tell you. Colin just—cleared out—this morning. I didn't know where. But Bret thinks he's up on Jungaburra somewhere. If he did go there he might be—hurt. He—he wasn't in a fit state——"

Millicent felt relief and a new anxiety run together in her mind, a strange mingling, as of a warm with an icy stream. She said:

"Didn't Bret take any one with him?"

"No. He was going to signal if he needed help."

Drew demanded, breathing heavily:

"And Susan? What's the idea? Going off alone in the middle of the night——"

Margery said:

"I wanted to send Bill with her, but she wouldn't have him. I wanted her to wake you and get you to go."

"What I want to know," Drew said explosively, "is why she had to go at all? Taking my car God knows where—probably smashing it up even if she doesn't kill herself——"

Margery stood up. In the moonlight her face had, now, a ghastly pallor. She came up the steps holding on to the railing, and Millicent, at the top, put an arm round her only just in time. She said:

"There, darling, never mind. They'll all be safely home before long. You're worn out. Help me, Tom."

She thought, settling Margery down on the couch in the dining-room, that if she had not had, as she turned to come in, that momomentary glimpse of Jungaburra's vast bulk cleaving upward through the silver sky, she might have felt more able to believe herself in her own reassuring words. And, too, if she hadn't happened to remember it so vividly from the last time she'd seen it, forty—no, nearly forty-five years ago! Not that that was more than a blink in its existence, but all the same, reason as you might, it did seem strange and rather awesome to come back after years which had so altered other places to find that spirit place so utterly unchanged, dreaming its immortality away.

And on it, somewhere, Colin, Bret, Susan.

She asked, settling a cushion behind Margery's head:

"What made her go? Is that comfortable?"

"Thank you—yes, quite. She was anxious about Bret."

Ill and exhausted as she felt, she could not quite subdue the smile that her own words aroused. That, she supposed, was half of Susan's charm—that her beauty had, like a kitten's, so much of the comical in it; that you couldn't, without wanting to laugh, think of her, tiny and indomitable, setting forth at midnight in a car only smaller than a charabanc, to succour two large and strapping males. . . .

All the same, Drew's sudden jovial explosion startled her. It had, she conjectured, glancing round, startled him too! He began to explain hurriedly:

"Just the thought of her—little devil! What sort of a road is it? Does she know the way?" He looked at her abruptly, almost menacingly, and came across the room to stare down at her:

"Why wouldn't she wake me—to go with her?"

Here it was. Margery wondered whether she some day would forget that children, when they were no longer children, liked to be left alone. That their whole instinct, when they found themselves in any of the tight places of adult life, was to battle through by themselves or with help, if need be, from their own generation? That there should be, for parents, one vast Commandment—Thou shalt keep out of the way——

She found herself looking unhappily at Millicent, who said:

"They didn't really, don't you see, Tom?—want us to know anything about it. They didn't (a small smile which it hurt Margery to see, touched her eyes for a second) want us to be worried. So don't you think that perhaps the—the most tactful thing we could do would be—to go back to bed?"

Drew looked at her and then at Margery. He was conscious again of that newly acquired (or perhaps it was only newly realised?) perceptiveness of his. Not that it was much use to him as a faculty; it felt, he thought with wry humour, rather like trying to play golf with a new club which you hadn't quite got the hang of yet! It was like a light just bright enough to show him that there were matters here which he didn't understand, but too dim to enable him to analyse them. So he looked at Millicent who, he now remembered, had often seen her way, and incidentally his, through difficulties before which, like an angry elephant at a closed gate, he had thundered and trumpeted and made ready to destroy.

So that if, in spite of the fear he could see so plainly written on her face, she decided to go back to bed, to say no more, do no more, behave as if it were the most natural thing in the world for one's children to go gallivanting about on a dangerous mountain in the middle of the night—well, no doubt she had a reason, and a good one. And he hadn't missed, on the tired face of his son's wife, a little quiver of very evident relief.

So the old people weren't wanted.

Well, he supposed there wasn't anything to stop him watching the bit of the road that was visible from their bedroom window?

It was, as his weary arms testified, a darned heavy car for so small a person as Susan.

"Not in a fit state," eh? Still, that was this morning.

Supposing he *was* in trouble—could Bret——?

Good chap, Bret; he would do all he could.

But then *he* might——?

Susan——

Millicent, from the doorway, said questioningly: "Tom?"

He bent down and patted Margery's hand.

"Well, we'll go off again. Sure you'll be all right now? We'll probably hear them when they come in. Not a word to Colin, eh?"

She pulled his head down, suddenly, and kissed his cheek.

CHAPTER TWENTY-THREE

I

HALF strangled by the thought that a sudden noise might alarm her and cause her to lose her balance, Bret's sharp cry of her name reached his lips only as a smothered and incoherent exclamation. But she heard it and looked up with a startled backward fling of her head.

She said dubiously after a moment:

"I don't think my legs are long enough."

Colin, still out of sight round the bend, called, "What's up?" And Bret, amazed at an unnatural quality in his own voice, replied:

"Susan's here."

He added shortly, to her:

"Get off this ledge. Go back to the chimney. What the devil did you want to do this for?"

She turned without a word and walked back. It didn't, he had to admit, seem to bother her; but all the same he let go a breath he didn't know he'd been holding when she faded into semi-obscurity at the end of the ledge. He said over his shoulder to Colin:

"How about this gap? Are you all right?"

"Yes; go ahead."

Bret stepped. It was easier coming back, he decided, turning; the wall didn't jut out so and there wasn't the shadow to confuse you——

Colin, the moon making a silvery halo round his head, was crouching on the other side with one hand over his eyes. Bret said sharply:

"What's wrong?"

Colin, subsiding on to his knees, answered without looking up:

"Must have shaken myself up a bit. Never had a head before. Chuck me an end of the rope."

Bret uncoiled it wondering what chance he'd have on a narrow ledge of holding Colin's weight if he did fall. He threw an end. Colin's groping hands found it and tied it in a bowline under his arms. He didn't lift his head; Bret suspected that his eyes were shut. Colin said:

"Go along the ledge about five yards or so; there's a jutting-out bit of rock about as high as your waist. Get a belay round it and you could hold anything that didn't break the rope. I'll be all right—but hurry up——"

Bret wondered, squatting on one heel, holding the rope round the rock, watching Colin get up, rather waveringly on to his feet, whether "head" might not be catching——? Whether perhaps the sudden faint malaise he himself was feeling might not turn irresistibly at any moment into a sickening giddiness, nausea, vertigo——

Colin standing on the edge of the gap, said, "Take in the slack, Bret." And he took it in mechanically, his eyes on the dark, silver-edged figure. It stood there, he thought, for so long that it made the whole situation seem to pass from reality into some other realm of immobility, or rather, perhaps, of indefinitely arrested movement. When it came forward at last it seemed like the whole world leaping at him, so vast and black and momentous was it, so fraught with dreadful and unspecified possibilities. One corner of his mind, defying desperately the invading confusion of the rest, told him it was Colin. Colin, safely across. Colin on his hands and knees only a couple of yards away, breathing heavily like a man exhausted.

Susan's voice from the darkness on his right:

"Can't I help, Bret?"

He answered shortly, "No." But Colin, always with his face down and his eyes shut, called:

"Head all right, Susan?"

"Yes, perfectly."

"Come and get one end of the rope, then. Take it back to where you are and hitch it round something. Bret can hold this end over the belay and I'll use it as a handrail. Quite soon I'm going to be sick."

Bret opened his mouth to speak. He wanted to shout furiously to Susan to stay where she was. Not on any account whatever to move. Not to dare to come out again on to this damnable ledge which, to his fast crumbling nerve, looked every moment narrower, more sinister, more surely a place for shaking hands with death. But he had reached actually a stage in which even speech had become impossible. The very movement of his lips would have seemed an earthquake to jolt from its tight rope his precariously balanced self-control. He could only watch, dumbly, Colin crawl beside him and unfasten one end of the rope from round his waist. He could only see, with a depth, an agony of fear he'd never conceived possible, Susan walking along, taking up the end he threw her, retreating with it into the darkness again. When she'd vanished he was aware that some unbearable oppression had gone from him, but he hadn't time or mental energy to spare for the considering of it. He tightened his end of the rope over the rock, felt Susan pull on hers, watched Colin, looking tiny and distorted as people look when one is ill and feverish, receding along the ledge between the rope and the wall. Then he was out of sight, and to Bret it was as if, with his vanishing, he had ceased to exist. He sat still feeling dazed and stupid. He found himself wondering why Susan had looked queer—unfamiliar. He discovered too, with some surprise, that he was in the middle of a vast yawn——

Colin called:

"Are you right, Bret?"

He stirred unwillingly. There was still that long silver streak. And there was still a tightness in his head and a strange emptiness in the pit of his stomach. Susan called cheerfully:

"Colin's been most beautifully sick. He's a new man!"

Bret snapped out:

"*Don't!*"

His forehead was dripping. His ears began to buzz. Purely by instinct he threw himself forward face downward on the rock. His whole inside seemed to tear itself away from him, and the blackness behind his eyes was suddenly lit with stars and sparks.

He felt a hand on the back of his head. Susan said, "Bret! Bret, darling! Oh, Bret, sit up and put the rope round you! Look, it's here. Let me——"

He sat up and swore at her:

"Blast you, Susan, get off this ledge and stay off it. I'm all right now. I'm coming. Here, hold the rope as you go. I'll follow you."

"I don't need—oh, very well. Will you tie it round you when I'm back?"

"All right—*all right!* Only be quick. Good God, you little fool, don't *run*!"

She said angrily, regaining the shadows:

"I wasn't running! What do you take me for?"

Bret stood up, holding the rope. He felt surprisingly better. It crossed his mind that perhaps the everyday normality of a squabble with Susan had had a steadying effect. He walked slowly, holding the rope while Colin and Susan took it in. When he stood at last beside them in the dark, she burst suddenly into a dreadful storm of weeping.

Bret offered her, gloomily, his last cigarette. For an hour or so he'd been living, he realised, a restful life of uncompromising simplicity. A life which had been composed, really, of nothing but the necessity for maintaining a physical equilibrium, and the sudden return to an existence bristling with emotional complexities depressed and disturbed him. He was aware too, unwillingly, that these same complexities had, in some mysterious way, altered since he had last examined them. Something had happened—something had changed; but, he told himself resentfully, he was damned if he was going to worry his head about it now. He was too dog tired; and an arm that he'd cut on some sharp grass coming down the cleft had begun to smart and throb. Or perhaps it was only now that he'd had time to notice it; he saw, surprised, that his wrist and hand were dark and sticky with half-dried blood.

Susan said:

"No—I don't want it," and wiped her eyes with her sleeve. She had stopped crying as abruptly as she had begun, and Colin who was coiling the rope said casually:

"That was a good idea of yours to use the spotlight."

Bret turned. He realised now that he'd been puzzled

when he was on the ledge by an impression of bright light somewhere below him. Now he could see, when he walked a few steps across the platform, that the chimney and the underneath of the chock-stone were illuminated. He said sharply to Susan:

"How did you get here?"

She stared.

"I brought the Madison, of course."

"You br——"

He began to laugh. It didn't seem possible, he thought, that down there on a crazy, unmade bush track with its head and spotlights trained on a wild, dark mountainside, was the same car which had stood only this morning, resplendent and urbane, on the concrete highway of Ballool. But in the next breath he was conscious again of irritation.

"How did you get up that chimney and over the chock-stone?"

She answered sulkily, like a reprimanded child:

"It wasn't hard. What's the chock-stone? Oh, that rock? I didn't get over, I crawled under it."

Bret thought:

"Good God, I must be tired! Or ill, or something—"

He had never felt before this crazy wavering between amusement and ill-temper. It seemed now definitely humorous that where he and Colin had to strain and squeeze and pull in the narrow chimney, Susan, light and unhampered, could go up easily; where they had to make a dizzy outside leap at the chock-stone, she like a rabbit could creep beneath it——!

And then, as though his emotions were swinging helplessly on the end of a pendulum, he was angry again. A midget like that to bring so huge a car out at night along a dangerous track—to——

He said harshly:

"You had no business to come. It was idiotic. You might have made a whole heap more trouble and you couldn't possibly have done any good. I thought you had more sense."

She turned on him; for one moment he saw her face flaming with anger unexpressed. It was streaked with tears and the moonlight made it look very pale; her eyes glittered like dark water. She stared for a moment and then turned her back on him. So quickly that he hadn't realised what she was doing she disappeared down the cleft behind the chock-stone. He started forward, swearing under his breath, but Colin said:

"Leave her alone; she's all right. The thing's as bright as day and the handholds are like stairs. Besides she knows it."

"Knows it?"

Colin said casually:

"She came to the top of the cleft with me one day. And she and Jim used to poke about here pretty often. Will you go next or shall I?"

"I'll go."

"All clear, Susan?"

"Yes."

"Bret's coming. Stand aside in case of stones."

"Right."

Bret found her standing on the sloping rock in the full blaze of the spotlight. Her hair flamed in it. As his feet came down on to what was, to all intents and purposes, firm ground again, some tension in him relaxed and he gave an involuntary shout of laughter. Susan, usually so immaculate, with riding breeches slipped down round her hips, with hands vanished up the sleeves of Margery's jumper, with white sandshoes that seemed to double the length of her feet! He laughed helplessly, leaning his shoulders against the wall, and she stood, a grotesque small figure, and scowled at him from under her black brows and her wild red hair.

Colin joining him, said:

"What's the joke?" but it was Susan who answered shortly:

"I think it must be me."

Colin let out a brief brotherly guffaw.

"You do look a sketch. Go on, Bret, you go down first and catch her if she falls. I'll give her a hand from above."

Bret, clambering down the last wall, felt a kind of contrition sobering his mood. He thought, cursing under his breath as a sharp edge set his arm bleeding again, that perhaps it hadn't been very kind or very tactful to laugh at her like that. Although, God knew, there hadn't been any malice in his laughter. Not even, he decided, jumping the last few feet to the ground, very much real amusement. It had been, most likely, only a form of letting off steam, a——

A white sandshoe just above the level of his eyes waved about exploringly.

Susan said crossly:

"I can't find anywhere for my foot."

He told her, "About six inches farther down," and she snapped, "Don't be silly. I'm stretching as far as I can, now."

He said:

"Oh, all right. Can you give me a hand and jump?"

She released her left hand and turned, holding it down to him. He could only just reach it, and the sudden impact of even her light weight made him stagger a little as he caught her. He put her down, and she gave him a savage and ceremonious "Thank you" before turning away.

Colin, above, called:

"I've left the rope up at the foot of the chimney. I won't be a moment."

But Bret was staring at Susan. One side of her face was wet and crimson. He felt his heart turn over with anxiety, compassion, remorse——

Something else? Something more? He said:

"Susan? You're hurt?"

He took her by the shoulders. She said vaguely:

"Hurt? No–I don't think so–where?"

He touched her cheek, leaning forward to peer at it. She put up a hand with a handkerchief in it and rubbed vigorously. The blood vanished leaving a smooth and unscarred cheek. He laughed, and glanced down at his own arm.

"It was my blood! Sorry!"

She cried:

"Oh–*you're* hurt——!"

Something overwhelmed him. The pent-up strain, excitement, anxiety of this strange night made it seem, in a mind working hazily, lethargically, quite fitting that it should culminate in an unfamiliar burst of a hitherto quite unknown emotion. She stayed in his arms perfectly still. There was no response in her body, her lips, and yet no resistance. She seemed almost to be listening. Dimly he remembered that once, somewhere, somehow, he had stood still and seemed to listen too. Colin called:

"Are you there? Rope coming down!"

It fell beside them. They stood apart, staring down at it stupidly. Then Susan, wordless, went away and vanished into darkness behind the headlights of the car, and Bret, breathless and bewildered, stooped slowly for the rope.

3

When they got home, Margery had coffee and sandwiches made for them. Susan shook her head and went off silently to their room. Bret, half stupid with weariness but very hungry, ate a few sandwiches and drank a cup of coffee. When they spoke it was in low voices so as not to disturb the sleepers, who were not asleep; it all seemed to Bret, through a haze of fatigue that dimmed his perceptions as a fog dims the vision, more like a scene from a rather bad play than a slice from normal life.

When at last he went out to his stretcher on the veranda it was nearly two o'clock. They'd had trouble coming home—lost the track twice and got bogged in the soft mud on the creek bank. He stood up for a moment winding his watch mechanically, fairly swaying on his feet with weariness and looking at the faint blur of Susan's head through her mosquito nets. His last conscious thought when he was at last in bed was that there was something concerning her which he must remember to think about in the morning.

CHAPTER TWENTY-FOUR

I

SUNLIGHT across his closed eyes woke Bret next morning to a magpie chorus so intoxicatingly lovely that without opening them he lay while it lasted, listening. The sun on his face was warm, his body relaxed and rested. Plunged from unconsciousness straight into this ecstasy of sound, he did contrive to keep, for a few blissful minutes, that delicious blankness of the mind which, upon waking, is usually so ruthlessly destroyed. He felt too, an awareness of some new well-being, a realisation of beatitude, waiting patiently just beyond the closed door of his consciousness until he should be pleased to admit and enjoy it.

The sun on his face made a red dazzle behind his lids; he lifted a hand and laid it palm outward across his eyes. But the movement, and its accompanying pain, woke his idle brain to coherent thought, and sharply disturbing memory.

Yes, disturbing certainly, but a new and less painful disturbance—— His thoughts had sped, by way of the stiff aching of his cut wrist, straight back to Susan with his blood on her cheek, Susan the next moment in his arms——

And the sensations which went with that memory were, he discovered, unaccompanied by the instant alarums and excursions, the warring and jarring, all the mental turmoil, stress and confusion to which he had become, in this last year, unwillingly accustomed. So accustomed, he marvelled that the very relief which their absence roused in him was a shock which in itself amounted almost to suffering. The kind of shock, the agonising relaxation which one might feel beneath the gallows at an eleventh-hour reprieve!

Warily, like one who having once pulled the tiger's whiskers with impunity makes ready for a second attempt, he let his thoughts slide back to that strange overwhelming moment. He found nothing there but a medley of pleasantly poignant sensations, small things like the roughness of her woollen jumper on his arms, the sudden flutter of her lashes against his cheek. Things, he thought, that he'd felt often enough —too often—before, but always with the background of his own inhibitions to spoil them. Things that he'd felt, not with last night's grateful simplicity, but with some inner whisper not to be subdued, which had made of them temptations and beguilements, woven about them and about him in his moments of nauseated capitulation, a veil of illusive and resentful shame——

That, he thought soberly, opening his eyes and blinking them in the dazzling sunlight, was a silly word to use, to think of, in any relation to Susan. And he stirred, turned over on his side, peered across the veranda through his mosquito nets at the other white shrouded bed in the shade of the wall.

She must be still asleep. He looked at his watch, and sat up suddenly. Half-past nine! Good Lord, they were to have been on the way by eight! He got out of bed and went over to wake her, but nothing was visible except a heap of curls which in the shadow looked, he thought, the colour of dead pine needles. Disarming curls;

disarmingly small, the huddled lump under the bedclothes; he turned away and went inside to have his shower.

He thought, shivering under the cold well water, that quaint as it appeared, he'd only seen her asleep half a dozen times in his life! And all those times had been on their quite fantastic honeymoon! And at the thought of that honeymoon he caught himself smiling a little, because it had really been rather funny in its way—a fun they had both, thank heaven, been able to appreciate!

He discovered that his hair was full of grains of sand and grit that had fallen into it last night on Jungaburra, so he put his head, too, under the shower and soaped it vigorously, thinking with one corner of his mind that the frothy and feathery touch of soapsuds down one's back was strangely pleasant, and with another of his wedding day.

He'd sat on the railing of the hotel balcony, watching the sea and the faint pathway across it of the rising moon. Everything, he supposed, had contributed to the strange alertness which, even now, he could remember as having been his predominant sensation. If he'd been a dog, he reflected, he'd have had his nose in the air, sniffing, his ears pricked! Keyed up, mentally, physically and emotionally to an unfamiliar atmosphere. Salty air from the sea instead of the indefinable country scents to which his nostrils were accustomed; a deep incessant thunder of surf instead of silence; and there behind him in a room whose light made a bar of yellow across the balcony, that disturbing, red-headed stranger who had so suddenly become his wife——

He'd admitted to himself that it was she, actually,

who had saved the whole preposterous day from being the nightmare it might have been. Standing alone that morning at a street corner waiting for her, he had had an interval of sheer ignominous panic. What he was doing had still seemed the only possible thing to do; not the action itself, but its details suddenly alarmed him, and it was in a state as far removed as was possible from his usual self-possession that he had seen her at last walking towards him with her father and mother. Well, she'd been cool enough, anyhow! Cool, calm, friendly, business-like! The ceremony in the registrar's office might have been the signing of a lease! He'd taken, thankfully, his cue from her; Millicent had been, with a dignity which not even this bizarre and painful situation could shake, indomitably herself, but Drew had been sweating at every pore! His trouble had been, of course, that the Book of the Rules by which, unconsciously, he formed his behaviour, was in this case disconcertingly useless. He couldn't greet with a jovial word and a slap on the back this son-in-law so obviously malgre-lui; he couldn't beam paternally; couldn't wish them happiness——

He couldn't even, Bret realised, his faint grin fading, expect it for them. And on that thought he'd turned his head towards the lighted window, his forehead creasing, his mouth tightening with a perplexed anxiety, a mental bracing of himself to a difficult job. He'd told himself for the fiftieth time that whatever you thought of her you couldn't deny her pluck. It hadn't at that time struck him as being ominous that he should find it necessary so often to dam back the tides of his resentment, his dislike, with this one frail barrier of approval.

Not that there weren't other things to be said for

her. That day, their wedding-day, had shown him quite a lot of them. There was something, he had reflected, beginning to stroll up and down the balcony, essentially sporting in her whole attitude to life, to himself—— A game with, according to your skill, prizes or penalties. He, himself, he had supposed ruefully, was her penalty, and he couldn't but admit that she'd accepted him gamely enough. Of that strange confession—or assertion—of hers the other day among the spinach and the cabbages, he had tried to think as little as possible. It couldn't be true, of course; she was very young, very distraught at the time—hysterical probably. Didn't girls get queer spasms of affection for people——? "Crushes" or "pashes" or something——

And there hadn't been, since that moment, any suggestion in her manner that she regarded him as other than an accident in her life, as she was in his, to be accepted as philosophically as possible!

He'd said abruptly as they drove:

"I've engaged connecting rooms and a bathroom. I shan't bother you."

The corner of his eye had caught a fiery glinting streak as her head came sharply round to him. In the momentary glimpse he'd had of her face before he fixed his attention on the road again, he'd seen her cheeks flaming, her eyes bright with a kind of angry pride. She'd replied instantly:

"There was no need for that."

He'd shrugged, and after a mile or so she'd said rather wearily, "Thank you," and gone on to pleasant and trivial remarks about the road, the car, the scenery——

So now, he'd thought, pausing in his stroll and

leaning his elbows on the balcony rail, it was up to him. He glanced over his shoulder at the lighted room where she was unpacking. He had cleared out and left her to it simply because he could think of nothing to say to her. Emotions, he admitted grudgingly, were funny things. The last few days, wrenched out of perspective by the shock of his brother's death, seemed now to be like a separate, distorted life between one orderly existence and another at whose beginning he stood perplexed. Emotions which had seemed in that fevered interlude to loom overwhelmingly with the unchallenged permanence of Mont Blanc, now seemed, to his uneasily roving mind, less inevitable, less fundamentally changeless. It wasn't any good denying to himself, for instance, that in there, after dinner, he'd felt——

Well, what it amounted to was that a mock-marriage, even in such circumstances as these, wasn't going to be easy all the time. That didn't mean, he told himself angrily, that it was impossible. When the child was born, he realised (without feeling in the very least called upon to analyse his conviction) things would be different. That was the way he happened to be made. Until then——

Suddenly, as if accepting a challenge, he had walked along to the lighted door and knocked. A very composed voice told him instantly to come in.

Here again, a year later, with his head under the shower, Bret found himself smiling. He found, too, in his memory a picture so bright, so detailed and clearly defined, that he wondered fleetingly that some unconscious self should have stored and guarded it so jealously.

She was in bed, reading. He had wondered, amused

and rather touched, if she had been trying to make herself unalluring. She had scrubbed her face, and her nose had a shiny high-light down the middle of it. Her hair, damp round the forehead, combed back relentlessly, looked darker, less like a war-cry than usual. She was wearing a very plain white dressing-jacket that covered her from throat to wrists.

He remembered now the sound of his own sudden laughter. He had felt genuinely what he had been acting all day—friendly and light-hearted and matter-of-fact. And amused. Amused by an only-just-realised mental picture he must have built up somehow of a lovely unscrupulous Susan, subtly sophisticated, delicately rouged and powdered, dangerously versed in all the arts of seduction; a very different Susan from the one who was looking up at him over the top of her book with a smile whose valiance did not quite hide its hesitation, its hint of appeal——

He sat down on the edge of her bed.

"What's the book?"

She showed him.

"It's rather good. Do you like his books?"

"Yes, as a rule."

He had looked at her curiously. It had struck him for the first time that there might be qualities of companionship in this rather unpromising marriage. He said:

"I wonder if our literary tastes are alike." But she only answered non-commitally, "I wonder."

"There are," he stated, looking at her, "quite a lot of things we have to find out about each other."

"Yes."

He saw that her hands were shaking, and he went on quickly:

"I've found out one about you already."

She said, "Have you? What is it?" looking slightly nervous and avoiding his eyes.

"You have a shiny nose."

She laughed, her head back, her teeth gleaming in her red, half-opened mouth; he added:

"And that schoolgirl complexion."

She stopped laughing and a faint wave of colour ran up in her cheeks. He said on an impulse:

"I hope—I haven't persuaded you into something that's going to make you miserable."

She said quickly, brightly:

"Oh, no! I'm sure it—it will be all right——"

She had taken the book from him and begun to turn its pages. He saw, compassionately, that she was perilously close to tears and stood up with a yawn which, artificially begun, ended in a spasm of intense and genuine weariness. He said.

"Good-night. Can I get you anything?"

"No, thank you. Good-night."

So he'd given her back a little pat, her nose a little tweak, and gone outside for a pipe before turning in. . . .

2

Margery knocked on the door.

"Bret?"

"Hallo?"

"Grilled steak or bacon and eggs?"

"Both."

"Hog. How do you feel?"

"Fine."

Fine! He began to be aware, as if his body had been awaiting verbal confirmation before asserting itself, that he really did feel very fine indeed! He was in a most tremendous glow, a glow only partly accounted for, he felt, by the sting of cold water. That climb last night. A good feeling! Rightly or wrongly, one got a kick out of flirting, now and then, with danger! He felt now a kind of delayed mental exhilaration—what he should have felt last night if his body had not been so rebelliously exhausted! And not only that either. He felt . . .

Well—happy!

Happiness, he told himself, towelling vigorously, is a state of the emotions. So that here he was feeling physically, mentally and emotionally fine!

Why?

No, hang it all, when you are fortunate enough to achieve, even for a little while, such a condition of beatitude, you don't stop to ask why! A waste! A crime!

He sang:

"*I want to BE happy, but I can't BE happy*
Till I make YOU hap——"

The word died abruptly on his lips. He stared absently at the wall for a minute while he put on his dressing-gown. Why are popular songs popular? Because they're true? Truisms? Obvious things, fundamental things that come into every one's life? Love—"*One alone to be my own . . .*" Hopes and imaginings—"*Somewhere the bluebird is singing and winging his way to you.*" Sentimental yearnings—"*Oh, God bless you and keep you, Mother Machree!*" Plain truths of human psychology. The A B C of the human animal in love—"*I can't BE happy till I make YOU happy too!*"

So he said to himself, going back along the hall to their bedroom, "Well, well, fancy your discovering that!" and paused inside the door looking speculatively at Susan's belongings strewn about the room, as though he imagined that, in the light of his new understanding, they might take on a new significance.

And in a way, he thought as he dressed, they did. That morning, for instance, the first morning of their honeymoon, he had looked at them with a feeling quite different from his present feelings.

He'd wakened, he remembered, to a rather pleasant sensation of holiday. He could hear through his open window voices and laughter, early-morning surfers returning to the hotel, and he had begun calculating idly how many years it was since he'd spent whole days sprawling face downwards on the sand, feeling the sun beating into his body. He had wondered, too, if Susan liked surfing, if she liked sunbaking, if she liked a swim before breakfast; and whether, perhaps, they had created a record in that they had married each other without ever having had, in the true sense of the word, a conversation.

He'd got out of bed, into a dressing-gown and slippers, and leaned his head out of the window into the brilliant sunshine. There were still half a dozen bathers left on the beach; two girls, one in green and one in scarlet made, he thought, a rather charming patch of colour on the long creamy beach with the turquoise, white-ridged sea behind them. But all the time behind his conscious thoughts and observations, there had persisted a chain of rather intriguing guesswork about Susan, a new small hope that she might be quite a good companion; and that there was no reason he could see why good companionship should not take, quite successfully, the place of love——

Rather anxious, perhaps, to begin testing his theory he'd knocked at the door of her room, but there'd been no answer, so he'd opened it and put his head in. Her bed was empty but he could hear her splashing in the bathroom, so he went over to her window which commanded a view of the road and the hotel garden, and stood there with his elbows on the sill watching a car load of picnickers setting out for the day.

Her voice came, presently, from behind him.

"Hallo!"

He had turned, slightly dazzled by the glare of the sun. She was hanging up her towel, looking, he thought, in her stockinged feet, and white slip, with her hair damp and ruffled, like a child of fourteen. He said "Good-morning," and felt that it had sounded like an uncle to his niece, so he added hastily, "How's the head?" and decided irritably that that had, if anything, deepened the avuncular effect. She had answered politely, sitting on the edge of the bed and putting on her shoes.

"Quite well again, thanks."

So then he had prowled across the room and had found her odds and ends rather intriguing. He had been amused, for instance, by her hairbrush, a stout wooden affair with intimidating steel-bristles sprouting from a rubber base. A queer thing! There was something, indeed, that appealed to him about all her belongings—they weren't the expensive, monogrammed fal-lals which she could, undoubtedly, have afforded, but oddments which gave the impression of having come with her from her childhood. A long, Japanese-looking, wooden box with handkerchiefs in it; a good but small and old-fashioned hand mirror, ivory-backed; a plain black comb. Her suitcase was open on a chair; he could see stockings neatly rolled, and stacks of things that looked soft and silken; a blue linen dress was lying across the foot of her bed.

She had asked:

"Are you going to have your bath now?"

He said, "Am I in the way?" And she looked up swiftly, almost guiltily, and protested, "Of course not. I didn't mean that. But—aren't you hungry?"

He laughed.

"Why, are you?"

"*Starving!*"

"Now, I come to think of it, I am too." He had watched her for a moment. "Is that a good kind of brush?"

She'd paused with it half-way to her head and studied it with a faint surprise.

"I don't know. I've always used one like this. What's the joke?"

"I was wondering how you get that soap-and-goodwill shine off your face."

The sudden impishness of her smile made him remember vividly the Susan of his first acquaintance.

"If you'll bring me my powder bowl from over there I'll show you presently." He picked it up. Its extraordinary beauty of shape and colouring impressed him. It was very heavy, very smooth, brilliantly blue. He had wondered as he brought it to her, what it was made of

"Where did you get this lovely thing?"

Her hand had stopped its rhythmical movement.

She had pushed her hair away from her face and met his eyes.

"Jim gave it to me."

He had put it down carefully in front of her. He realised with sharp dismay and consternation that the mere mention of his brother's name had been enough to destroy in a second the sense of well-being, of pleasant companionship which had just now enwrapped them. Suddenly aware of his own silence, of the small preoccupied frown that was creasing his forehead, he had glanced at her. She was looking out the window, but she turned at once to meet his eyes again. He said with an effort:

"Well, I'd better have my bath. I won't be long. But don't wait for me if you're hungry."

3

Dressed, he brushed his damp hair and stood for a moment staring soberly at the dressing-table. Yes, that was how he had felt, that was how he had reacted on that day which seemed so long ago, to those same trifles which now lay there before his eyes, the same—and yet, actually, so different!

The brush was still the same comical brush; the box still had handkerchiefs in it, and the powder-bowl which Jim had given her was gleaming with a lovely luminous blueness in a streak of morning sun. Somehow it didn't hurt him now. Somehow those things had acquired a rather precious and familiar air; from becoming the personal belongings of a stranger they had slipped somehow into the pattern of his life. . . .

He went out on the veranda, lifted the mosquito net away and pulled one of the russet red curls gently.

"Wake up, Carrots."

She sighed and grumbled and came up from under the bedclothes, yawning and rubbing her knuckles in her eyes.

CHAPTER TWENTY-FIVE

I

As she turned over, yawning, her warm cheek came down on his hand where it still lay on her pillow. She opened her eyes, squinted down at it, and then quickly up at his face. She said, "Oh—hallo," in a voice still slurred and blunted with sleep, and he saw her feet thrust down under the bedclothes and her whole body stiffen like a cat's in one vast luxurious stretch.

There in the shade the air was keen; his movement was as instinctive as the spreading of chilled hands to a fire, as the bending of one's head to a scented flower. When his arm was half round her and his face against her cheek he remembered a puppy which had followed him once in the city. It had been an endearing small thing; his hands, on that cold day, had found a certain pleasure in patting it, in burrowing into the soft folds beneath its chin; he'd been amused, for a few idle moments while waiting for his tram, at its eager, absurd, passionate adoption of himself. And he'd wondered rather uneasily, catching his last glimpse of it as the tram rattled off, standing with its head lifted, and its tail drooping, its eyes full of the incredulous misery of the forsaken, whether his caresses, his careless acceptance of an illogical devotion, hadn't been rather a low-down brutal sort of kindness. . . .

He found his impulsive movement slain suddenly by this memory. For a second he remained there, thinking with a smile in the thought, that she was really even warmer and pleasanter than a puppy, and then, with the smile vanishing, that she probably had, also, an even greater capacity for being hurt. But as, with a sigh, he began to pull his arm away, he felt her suddenly stroke his hair back from his forehead with a touch so gentle, so loving and compassionate that it seemed to clarify and bring to a single focus of misery all the vague doubts and nebulous fears which had been for so long overshadowing his mood. She said:

"Poor old Bret!"

He asked slowly, staring at her.

"Why 'poor'?"

She smiled and gave his cheek a pat as he straightened up.

"Well, aren't you?"

He said vehemently:

"I don't know. I feel it sometimes. Perhaps—what made you say it, anyhow?"

She sat up, pushing her hair away from her face.

"Sometimes I used to feel that way about Jim."

"What way?"

"As you felt just now. I was awfully fond of him. Sometimes I used to feel inclined to stroke his hair because it had a nice crinkly feel—and sometimes I used to want to hug him—just because he was young and healthy and strong and good to touch—but I couldn't because I was always afraid he'd think it meant more than it did mean. . . ."

Bret sat quite still looking along the veranda to the green of the paddocks and the cobalt shadows on the hills. He sat for so long saying nothing that at last Susan stood up on the bed in her pyjamas, jumped down on to the floor and went off to her bath. And still Bret sat there thinking.

He thought that probably she was right to insist so on her relationship with Jim. That uncompromising determination of hers to stress at all times the strange parallel of his present attitude to her with her past attitude to his brother might be, according to her code of honesty and pride, her only possible course. What was it, after all, when you brought it down to its simplest and crudest terms? Simply that she saw Jim quite clearly as the barrier between them. Simply that she saw, in his evasions of the subject, in his tortured desire to forget or ignore it, an attempt to creep round the barrier and leave it standing—no longer between, but everlastingly before them. Wasn't she right to fear that?

He stood up and went over to the railings where he had stood last night, and wondered when he got there whether that physical movement might not have been a subconscious effort to find again the mood he had so deeply felt there, and so swiftly lost.

Jungaburra, he thought looking up at it, had lost its midnight air of menace; it seemed actually to have moved farther away, no longer lowering blackly almost over his head, but withdrawn by some magic of colour and light, its lavender and amethyst and lichen-green washed over by pale sunlight, and its peak showing faintly through a veil of mist. It wasn't likely, he thought ruefully, that here in daylight, chasing it with the blundering clumsiness of conscious effort, he would recapture the fugitive impulses of an emotion that had come like a moth out of the dark, and returned . . .

He seemed to see her vanishing past him into the dusk in her pale wide-spreading dress. He'd thought her like a moth then.

"*If I were your sister.*"

Never, he told himself rather irritably, had he done such an infernal amount of thinking and feeling and worrying and wondering as he had done since he married Susan! There was hardly, hang it all, an hour when he could be comfortably and stolidly himself, doing a definite job with a clear and easy mind. He couldn't, he realised with amazement and trepidation, get up and walk across a veranda without beginning to analyse his motives like some blasted be-spectacled highbrow dabbling in psychological bunk!

And yet he was aware, uneasily, that contempt and profanity would not explain, far less banish or subdue the strange disturbances of his mind. They would not obliterate the knowledge that he had for nearly a year past, and especially last night, been cast adrift upon his emotions like a cork on a stormy sea. He'd felt fear and anger and loneliness and relief all with ten times the intensity he had ever known before. He'd been wildly excited, furiously angry, triumphantly glad. He'd sworn at Susan in one breath and laughed heartily at her in the next. No wonder his feet had, literally, stumbled with weariness last night, as he went to bed; no wonder he had slept so soundly!

No wonder——

But there he stopped, his thoughts baulking, trembling on the verge of a discovery. Thoughts seemed to be like that. If you kept them, drove them like horses on the roads—well, the roads were all you ever saw. But if you let them range they brought you to new places. They had brought him once already that morning along the trivial by-path of a song to an elementary fact which he had never realised before.

And here they were again showing him the end of a sentence he had unwittingly begun.

No wonder he'd wakened feeling so good!

Well, this also was kindergarten stuff, he supposed. After all, everybody knew that to keep any living thing in good working order you had to allow it the full exercise of its natural functions. Funny that he'd never realised before that your emotions needed exercise just like your muscles, that the healthy human being had the waste products of his feelings to get rid of as well as the waste products of his digestive organs! And he thought with a kind of alarmed amusement:

"Good God, I've been constipated!"

There again, following the irrational and flippant wanderings of his thoughts he found a truth which dumbfounded and wickedly delighted him. He dashed into the bedroom and grabbed Susan by the shoulders. He said:

"My child, I've discovered what love is. It's an aperient. Don't stare like that, idiot. Kiss me every morning and—who knows——? It's the little daily dose——"

She began to laugh helplessly. They found themselves waltzing round the room.

2

Drew, Millicent and Richard ate their breakfast at the veranda table in the sunlight. Rich smells drifted out through the open kitchen door, smells of bacon, and coffee and of steak cooking over an open flame; they mixed, Drew thought, very pleasantly with the damp country smells of the paddocks. The paddocks indeed, kept his eyes from his porridge plate. Every blade of grass had its drop of dew, and every drop of dew was like a diamond. The whole scene, the very day itself had a diamond-like quality—cold and keen and polished. . . .

He said to Margery as she came out with a rack of toast and sat down opposite him:

"This is a fine scheme of yours—breakfast in the sun. There's a nip in the air."

She smiled absently, moving Richard's plate a little nearer to him. Her eyes were heavy, Millicent thought, glancing at her, and she was pale from want of sleep, but she looked—more alive, as if a few years of lost youth had been handed back to her in the night. Colin, too, in their brief glimpse of him early this morning, had looked happy and vigorous.

He'd stuck his head round their bedroom door and called:

"Hallo, family! Sorry I wasn't here to welcome you last night. Sleep well?"

Millicent took her cue.

"Splendidly, dear. What time is breakfast?"

"Any time you're ready. I've got to ride over to see Miller about some sheep before I have mine, but I won't be long. See you later!"

He'd disappeared. She had looked down at Tom, and begun to laugh helplessly. The children were always doing that to him. Taking a situation out of his hands with a few swift nondescript, even idiotic sentences, so that before he had had time to consider far less to speak weightily, the matter was dealt with, the subject closed! And he always looked, poor dear, so bewildered! She had bent with loving compunction and kissed his creased forehead.

"It's no good, darling. That's *that*!"

He'd shrugged ruefully, running his hand through his greyish hair, and said:

"I suppose it is."

And it was. They had dressed and come out to find, in the clear morning light, a household very different from that whose strange atmosphere of tension had so worried them last night. Margery, brisk and efficient, set the table on the veranda, told them brightly of Richard's latest escapades, answered Millicent's questions on small domestic matters, put her one maid on the right track with the cooking of the breakfast.

So, Millicent thought, lifting Richard on to his chair and tying his feeder round his neck, if they wanted, she and Tom, to indulge in any more guiding, helping, directing, guarding of young lives, they'd have to wait for grandchildren! Well, one was easily consoled! She was amused to realise that even this trivial service to small Richard gave her a pleasure she had not felt for many years. Colin, bless him, was going to paddle his own canoe; Susan, bless her too, was going to deal somehow with her own strange problem. But there was still, thank heaven, Richard's feeder to be tied!

And she said sadly to Drew:

"Parents are very selfish creatures, Tom."

He protested indignantly:

"Selfish? Nonsense! Give up their whole lives to a pack of ungrateful brats! Get nothing in return! Selfish be damned!"

She shook her head.

"There's nothing we ever do for them that gives them half the joy they give us—just by existing."

Margery came out with steaming plates.

"Do you mind eating this while it's hot? I'll come out presently, but I just want to see that Annie doesn't burn Bret's steak to a cinder."

Drew asked:

"Where is he? And Susan? Aren't they up?"

Margery said, her head bent over Richard:

"I thought we'd let them sleep. You—you aren't really in a dreadful hurry to leave. . . .?"

Millicent answered swiftly:

"No—oh, no, not at all. What a pretty plate that is of Richard's. . . ."

Drew, on the edge of a protest, on the edge of some remark about the weariness of Bret and its cause, found again that he was too late. He surprised in himself a faint amusement and admiration at the deft way in which a very chasm of strange and sinister happenings had been covered by a few airy words, an attitude of matter-of-factness, as an elephant pit is covered by thin boughs and leaves. All very well, he thought, for Millicent, for Colin, for Susan, who were practised in treading lightly! For himself, as he admitted grimly, he was, conversationally, a born elephant. Well, even an elephant could keep away from the trap if he knew where it was.

So he said:

"Sit down and have your breakfast, Milly. Well, young Richard, how about taking us for a walk when we've all finished this enormous meal?"

But Richard's answer was lost to him because he could see, far away across a couple of paddocks, Colin cantering home.

3

Colin was thinking, with unregenerate enjoyment, that something nearly always turned up to help the undeserving. This early-morning ride of his had been Margery's idea—and a good one too. The sharp air and the exercise had cleared his aching head, and he guessed from the tingling of his cheeks that some of the yellowish pallor which he had seen that morning in the mirror had probably disappeared. And of course if it hadn't been for this entirely heaven-sent bit of news he could have stayed away longer—arrived back at Kalangadoo with time for not much more than farewells.

It wasn't, he protested to himself, dismounting and leading his horse through the second last gate which was sagging on its hinges, that he didn't want to see his parents. Only that as things were at present he didn't particularly want them to see him. Parents, from lifelong habit, perhaps, were too darned proprietary. If they thought you were doing something you shouldn't they considered themselves privileged to rebuke you, as though you weren't yourself an adult, as though you couldn't see for yourself where folly was and where tragedy and ruin lay in wait. . . .

As though they couldn't realise that from the moment you took a wife and begot a child, you ceased to be part of their microcosmic existence and became a new being with a new set of human relationships.

And as though, he thought with a sudden scowl which made him look for a moment very like his father, he couldn't manage his own life himself! For he could and he would and he *was* managing it! Yes, in spite of yesterday, in spite of the blind drunken fury and despair which had sent him up the mountain, and which instead of ending in tragedy as it probably should have ended, had fizzled out so quaintly with the small Susan and the large car as rescue party!

What they didn't understand—none of them except Margery, and even she had failed yesterday—was that if his drunkenness meant failure his soberness meant triumph. A batsman wasn't judged by his one duck but by his many centuries; an airman not by his few forced landings, but by his long successful flights. And he, with his always increasing intervals of sobriety, had felt himself—no, hang it all, *did* feel himself—as one slowly gaining ground in some long and fiercely waged battle. And he wasn't going to be frowned on, or advised, or rebuked or sighed over. No one knew, no one even began to realise how precious a weapon his own self-respect was to him. Nothing sustained him sometimes but his own convictions that he would win; it was like a small candle-flame in some black labyrinth—his only comfort, his only hope of finding, at last, his way back into the daylight. So that it had to be guarded and cherished and shielded; so that, on the bad days after each temporary defeat it flickered and guttered, and disapproval, he thought, like a draught of wind, might well come near to extinguishing it altogether. . . .

No—what he wanted now was breakfast, a kiss from Margery, the swift hug of Richard's arms as he lifted him to say good-bye; and then a day's work. A hard day's work. So that he'd sleep to-night like the dead and wake to-morrow with that day and night of righteous toil and rest standing like a buffer between him and his day of failure. That was how he managed.

From there his start was clean; he could go ahead with confidence and add another week—another month—even several months to his previous record. In that way, he reflected, you could invest it all with something of the character of sport—you could take, even, a kind of gambler's interest in yourself as the days went by, laying odds on your chances, waking to each day with a speculative interest, a wonder which was partly fearful, partly cynical, partly amused!

Not, perhaps, in the best heroic tradition. Not even, possibly, in the best taste! But God preserve us, his strained nerves cried out, from solemnity! God save us from vows and repentances, from self-abasements and despairs!

Nothing—*nothing* he thought, riding his horse up to the last gate and leaning forward to open it, was ever the better done for being done heavily. You could make a resolve flippantly, airily, as though it were a wager, or you could make it with awesome oaths and prayerful vigils; it wasn't how you made it but how you kept it, that mattered.

And when you didn't keep it, repentances were a waste of time. You had yourself for your only weapon—you weren't going to abandon that weapon to humiliation, to brooding, to sickened self-contempt. Things that would be to it like rust to a sword——

So he snatched his hat from his head and brandished it, dug his heels into his horse and came thundering up to the veranda shouting, "Whoopee!" in his best cowboy voice, and preparing his news gleefully to fling at them, like a small boy holding a throwdown behind his back.

4

Bret said:

"Hallo, you're early on the job." And Susan with her mouth more full than it should have been, scoffed:

"Early! This is supposed to be breakfast but as a matter of fact it's nearly lunch. Yes, I know I'm exaggerating."

Margery asked:

"Was it all right about the sheep? Because we put a call through to Miller just after you left."

Colin looked at her quickly. Had that confounded girl, Annie, listened in? And if so had she told——?

But Margery added:

"I thought perhaps your buyer had changed his mind."

Colin said nonchalantly:

"No, it wasn't that. It was his aunt ringing from Coonabarrabran. Wondabyne's for sale again. Old Mortimer's dead."

CHAPTER TWENTY-SIX

I

It was nearly half-past eleven when Drew, looking thoughtful and driving silently, swung the car on to the main road again. He hadn't said a word about the new dent on one of the front mudguards, nor about the great horizontal scar along the once immaculate paint-work of the bonnet. And when he'd found a coil of rope lying on the floor at the back he'd just taken it out and handed it to Bret without a word. Any one else but Bret, Millicent thought, might have looked a little sheepish. But when it came to sheer immovable woodenness of expression, Bret stood quite alone.

She admitted to herself as she settled back more comfortably into her corner that she was glad to have left Kalangadoo behind. And even, going suddenly further in her thoughts than she had intended to go, that she would be glad when they had left Coolami behind too, and were headed back, she and Tom, to Ballool. For somehow that news of Colin's which didn't really concern her at all had shocked her more than she cared to own. She felt danger then and wondered again, in a kind of panic, at her own fool-hardiness in venturing so far away from the safe, stagnant resignation of her life at Ballool. What did it matter to her, she thought angrily, that Mortimer was dead? It had, for her, no significance at all, and yet, like some submarine eruption it had flung to the surface of her mind a long-drowned picture of her home. She realised now that she had been looking at it all this time through depths; years, distance, an always accumulating mass of happenings. The remembered sounds of it had been muffled, its remembered outlines blurred and wavering. She had been safe in thinking of it when it lay so deeply submerged—so unattainable!

Now, quite suddenly, she was close to it again. The scents and sounds of it were all about her. Only a few hours driving would bring them, actually, to its first paddocks, and it was alarming, it was terrifying and exhausting to find in what minute detail her memory had treasured it.

Somehow if this man Mortimer hadn't died it would have been less poignant. He, an unknown owner, would have seemed like a buffer between Wondabyne and her irrationally persisting sense of possession. But now that he was dead there would be a kind of emptiness over all those sunlit acres. A waiting. An invitation. . . .

She shook herself and blinked her eyes rapidly to focus them again upon the road. She felt so tired, so disheartened and depressed that she knew she must really be getting old. Last night had piled a veritable mountain of age upon her heart. She wanted, now, nothing but to creep back to Ballool with her tail between her legs!

For, she thought, one was not made old by one's own many years but by the few years of the young folks about one. She herself, alone with Tom, was still simply Millicent, but surrounded by these unrestful young people and their problems she felt herself wading into old age on other names which took her deeper at each step; mother—mother-in-law—grandmother. If you could achieve anything, she protested silently, with these relationships it would not matter that they aged you; if you could, for instance, help your son and comfort your daughter-in-law and do something more for your grandchild than tie his feeder!

But you couldn't, you couldn't. You must only hover tactfully on the outskirts of their lives while they, growing up or growing older themselves, pushed you back relentlessly into old age. Unless you escaped.

Escape one's children? Ridiculous! And yet a faint fear assailed her. She realised that, unwittingly, her mind full of her son and her daughter and the shaping of their lives, she had come suddenly upon a crisis in her own and Tom's.

One might say actually that they had no life left. All that had made Tom's, his work, his fight (which had been less a battle for money than for a vindication of himself to himself) was over. All that had been hers – the children – had suddenly been taken from her. Nothing remained, really, but an existence and a host of material possessions.

She saw this journey now very much in the same way that Susan had seen it for different reasons – as a kind of interlude between two lives. To-night they would sleep at Coolami. To-night and to-morrow and thereafter her daughter's life would run a course diverging steadily from her own. A course in which new loves and new preoccupations would gently force out old ones – inevitably, rightly and beautifully as the spring leaves of some trees push off the dead ones of last year.

An existence and a host of material possessions. Could you make a life of those? She considered them dubiously like a cook considering some flour and a handful of raisins, and wondering if, by some miracle of culinary art, a cake could emerge from them? And she looked sideways at Tom's bent brows, speculating upon what he'd say if she told him she was a cup of sugar, and asked him to pretend to be an egg. . . .?

2

Bret, with his pipe in his mouth and his feet propped up on the two suitcases, stared at the greenness that was swinging and swaying past his half-shut eyes. He saw it just now simply as greenness, a colour restful not only to the eyes but to the heart and mind of a countryman. Without any reasoning it added a saving touch of contentment to a mood which had been vaguely ruffled for the last ten minutes by his thoughts.

He had been thinking about Wondabyne and comparing its fortunes with those of Coolami. It worried him rather to think that so magnificent a property was not having its just due. Long years of competent and uninterrupted management by the same man—or at least by the same family—was what it needed. Wondabyne, he reflected, had never really had a fair deal since the death of Millicent's father when he himself was about seven. Her brother had been at first too young and then increasingly too ill to run it properly. When he died and poor Agatha had tried to keep it on with a manager——! He made unconsciously a little noise of impatience and exasperation. It had been enough to make your heart bleed, he thought, to see the state it had fallen into then—the rabbits multiplying in thousands so that even Coolami had been quite seriously threatened; a wool clip that the old man would have been ashamed to see go out with the name of Wondabyne on the bales.

Into the end of that bad chapter of its history Susan had flashed so suddenly. Bret wondered for a moment if part of his instantaneous dislike for her might have been caused, quite unreasonably, by the fact that at that time everything and every one connected with Wondabyne irritated and annoyed him. The gentle ineffectual Agatha; Bailey the manager leaving ruin in his wake! His feeling then for the property had been the feeling of any humane man seeing a child or an animal badly used. Indeed he had been so concerned that he had actually suggested tentatively once to Jim that they should buy some of it—the paddocks that ran with Coolami—"just," he remembered saying uneasily, "to put it out of its misery!"

Well, times had been bad then, they had decided that it wasn't possible. But Mortimer had come along and bought it from Agatha soon afterwards, and in his slow and uninspired way he had been heading it back towards order and prosperity.

In time he'd have made a fine property of it again. But he was dead. . . .

Susan, leaning towards him with her hair blowing, asked:

"How's Desdemona?"

He answered:

"All right—why?"

"I want to do an awful lot of riding."

He nodded. Behind his unchanging expression as he leaned back in his corner his deflected thoughts began to unfold a new sequence of pictures. He saw Susan on one morning just after their return from that idiotic honeymoon. Still trying desperately to keep the thing on a practical and friendly basis he'd suggested a morning ride, and she'd come down in her khaki breeches and leather leggings and a white shirt, looking, he'd thought, particularly trim, and particularly fit. And then, without warning when they'd been walking their horses up the hill from the windmill paddock on the way home, she'd gone a greyish-yellowish colour very suddenly and shut her eyes. He'd steadied her for a few moments and she'd recovered quite quickly and said, "It's all right—it's nothing—I feel fine now. . . ." Not until the middle of the morning when he was up to his eyes in work had it dawned upon him that, in addition to the psychological difficulties which they were to share, she had physical ordeals to face. . . .

After that he'd been nervous about her riding. He protested, but she only laughed. The pleasant and friendly basis upon which they were building their life together began to show signs of cracking. His protests, from being honest expressions of concern, took on a tone of ugly accusation; her laughter became reckless and bitter, and all that came of the business was that she went riding with Ken instead. While he was there. But when he went away and Bret had been on the point of further protest or even command, she had given up riding of her own accord. She had behaved altogether, he had been forced to admit, sensibly and pluckily. She'd been careful, but she'd refused to mollycoddle herself. And she'd never for one second used her condition as a weapon against him, a defence from him, an excuse for any of her own less creditable words or actions.

And they had both behaved badly enough at times. His spurt of anger over the episode with Ken in the woolshed had given her a glorious weapon. And hadn't she used it! Not that you could blame her, he thought, when you considered what a cruelty, what an unbearable humiliation his whole attitude to it must have seemed to her. Natural enough for her to hit back at him how and when she could. She had, all the same, her own particular knack of putting a dash of spice and exhilaration into everything—even unhappiness! It was just as well, he thought grimly, that they had both been able to introduce into their squabbling something of the gleam and glamour of sword-play, for the ugliness of the things they had said and done to each other in those dreadful months could never otherwise have been endured.

And Ken, of course, had been vastly amused by it all. . . .

A sudden shock of something went through him so violently that he found himself sitting upright with his pipe in his hand before he recognised it as anger.

Anger? He told himself irritably that it was rather late in the day to start being angry now! Absurd to see Susan and Ken in miniature, bright and unreal like figures on a stage, dancing up and down the hall at Coolami to the music of a gramophone. Ridiculous to be enraged now by things which, at the time, had roused in him only a detached, impersonal disapproval. To be unable now, months later, to shrug as he had shrugged then, refusing to be goaded. . . .

Ken had played up to her. That was all there was to it. He hadn't cared at the time, and he was damned if he could see why he should care now. . . .

Drew called:

"Want to stop in Mudgee?"

Bret answered mechanically:

"No, thanks," but turned at a small sound to find Susan shaking her head at him.

She said reproachfully:

"My chocolates!"

The remnants of his anger seemed caught up suddenly in a blaze of some other emotion. He found that he was staring at her with a feverish intentness as one stares at something which is to be, in a moment, whisked out of one's sight for ever, and through a queer drumming in his ears he heard himself say in a voice which sounded almost threatening:

"You won't need those now."

Drew, cocking an ear backwards, said:

"Hey? What's that?"

Susan, with scarlet cheeks and startled eyes, was gaping at her husband. She looked so amazed, so unbelieving that Bret began to laugh. He said:

"I'm going to get them all the same," and called cheerfully to his father-in-law:

"Yes, stop just near this corner, will you? Susan and I are going shopping."

3

Susan walked beside him down the street. At school when she had had to go on the platform to receive prizes she had had just the same breathless uncomfortable feeling that she had now. A *stuffed* feeling. Words, she knew, if she had to say them, would come in jerks, and sometimes there wouldn't be enough breath left to finish them. It was all, she thought resentfully, very stupid and inappropriate that happiness should be able to rob you of your dignity and calm as misery never could. She felt that even if Bret really meant what he had seemed to mean, he'd only need one downward glance at her to make him recant, for so abruptly had her poise deserted her that she really saw herself for a few seconds in a thick shapeless navy blue tunic of her schooldays, in cotton stockings and flat-heeled shoes with the toes kicked almost out by hopscotch!

He said, "Come on!" and steered her abruptly into a shop.

She thought miserably:

"I suppose I'm being an ass. Why should he feel any differently to-day? Only yesterday he was still hating me."

She roamed about the shop and came back slowly to the counter. She glanced at Bret absently and then again sharply with amazement. He seemed to be buying everything in sight. The counter was littered with paper bags and the white-coated man behind the counter was looking dazed. Bret said:

"And I'll have a dozen of those."

Twelve mammoth slabs of chocolate in orange-coloured wrappings were piled before him.

Susan began to laugh, and the man glanced at them suspiciously.

"'Avin' a party, sir?"

Bret nodded gravely.

"A birthday party. For our triplets."

Susan turned her back too quickly for her face to betray her. She heard the man say genially:

"Well, well, that's unusual, ain't it? 'Ow old are they?"

Bret said:

"They're three." And added courteously, "The twins, of course, are younger."

Susan exploded.

She went outside and waited on the footpath in the sun, shaking. When Bret came out with his arms full of parcels they stood and grinned till their grins died of exhaustion, and they still remained there looking at each other's faces quietly and contentedly as if they had been parted for a long time. Presently Bret said:

"Come along—we must get back to the car. Here, carry some of your blasted chocolates or I'll spill them all over the street. Have one?"

She shook her head.

"I don't need them now."

He said gently, "Bless you!" And began to rummage in one of his bags. She watched him amusedly, thinking that in many ways he often seemed younger than Jim—younger even than herself——

He said:

"How about this one?"

She took it—a "conversation lolly"—heart-shaped and biliously pink, with "I love you" in crazy red lettering. She said lightly:

"Thanks, I'll have that," and then began to run ahead of him because her eyes were hot with tears.

CHAPTER TWENTY-SEVEN

I

DREW, mooching along at thirty, was telling himself that at his age a man should have less sense. He did not, actually express it in that way, but he was aware of a nebulous conviction that to every human being there belongs an inalienable right to behave wildly, ridiculously, at least once in life. And that if one has spent fifty-eight years being sensible one is due, if not overdue for an outbreak of lunacy.

For that, he warned himself, was just what it would be. Sheer, boneheaded madness. This was what came of stepping out of your routine. This was what happened when you yielded—just for a moment—to an impulse, a prompting from some not very often asserted self, and bought a fanciful geegaw for your radiator cap! He looked at it sourly. He knew now that it had been the thin edge of the wedge. Once you'd admitted to yourself, by buying it, the power of a thing like that, you had delivered yourself into its hands. It was only a step from there to seeing flowers where none existed. And only another step to finding music in queer names. And only one more to being bewitched by a map. And good God, what an unholily seductive thing a map could be! Black magic, no more, no less. For after you'd seen it the road you drove was no longer just a road, but a valiant little black line, weaving and threading and picking its way across plains and through vast tracts of bush and over wild

T

blue mountains. Your car wasn't just a car; you had, instead, an eagle's eye view of it as an infinitesimal speck moving along the black line, heading away from security into unimaginable adventures.

Names which you must have seen last night in small black print were like voices now, calling out of some primeval past; Yarragrin, Cobborah. They were like something you had forgotten a thousand years ago and to which you were returning now, not only in miles along a road but in spirit through a dissolving barrier of time. . . .

Time! Again he was aware, uneasily, of the difference even, sometimes the antagonism, between what one knows and what one feels. And he found himself suddenly abashed because he realised that until now he had always felt that this land of his had been born out of the womb of Mother England in the year 1770 with Captain James Cook for midwife.

Yes, he thought, feeling his way gingerly through unaccustomed mazes of surmise, the things you knew were perhaps only raw material out of which if you were wise—or lucky—there might some day blossom things you felt. Years ago, for instance, from the boredom of some otherwise profitless lesson you had saved and kept the knowledge that the grass-tree was one of the oldest forms of vegetable life. But not until this very moment had the meaning come to you of a sight you had seen only yesterday morning, and thought then, carelessly, nothing but, "Queer effect, that!" Now at last you had felt it. Now you could understand that gaunt hill-top with the tall spears of its grass-trees like an army against the sky. Now you could feel that its strangeness was the strangeness of Time arrested, Time suspended, so that there for an acre or two you might walk in a world of tremendous, of majestic antiquity. . . .

Back there on Jungaburra, he reflected, an ancient people had seen spirits God only knew how many centuries ago. In the mountains the records of a thousand years were written across the cliff faces; and in the gullies, through a dim green light and on soft earth that gave out a damp, rich smell, you might walk under tree-ferns whose ancestors had been tree-ferns before you grew legs and came to live on dry land!

He surprised in himself an urgent and compelling emotion—half attraction, half antagonism. He wanted to come to grips with this new world which he hadn't ever understood or even clearly imagined before. He wanted to grapple with it, as men and other male animals cuff each other and snarl or use rough words as signs of affection. For here was, he realised with mounting excitement, a glorious, an inexhaustible source of combat! In that other life he'd left so far behind that it now seemed incredible, there was nothing left to fight.

But fifty-eight . . .!

Millicent said:

"Tired, Tom?"

He became aware that he had sighed. He shook his head, his eyes straying to the surrounding countryside. Strange paddocks he thought, eyeing them; pitted and scarred and dotted all over with heaps of stones and rubble and barren-looking soil. Evil and forsaken. On one side of the road some kind of crop had been sown, but it had a half-hearted appearance, yellowish, dwarfed, uneven. Here and there, where it encountered one of those heaps, it seemed driven back, repelled, the wave of green thinning, scattering as it approached till it died altogether still yards away.

Bret said:

"We're just out of Gulgong. Take the road to your right."

Drew's eyes sharpened suddenly with interest. Gold! Of course! The grim heaps of stones, the tortured and mutilated earth became glamorous. He turned back to Bret.

"Pretty rich fields here once, weren't they?"

But Bret's unenthusiastic glance was the glance of the farmer who sees good land ruined for crops. He said:

"Legend has it that the children still go out after heavy rain and find gold specks in the streets."

Susan asked drowsily:

"Have I died and gone to heaven? Gold streets?"

"Not heaven, darling," Millicent explained. "Gulgong. Have you been asleep?"

She looked round at her daughter. Susan sat up and smoothed her hair and said, "Nearly, I think. It's so hot now," but she looked, her mother thought, more wide-awake, more alert and eager than she had looked for months. Well, young people were erratic and impulsive. What had happened to transform the stormy Susan of yesterday afternoon into the happy Susan of the present moment she supposed she would never know. Nor what had lit behind Bret's still imperturbable expression a kind of glow which even he could not quite subdue. Perhaps nothing at all. It was, undoubtedly, one of the prerogatives of young people to be wildly and deliriously happy for no cause whatever, and, she thought, one could not grudge it to them. For they could be with equal lack of reason, most gloriously and lusciously miserable. Not that you didn't rather envy them there, too! For that, really, is the measure of youth—the vigour and intensity of its emotions. Living hard, loving and hating hard, letting the stars hear its laughter, and turning its tears into temporarily immortal poetry. . . .

And there with that little gibe, she thought sadly, she was admitting her own lost youth. Easy enough to mock at an intensity and passion, the memory of which still has power to hurt you a little because you know it lost to you for ever! She heard Susan say:

"Quick, Bret—throw them!"

As she turned her head she saw a succession of orange streaks curving through the air. Shrill voices followed—yells, exclamations, a swelling pæan of joy. She hung over the door, looking back. The narrow street seemed literally paved with chocolate in orange wrappers, and children were springing from every fence and doorway. She wondered watching till a turn in the road hid them, if they had ever picked up gold in the streets which was more to their liking, and if there would come again, in the life of even one of them, anything so nearly approaching a miracle.

And yet, really, were miracles so scarce? Weren't they, as long as human beings lived and thought, and felt, and blundered along their precocious and audacious way, daily or even hourly commonplaces? What was it, for instance, but a miracle, which had kept Tom silent, back there in Mudgee, when he saw his quite sane and responsible son-in-law gravely emptying several pounds of sweets in assorted bags, and twelve cakes of chocolate in orange wrappers into the back of the car? Only yesterday he would have said a good deal, beginning probably with, "What the hell——?" And not only in him had miracles been at work. It didn't matter, she realised, that one's body sat quietly in a well-upholstered corner, and that one's tongue uttered, politely, trivial fragments of conversation. What counted was that in one's brain the strange alchemies of thought, the mysterious vagaries of memory and hope were going on all the time. So that you were not necessarily now the person you had been yesterday—or even half an hour ago!

She glanced almost timidly at her new husband. She thought that she might like him even better than her old one when she had had time to know him.

2

When they came at about two o'clock to a bridge over a creek, Drew stopped the car on the grass by the roadside and pulled his driving gloves from his hot cramped fingers. He asked idly:

"Any one hungry?"

Bret, getting out and stamping a foot which was nearly asleep, didn't answer. He was trying an experiment with himself, seeing, as he walked to the bridge and leaned his arms on it, Jim and Susan laughing and squabbling on the sandy bank of the creek below. He'd had that glimpse of them one day as he drove past on his way home from Mudgee. He'd spent a bothersome and profitless morning, he remembered, arguing with an obstinate ass of a chap about a tractor, and he'd been feeling rather disgruntled even before he swung round the curve on to the bridge and saw Jim's single-seater parked by the roadside, its bonnet faced towards Sydney.

He'd pulled up savagely, his tyres scraping and skidding on the road as he wrenched with unhabitual violence at his brake. For he'd needed Jim that week-end, and there had been no talk of a journey to Sydney when he had left the day before. He'd stood for a moment on the bridge looking down at them. Susan was trying to get some water in a billy and Jim was trying to stop her. Their laughter and carefree foolery, he remembered, had made him feel so furious that he'd stopped to light a cigarette and calm himself a little before he went down the bank to speak to them.

And it had all been very futile, anyhow. Jim, cheerful and unconcerned, had greeted him casually. Susan, quite silent, had stood motionless, her eyes, he remembered now, fixed rather intently on his own face. He'd said:

"Where are you off to?"

Jim, wiping his hands on a handkerchief, answered:

"Sydney. Where's the lid, Susan?"

She gave it to him. Bret asked:

"For how long? We're short-handed, you know."

There must have been some hint of his exasperation in his voice, because surprise had flickered in the glance Jim gave him, and there was a shade of conciliation in his reply.

"I'll be back on Monday. Did you get the tractor?"

"No."

And then he'd looked straight at Susan and asked bluntly:

"Is this trip quite necessary?"

It was then he had noticed how intently she was looking at him. But it was Jim who answered:

"Oh, absolutely! We're going to boil a billy. Won't you stay and have some tea?"

He'd snapped:

"No, thanks," and then he hadn't quite been able to repress a smile at the transparent relief on Jim's face. He'd said, "I'll see you on Monday, then," and distributed a casual "Good-bye" between them as he went back to his car.

But as he'd driven off again he had been in a black mood of rage against the girl who, standing motionless and saying nothing, could still take Jim so easily from him and from Coolami. . . .

He took his arms from the railing and turned back to the car. Millicent was spreading a cloth in the shade, and Drew was collecting driftwood under the bridge to make a fire. Susan with the billy in her hand was standing on the other side of the road, and as Bret turned, her eyes, which must he thought have been glued to the back of his head, moved swiftly away, and she flushed, beginning to walk down the bank to the water.

He followed and took the billy out of her hand.

"I'll get it. What were you staring at me like that for?"

She asked slowly, without looking up:

"Were you remembering . . .?"

He said:

"Of course I was. One couldn't very well help it, could one?"

"I suppose not."

He looked about.

"It's too shallow here. I'll step on to that rock. Hold the lid, will you?"

She said, taking it:

"There's a way you've looked at me sometimes that I've always—connected with this place. Because that day was the first time I saw it. Contempt—and hatred."

He straightened up with the billy brimming and stepped back on to the bank. She held the lid out to him mechanically, but he didn't take it, so that presently she looked up at his face.

He thought, staring down at her, that it was only to be expected that so mysterious and irrational an emotion as love should assail one in a completely sudden and illogical manner. And yet possibly not so sudden after all. Perhaps no more sudden than the overnight blossoming of a flower whose seed has worked underground, whose stem has striven upward, whose leaves have opened and toiled for just this consummation. He didn't know, or care really, how long there had been accumulating in him the feelings towards her which only to-day had been fused into the one grateful and beneficent gladness which now pervaded him. He didn't know why or how it was that he should find he could remember Jim without anger or resentment, and with no hurt beyond the hurt with which one loses any friend to death. And he wondered, watching Susan's dark, shadowed eyes wakening, coming to life, what this queer power was writing on his own face where once, in this same spot she had seen hatred written, and contempt.

He said:

"They aren't there now, are they?"

She shook her head. He thought with sharp anxiety that she looked exhausted, as though some flame which illuminated was at the same time consuming her. A realisation of the full misery, the full suffering, both mental and physical, of the year she had spent came to him with a shock of pity and remorse. He said gently:

"They never should have been. They never will be again."

3

Drew stirring his tea with a twig, caught sight of his wrist-watch and thought, "Nearly three o'clock. We should be there comfortably by sundown. Better put some water in the radiator perhaps." His mind filled with these idle thoughts, it seemed to be from some others, quite unauthorised, that there came the impulse which made him say suddenly:

"Where did Colin get all his information about Mortimer, anyhow?"

He drank, waited, and then with his cup half-way to his lips again, looked round at his son-in-law. Bret was lying on his back on the grass, his half-shut eyes on the lovely curves and spirals of his ascending cigarette smoke; his thoughts, quite evidently, had shut the world out. Drew repeated:

"Bret!"

But even then, it was not till Susan prodded his ankle that Bret came back to the present with a jerk and rolled over on one elbow.

"I was half asleep. Sorry; what did you say?"

"Who told Colin about this chap Mortimer? How did he know Wondabyne was for sale again?"

Bret sat up and stubbed his cigarette out carefully on the grass behind him.

"His stockman, Miller, got the news by phone from his aunt this morning. She's been housekeeping for Mortimer since his wife died. It's to be sold for the children, of course—little kids they are. About seven and five."

Drew grunted.

"What'll they ask for it?"

"Ask or get?"

"Both."

"Well, they'll probably ask a hundred and fifty thousand and get somewhere round a hundred and twenty thousand."

Drew said, "H'm!" and passed his cup to Susan. "Any more in the billy?"

She dipped it out with a pannikin, wondering in passing, half-absently, why Dad had seemed so glum all day, and whether he was really very pipped with her for having taken his sumptuous Madison out last night and scratched its paint and dented its mudguard. But she wasn't very concerned about it. There didn't seem to be room in her at present for anything else but an almost incredulous gladness, and already her parents had faded a little, blurred a little, diminished a little, as if they were figures she was leaving slowly behind her on a misty road.

She began to think eagerly, impatiently, of Coolami. There a mist seemed to be clearing away, as though all the unhappiness of the time she had spent there had obscured her vision of it; she felt that now when she came to it she would be able to love it as she had always wanted to—as she had never felt quite free to do before.

She began to think about it in detail—its solidity, its comfort, its rather exciting and queerly appropriate note of austerity. Bret's mother, she thought, must have loved the country very much to have grown such a house in it. For, as her own mother had said, it didn't look as if it had been built. It looked, really, with its lines and angles masked by trees, as if it might be only another and larger one of the great granite boulders whose outcrops dotted the paddocks here and there. She remembered that the first time she had seen it she had stood beside the car for a moment while Jim hunted for tennis-racquets, and she'd found herself thinking, "For ever and ever, amen!"

Her thoughts of it drifted down about her, shadowy and intangible like mist or smoke. They were less pictures than patterns of words which evolved themselves slowly and deliciously in her mind as though, childlike, she were telling herself stories of it. She told herself about the library where there was always a comfortable litter of things—— A chair with dented cushions and a newspaper on the floor beside it; a magazine open on the table; sometimes Kathleen's big dilapidated sketch-book with a couple of pencils and a cigarette-holder snapped under the elastic band; Bret's hat on the chair just inside the door.

She thought about the drawing-room with its row of long glass doors opening on to the flagged pathway of the inside garden. No one had used it much, except when Jim had rattled out songs and dance music on the piano. Ken sometimes strummed there, and it had been, for herself, a haven during the few long months of her married life. A room where other people didn't come very often, so that sometimes even if your cheeks were wet you didn't have to betray it to any one—not even to yourself. . . .

She thought of the blurred soft colours of cretonnes and chintzes dimly repeated in the mirror-like dark floor, and of the brass fire-irons at the far end gleaming against a fireplace like a cavern, and she thought of them quietly and gratefully without retrospective bitterness or grief.

When she left them and came in her thoughts to the small room across the hall which Bret called his office, she found that the words in her mind no longer made a pattern but a kind of inventory. It was that kind of room. Bare and plain and uncompromising, and yet without grimness. Wondering a little at the accuracies of her memory, she saw as clearly as if she had spent many hours sitting at it, the scratches on the once-polished surface of the desk, the burnt place at one edge where some one had left a lighted cigarette once and forgotten it. The revolving chair had a dark green cushion on it, and the curtains which were never drawn across the window were of the same stuff. There were papers and books and magazines. Bills and receipts on files, and a typewriter with a black tin cover over it.

And, very often, Bret himself. The window opened on to the inside garden, and from the balcony outside her bedroom opposite she'd seen him many times at night with his pipe in his mouth, writing or adding up figures, or typing with two fingers astonishingly fast.

And it had been there one night that she'd seen him through the uncurtained window with Ken; the night of that stupid, feverish, crazy hot day when he'd found Ken kissing her in the woolshed. She'd been sitting on the balcony rail in a thin silk wrapper, trying to get cool, when she'd seen the light go up in the downstairs window, and Ken, entering like an actor on a stage, putting a cigarette in his mouth, feeling in his pockets and then rummaging among the papers on the desk for matches. When Bret had come in too she'd known with a kind of dull indifference—an armour with which she had instinctively provided herself against too much and too acute unhappiness—that the brief sentences she could see, though not hear them flinging at each other, were sharp and hostile. She'd watched them idly, wondering even at the time how, without hearing their words, she could tell with such relentless accuracy the whole tone of their respective mental attitudes to her and to the episode they were so obviously discussing. She'd wondered, too, whether any actors could have achieved on a stage such a wealth of pantomimic expression with such an absence of gesture. And yet impersonal, armoured, carefully detached as she had been in her rôle of involuntary audience, she thought that nothing in all her life had ever hurt her, harmed her more deeply than the knowledge of Bret's reaction to that kiss. . . .

It had been rather like a poison to her; something she'd hardly felt at the time but which, as weeks and months went by, had spread and raged through her till no part of her felt any peace at all. For rail and jeer at jealousy as you like, she thought, there can be no love entirely free from it. Nothing before, not even his bitterest words and his most callous actions had so driven home to her the completeness of his indifference, and the essential ugliness of the compact they had made with such good intentions.

Memories! Dreadful things, dangerous things! She felt a little spasm of fear and pain contract her brow as though her thoughts had brushed like bat's wings across her face. How much of your life could you ever really leave behind you? Any of it? Any of it at all? What was it to forget? Just to thrust thoughts away like prisoners into dark dungeons under the surface of your mind. To leave them there, starved and dangerous—some day to escape!

No, no, that wasn't safe! Never forget things! Never lose them. Keep them there, however unprepossessing they may be, always under your eye, and make them work for you. For surely, she thought confusedly, labouring towards some comfort still hidden ahead of her in a fog of yet unformed ideas, that's what all your life is for? All of it, everything that has happened, good and bad, is only the material available to you for the building of your future? Then you can't afford to forget—to imprison—to waste——?

She looked anxiously at Bret. She had a dreadful momentary sense of frustration because she realised that the joy and fullness of bodily union can never be equalled by a union of the mind. Things interfere. Here, with her own mind abrim with inchoate thoughts, it just wasn't possible to talk to him—to find in his brain those complementary processes which might make of hers a whole idea, rounded and complete. And yet it must be, or it surely ought to be so? More vaguely because less calmly than Margery, she wandered among rather similar conjectures. She wondered why, when with their bodies in fusion, man and woman create a child, when with their souls or spirits in fusion they create a mysterious but far from illusory power called love, they could not—or did not—or did not seem to be able to create by a mental fusion anything whatever! Something wrong there, surely?

She drank a mouthful of her tea, but it was cool and she poured the rest out on the grass. She saw that Millicent was putting things back in the car, and that Drew was dipping more water from the creek into the billy. Bret said, scraping mud from the sole of his shoe with a twig:

"You wouldn't expect us to forget things altogether, would you?"

She jumped.

"Why do you say that?"

"You were doing some remembering too."

"Yes. And I wouldn't *want* us to forget them."

He threw his twig away and looked at her thoughtfully.

"You may be right. Anyhow, it doesn't matter."

She said dubiously:

"Can things happen so suddenly? Can people change —overnight?"

Quite unperturbed he answered, "Apparently," and went on after a moment:

"Not suddenly. Not overnight. Very gradually, really—so slowly and unobtrusively that you don't know till it's all over that it's been happening at all."

He added presently:

"Don't be so doggone sceptical."

She retorted swiftly:

"Can you blame me when the only declaration I've had from you has been in bilious-looking red letters all running together on a darned messy pink bit of fifth-rate confectionery. . . .?"

He laughed, getting up and stretching.

"What do you want, ass?"

She said quickly, standing beside him:

"Nothing. Nothing on earth."

4

Drew, with the brimming billy on the road at his feet, was unscrewing the radiator cap. He flipped the little silver figure round and round with a kind of vengeful and sardonic humour. It spun wildly, glittering, its head lifted, its outstretched arm awhirl, like a fanatical high-priest at the climax of some triumphal dance.

Drew thought grimly as he stooped for the billy: "All right, all right! You win!"

CHAPTER TWENTY-EIGHT

I

THEY drove silently through an afternoon hot and rich with sunshine. Their thoughts lulled by it, and by the faint, powerful purring and the rocking movement of the car, became less thoughts than day-dreams, disconnected and unfinished. To them all in different guises there was coming a strange delicious mood of almost languorous acceptance. A luxurious fatalism. A sense of waiting in some web of fairy-tale enchantment for some long-delayed but quite inevitable moment of fairy-tale release.

Somewhere not so very far ahead now, lay the end, and at the end they would each find, they dimly felt, a new beginning. The car had become less a mechanical means by which they voluntarily travelled, than a mysterious and omnipotent force bearing them, passive, tranced and pleasantly comatose, towards some destiny which they would not if they could avoid. Even Drew, driving with the sureness of many years' experience, was actually very far from the ingenious gadgets which his hands and feet so efficiently controlled; and to him also, in a state of hypnotised beatitude, the grassy hill slopes, the trees, the wheatlands, the endless road, seemed to be flowing towards them out of some inexhaustible legend.

What thoughts they had as the miles slid past were all drawn to it as to some vast magnet. It was as if each car-length of road they left behind faded and dissolved into nothingness; as if they were all the time just one jump ahead of an illusory past, with a future coming endlessly upon them which was still not quite their future. So that in a dreamlike way their thoughts seemed actually to leave their bodies, to hover before them, even to fly forward until, grotesquely, they took shape—the shape of the glinting urgent figure on the radiator, lifting its head and pointing its urgent finger to the west.

On this halcyon sea of shared and unspoken sensations they seemed indefinitely becalmed. But as there might come from the sea itself releasing winds and tides, there came suddenly, towards sunset, out of a golden haze of dust in front of them a slow-moving mob of sheep. Spreading, undulating from fence to fence, its rearguard melted out of sight, almost as if it were made up of incorporeal shapes born of the sunlight and the dust which rose from its softly thudding hooves. Drew put his brake down and crawled forward. Some part of him, still bemused by their strange mirage-like appearance, half expected them to fade into nothing as he reached them, but as they closed round the car the dust, and the heavy smell, and the faint occasional bleating of a lamb forced momentarily from its mother's side, brought him back with a grateful sense of awakening to a solid and tangible world.

The mob parted clumsily to left and right. Sometimes a sheep, safely out of the track, floundered across it again, driven by some obscure panic, and there came, once or twice, the faint bump of a fleecy body against the mudguards of the scarcely-moving car. On the heels of the mob two dogs moved swiftly—lean and black and indefatigable, with their pink tongues hanging out. Two more walked beside the drover, who, leading his pack-horse and flicking flies idly from about his face with a switch of gum-leaves, looked, Drew thought, half asleep on his ambling grey mare. But somehow, from beneath his hat-brim, he saw Bret, and his hand lifted in recognition quickly enough.

Drew asked when they were through:

"How many in that lot, Bret?"

Susan said quickly:

"Let me guess. Two thousand?"

Bret looked at her and said, "How——?"

Faintly as the shadow of a veil he saw a sharp remembrance, a momentary apprehension cloud her face. He said quickly in a low voice, "Who taught you that? Jim?"

She nodded, her eyes still on him. He said teasingly:

"Rats! It was a lucky guess!" and leaned forward to answer Drew who was demanding over his shoulder:

"Eh! How many did you say?"

"Susan was right to the last sheep. I happen to know them—they're on their way down to Mudgee from Nariel, Keith Browne's place."

Drew asked:

"When'll they get there?"

Bret answered him absently, "About a fortnight," for he was watching the top of the hill at the foot of which the Madison was gathering herself together for a charge. About half-way up there would spring into view over the skyline the top branches of a vast yellow box, and always from childhood he had watched for it. For it was the first glimpse of his own land, growing there and perversely flourishing on a hilltop while others of its family sought the river banks; as if it enjoyed growing there; as if it enjoyed holding aloft, like a flag of welcome, the first glimpse of a green nourished in the soil of Coolami.

He said suddenly on an impulse, to Susan:

"Look! There where I'm pointing. You'll see the top of a tree. There! That's the first glimpse you have of Coolami."

As he said the words he felt their staggering importance. Not even to Jim had he dreamed of mentioning that childish custom of his. Not to any other living soul could he so far have betrayed in words the strength, the violence even, of his feelings for his home. Some last barrier in himself had broken away with that impulsive confession, and he was amazed by the suddenly unimpeded torrent of his emotions. Not looking at her, not touching her, he became almost agonisingly aware of Susan, and as the car soared over the crest of the hill and all the visible world became in the flash of an eye his own, he felt with a shock of joy some mysterious fusion, some new and infinitely precious sense of completion and fulfilment.

Susan and himself and Coolami. Of course! He leaned forward looking out across the three thousand acre paddock wondering if old Job the dog man had been working there to-day, and if so what his total bag of rabbits had been, and all the time, behind the pleasant preoccupations of his thoughts for his land, he was aware of gladness and excitement in a warmly mounting tide.

2

Millicent said to her husband:

"This is the beginning of Bret's land, Tom."

He looked round at it as he drove. He was glad that now he could consider it all soberly and objectively as a hard-headed man of business should. He was relieved that he had been delivered out of a mood in which it would probably have swum before his eyes in a haze of sun-bewitched romance, rousing in him nebulous dreams and unsatisfactory imaginings. And yet out of the strange mental experiences of the last two days, something remained to him. He was like a man who through long hours of delirium has made strange journeys, and who with returning health, remembers them as dreams but can never altogether escape from them. He drove steadily at thirty-five, considering Bret's domain. Queer, he thought, who had never before known any one who owned more than a dozen acres or so, to watch his speedometer telling out mile after mile of Coolami!

He said abruptly to Millicent:

"Would you like to come back?"

"Back . . .?" She looked at him uncertainly.

"Back here." He took one hand from the wheel and waved it in a vague, explanatory gesture. "To the country. To Wondabyne."

She wondered for a moment if perhaps through the noise of the car she had not heard him properly. She repeated stupidly:

"To Wondabyne? How?"

"I was thinking I might buy it."

For the first time in her life she looked at him with

actual dislike and repugnance. For her instant wild impression was that he could not conceive this beauty about him save as another something to be bought with his all-powerful money. That he had seen in this coincidence of Mortimer's death his own picturesque chance for the ultimate conquest of his rival. And she had imagined him changed! "*I might buy it*!" Well, it was his moment of victory, perhaps—but would it satisfy him? So paltry a triumph? She stared in front of her, a tide of anger drumming behind her eyes.

And yet, on its ebb, there came another tide of juster thoughts, steadily and quietly flooding her heart with gladness and remorse. For she saw now that what she had imagined was a change in him, was only the long-delayed awakening of something always dormant, something her instinct had felt but never found before. She recognised with relief and gratitude that he was still Tom; that there remained essentially untouched by the strange experiences of this most eventful journey the sober and practical and hard-working man who would never fail her—or himself. Or Wondabyne . . .?

She found that her hands were clutching each other tightly in her lap. She thought with nervous amusement that surely no more alarming and disconcerting a thing could happen than to have one's heart's desire suddenly handed to one. For she recognised it now that it was before her as a dream so lost in the background of her mind that she had never been aware of it before. So preposterous that the practical Millicent of these thirty-odd years would never for one moment have considered it. Tom at Wondabyne! Its absurdity was grotesque. A man did not, at fifty-seven, forsake the City, abandon his clubs, his golf, his bridge, his first nights at the theatre, his summer surfing holiday, his vast circle of congenial friends and acquaintances – to buy a sheep station! But perhaps he hadn't intended . . .

She said doubtfully:

"Do you mean – to live there? To – to run it?"

He answered shortly:

"Why not?"

She remained for half a mile or so staring dumbly at his arrogant profile. Then she felt laughter beginning to waken in her, deeply and silently, so that her face suffused and there came a slight aching round her ribs. It was really less amusement, she reflected, than a wild and triumphant exhilaration because she saw now how unerringly the wilful and impetuous Millicent of thirty-seven years ago had recognised her mate. Hadn't she felt only yesterday that he wasn't really a runner round in circles? Wasn't this the juggling with points which she had imagined, and wasn't he off now, with a reckless adventurousness at which even she drew a breath of anxiety! "Why not?" indeed!

She said rather breathlessly:

"Darling, you're game!"

He took the car carefully round a bend before he looked at her with a faint grin and then back at the road.

"I suppose I'm not too old to learn, am I? And anyhow Colin could do most of the work."

She said doubtfully as if testing the idea:

"Colin?"

And again he answered briefly:

"Why not?"

She thought more soberly this time. All very well to be reckless with one's own life, but one's children's were more precious. She thought slowly and carefully, placing her conclusions neatly in a row for final analysis. She could feel in each argument as she dealt with it that Tom had been there before her, and she glanced at him gratefully, contentedly, feeling security in the knowledge of his shrewdness, gladness that not even she herself could plan more selflessly for their children's good. But was it safe to plan at all? Was it any good to set up in array a dozen—or a hundred—undoubted advantages if they were to be, as they very well might, overborne by the one ruthless and definite "No" of youth?

She heard the sadness in her own voice and was shocked by it.

"He mightn't want to, Tom."

His left hand came down on to hers, and then went up again to shield his eyes from the setting sun.

"Then he won't have to. I don't doubt we can run it ourselves, with a good manager perhaps, and Bret at our elbow. But I think he will."

He added presently:

"That girl Margery has lots of sense. And she wouldn't be sorry after last night to get him away from that damned mountain. . . ."

Susan called from behind them:

"Daddy, we're nearly there. You'll be able to see it from the top of this hill."

3

As they came roaring up to its crest Susan's thoughts flew backwards, wondering, awed, to re-discover other thoughts which had absorbed her such a little time ago. Only yesterday morning? It didn't seem possible;

and yet in a way it was comforting to know that things so definitely true, things so austerely provable by calendars and clocks could seem impossible. For then it was easier to believe in other miracles—in the miracle, for instance, which showed those imaginings of yesterday at once so accurately fulfilled, and at the same time to grotesquely denied.

For there was Coolami. "*About sunset they'd come to it—up to the crest of a long hill with the sun in their eyes, so that until the car began to swoop downward they couldn't see anything. And then like magic it would all be there, the great valley glowing with opalescent light, the wheat-fields quivering and flowing to the current of a vagrant breeze, the river like a mirror beneath a green deluge of weeping willows.*"

Could you have imagined it so clearly? Wasn't it, in this new awareness of mysterious forces, almost easier to believe that your longing, your hunger, your love for it must have run ahead of your body, which, even in a Madison, had come so slowly—so very slowly—home?

Yes, up to here (if they were imaginings) they had been accurately fulfilled. But it was hard now to imagine a darkness quite so heavy and impenetrable as that through which her further thoughts had stumbled yesterday. For she had said the name over and over to herself, "Coolami, Coolami," rubbing the back of her hand across her forehead as though she might clear in that way the obscure confusion of thought that the name roused in her. *What did it stand for, that name of her husband's home, beyond the lovely picture that it flashed instantly to her mind—beyond her memories of Jim—beyond the unbelievably carefree months of her romance, the freezing horror of its ending, the dreary and humiliating mess which had somehow grown out of what had seemed so lovely and so gay. . . .*

Inconceivable now, that one should ever have been so dreadfully in outer darkness! That one shouldn't have felt oneself struggling from futility towards usefulness—that one should have been as blind as a man lost in some underground tunnel, groping instinctively towards a light he cannot see.

For it was so easy to know, to understand now that there was no crime like the crime of stagnation—unproductiveness. With a creative trinity, mind, body and spirit, one must yield something back to the generous earth. And that was Coolami. The generous earth.

The car swung round towards the house, hardly recognisable as a house except for the blue smoke thinly and steadily ascending from its chimneys. A happiness which was almost vertigo so overwhelmed her that the joyous barking of dogs seemed to come from far away, and she saw only mistily the warm light from an open doorway. She felt in the detached manner of a dream the slowing and stopping of the Madison's great bulk, realised dimly the fading into silence of its rhythmic sounds, so that it seemed, in the general confusion of her senses, like some vast and friendly monster ceasing to breathe, bewitched now that its task was ended, back into gross and inanimate metal. . . .

She looked round and found Bret smiling at her. So that when he had opened the doors she got out and faced the house, thinking that now she could return to it gladly and confidently—a potential bringer and receiver of gifts.

4

Drew, looking across the room at his wife, demanded:

"Any hurry for getting back—to Ballool?"

But Millicent, unpacking his pyjamas and laying them on the bed, refused to be startled. Here at last was the game which she had once vaguely imagined that matrimony might be. You were both sudden and unexpected; you dashed off delightfully upon wild and unexplored byways; you talked nonsense and you did erratic things. And of course whichever one of you disconcerted the other most frequently was the winner.

So she only smoothed his pyjamas and answered warily:

"No dear—not so far as I'm concerned."

"Like to go on a bit?"

"On? Where?"

He made a vague magnificent gesture.

"Oh, just—on."

She glanced at him admiringly. How well he played! She nodded.

"I'd love it, Tom. Broken Hill, do you think?"

He eyed her sharply.

"Well—possibly. I had Alice Springs in mind."

She began to laugh.

"You win, darling. I refuse to die of thirst with a new-chum in the middle of a desert." She sat down on the edge of the bed and looked at him.

"Have you talked to Bret? About Wondabyne?"

Drew grinned, brushing his thick grey hair at the mirror.

"I've listened to him talk to me. He thought I was mad."

"So you are, darling."

"Possibly. Probably. Oh, of course, I am. Who cares?"

She said, "Not I!" watching him contentedly in the mirror. But the day in the open air had made her sleepy so that with the heaviness of her eyes it blurred and became alive with formless and fluidly-moving shapes. Fluidly-moving, melting and merging into a kind of coherence, so that at last they became a mud-bespattered car facing west with yet another rising sun behind it.

5

Bret came out from the library where he had been arguing with his father-in-law, on to the flagged path of the inside garden and looked up through the dusk to Susan's room. There was a light there, but almost as he saw it he saw her too, a dark blur at the end of the balcony, leaning her arms on the railing, looking down across the paddocks towards the river.

He wanted very much to run up the steps and tell her all about Wondabyne. He wanted to enjoy with her the rather gorgeous and intrepid lunacy of her parents, who after more than thirty years of matrimony were determined and eager—to start all over again. He wanted to share with her his delighted amusement in them—as though, he thought, they were the children and he and Susan indulgent but disillusioned adults. How long had they been hatching this? One day! One day to upset the carefully built structure of thirty-seven years! What had happened to the old chap to make him run amok like this?

He sobered, thinking, his eyes still on the fading outline of Susan's head and shoulders against the darkening sky. A funny journey it had been. After all, in a sense, he'd run amok himself. And yet nothing had happened. They had all been calm and civil and matter-of-fact and very nearly monosyllabic as one usually is. . . .

Danger, perhaps? Physical peril? Yes, there might be something in that. For twice during that journey he had felt his own life and Susan's as brittle fragments of some exquisite and complicated piece of craftsmanship entrusted to the care of people not able to appreciate their value.

Something in him then had cried out for another chance, protested in a blind panic which was less fear of death than fear of waste, against the destruction of beauty before its blossoming.

And now he could hardly see her at all. He called:

"Susan!"

The darkness moved a little where he was watching it. She came along the balcony and stood at the top of the steps peering down at him. Suddenly he knew that he didn't want to tell her about Wondabyne now; he didn't want to discuss anything or to explain anything. Words were heavy things, tearing, destroying things like stones flung through a cobweb. He saw her hand lying near the top on the wooden bannister of the steps, and he looked down curiously at his own resting against the post at the bottom. It occurred to him that there had never yet been so much as a meeting of their hands in perfect kindliness, and he looked up at her again, troubled and now irrationally ashamed of those things in himself which had made their life together so barren and so hard.

She came down one step, but still he did not move, delaying purposely, postponing for the sake of the strange half painful joy it gave him, a moment for which he now felt he had been waiting all his life. She said his name suddenly on a note of desperate appeal, and he realised with sharp contrition that her faith in him had been tried very high that day.

Until he saw his hand come down on hers, he hardly knew that he had moved.

THE END

Also Published in the Imprint Classics Series

For Love Alone

Christina Stead

Against a background of two cities—Sydney, thick with genteel sweat; and London, grim, dark and depressed—*For Love Alone* tells the story of Teresa Hawkins, high minded, passionate and independent, who knows only one commandment: Thou Shalt Love.

Obsessed by love and a sense of her own destiny, Teresa turns her back on Sydney and its suburban horizons, and sets off on her 'grand, perilous journey'. Following the self-seeking and contemptuous Jonathon Crow, whom Stead gives to us here in an unforgettable portrait of misogyny, Teresa arrives in London to a world in which she does indeed seem fated to belong. There she meets James Quick and discovers another form of love, and her own power as a woman.

This new edition of *For Love Alone* is published with an introduction by Peter Craven.

The Timeless Land

Eleanor Dark

First published in 1941, Eleanor Dark's classic novel of the early settlement of Australia is a story of hardship, cruelty and danger. Above all it is the story of conflict: between the Aborigines and the white settlers.

In this dramatic novel, introduced here by Humphrey McQueen, a large cast of characters, historical and fictional, black and white, convict and settler, brings alive those bitter years with moments of tenderness and conciliation amid the brutality and hostility. All the while, behind the veneer of British civilisation, lies the baffling presence of Australia, a timeless land that shares with England 'not even its seasons or its stars'.

ALIEN SON
JUDAH WATEN

'As soon as they saw me they burst out laughing and pointed to my buttoned-up shoes and white silk socks. I was overcome with shame and ran back into the house where I removed my shoes and socks and threw them away. I would walk barefooted like the other boys.' With such a gesture a child can adapt himself to a new country and new people, even though for some time he may not 'know a word of what they were saying'. For the older generation, however, things may not be so easy...

Judah Waten's classic story of a Russian family settling in Australia in the years before the First World War is published here with an introduction by David Carter.

'*Alien Son* is a real contribution to Australian literature...It even has some of the descriptive simplicity of Chekhov and Katherine Mansfield.'

Sydney Morning Herald

'This book pioneers a rich field for the fuller imaginative interpretation of Australian life. *Alien Son*, sympathetic, penetrating, shows us many possibilities...'

The Australian

'In *Alien Son* the child, the parents are two additions to the short list of characters in Australian fiction who deserve permanent life in our imagination...They are fully, grubbily alive. Mr Waten's ruthlessly realistic picture of them is nevertheless wonderfully tender.'

The Age

WATERWAY
ELEANOR DARK

This sparkling novel, set on the edge of Sydney harbour, follows a small group of people through the intricacies of a single day; a day that reaches its climax on the harbour when the ferry bound for Watson's Bay collides with a liner and sinks.

How will the accident change the life of Winifred, married to vindictive Arthur and in love with Ian? Will the events of the day alter the resentments of Jack Saunders or the vanities of Lorna Sellman? Is there any reason or morality when it comes to accident and death?

First published in 1938 when Eleanor Dark was at the heart of her powers, and reprinted here with an introduction by Drusilla Modjeska, *Waterway* is as brightly patterned as the harbour and as full of life as the people it describes.

RIDE ON STRANGER
KYLIE TENNANT

Civilisation is mad and getting madder every day.

So says Shannon Hicks in Kylie Tennant's marvellous, harsh, satiric novel. Arriving in Sydney just before the Second World War, Shannon, a dreamer and idealist, takes on the world of politics, business, religion... and men. The consequences are challenging and unpredictable.

Ride on Stranger is introduced by Kerryn Goldsworthy, and is a classic in contemporary Australian literature.

'...a witty comedy of manners.'
The Australian

'A quintessentially and uniquely Australian writer...'
The Sydney Morning Herald

'Tennant's work will endure?'
Paul Carter, *Age Monthly Review*